[redacted]

CiTY OF CLOWNS

CiTY OF CLOWNS

Daniel Alarcón · Sheila Alvarado

Riverhead Books

New York

2015

RIVERHEAD BOOKS
An imprint of Penguin Random House LLC
375 Hudson Street
New York, New York 10014

Library of Congress Cataloging-in-Publication Data

Alarcón, Daniel, date.
[*Ciudad de payasos*. English]
City of clowns / Daniel Alarcón, Sheila Alvarado.
p.   cm.
ISBN 978-1-59463-333-1
1. Journalists—Comic books, strips, etc.   2. Lima (Peru)—Comic books, strips, etc.
3. Graphic novels.   I. Alvarado, Sheila, illustrator.   II. Title.
PN6790.P43A43313   2015   2015013506
741.5'985—dc23

Printed in the United States of America
1   3   5   7   9   10   8   6   4   2

Book design by Alvaro Villanueva / Bookish Design

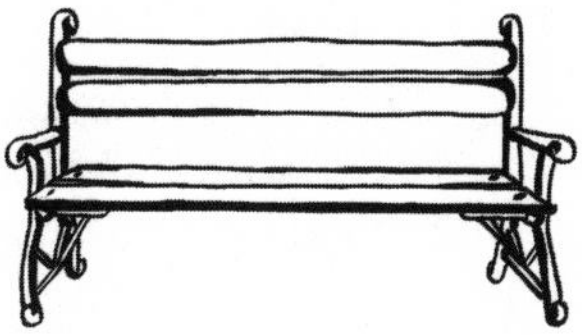

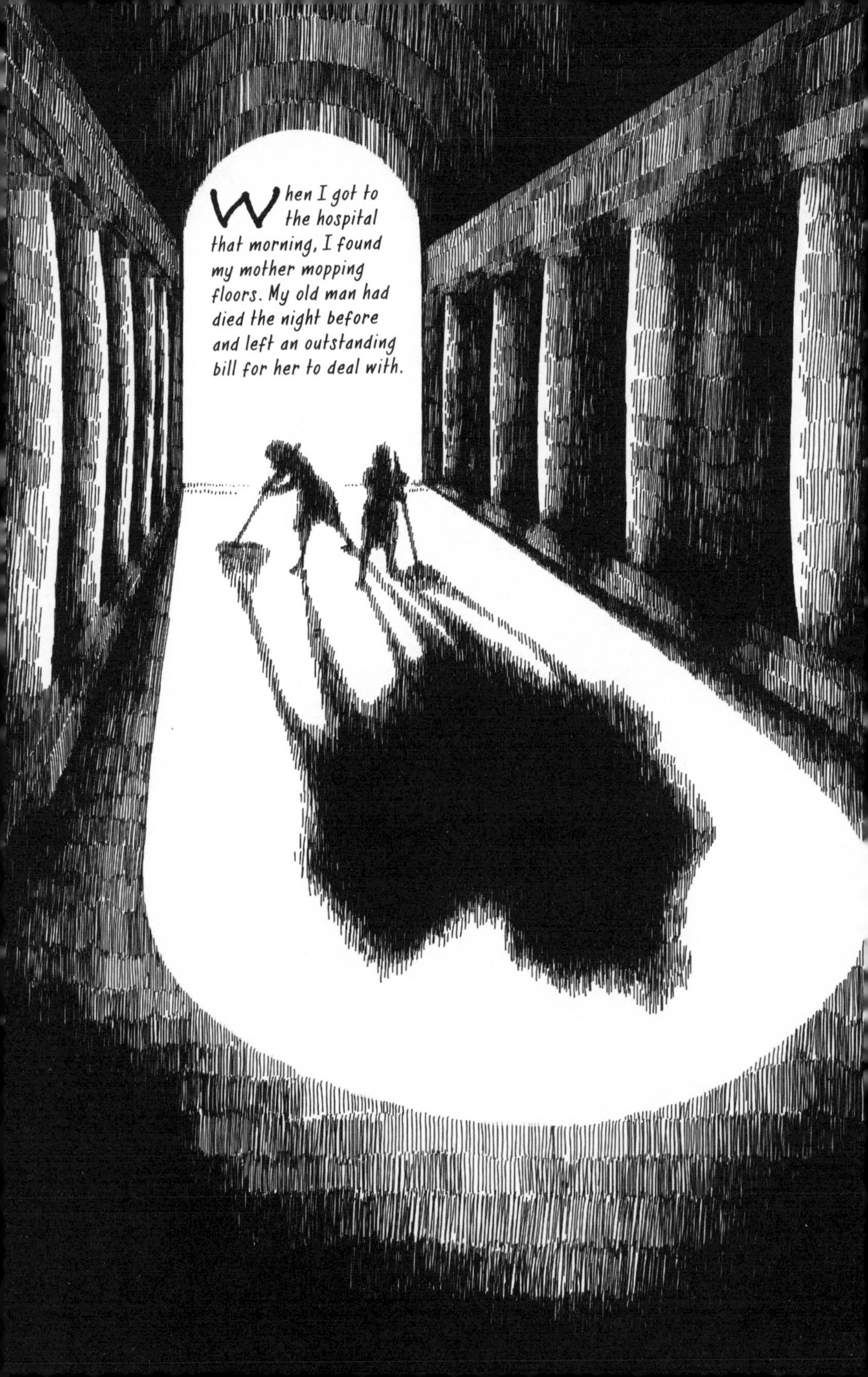
When I got to the hospital that morning, I found my mother mopping floors. My old man had died the night before and left an outstanding bill for her to deal with.

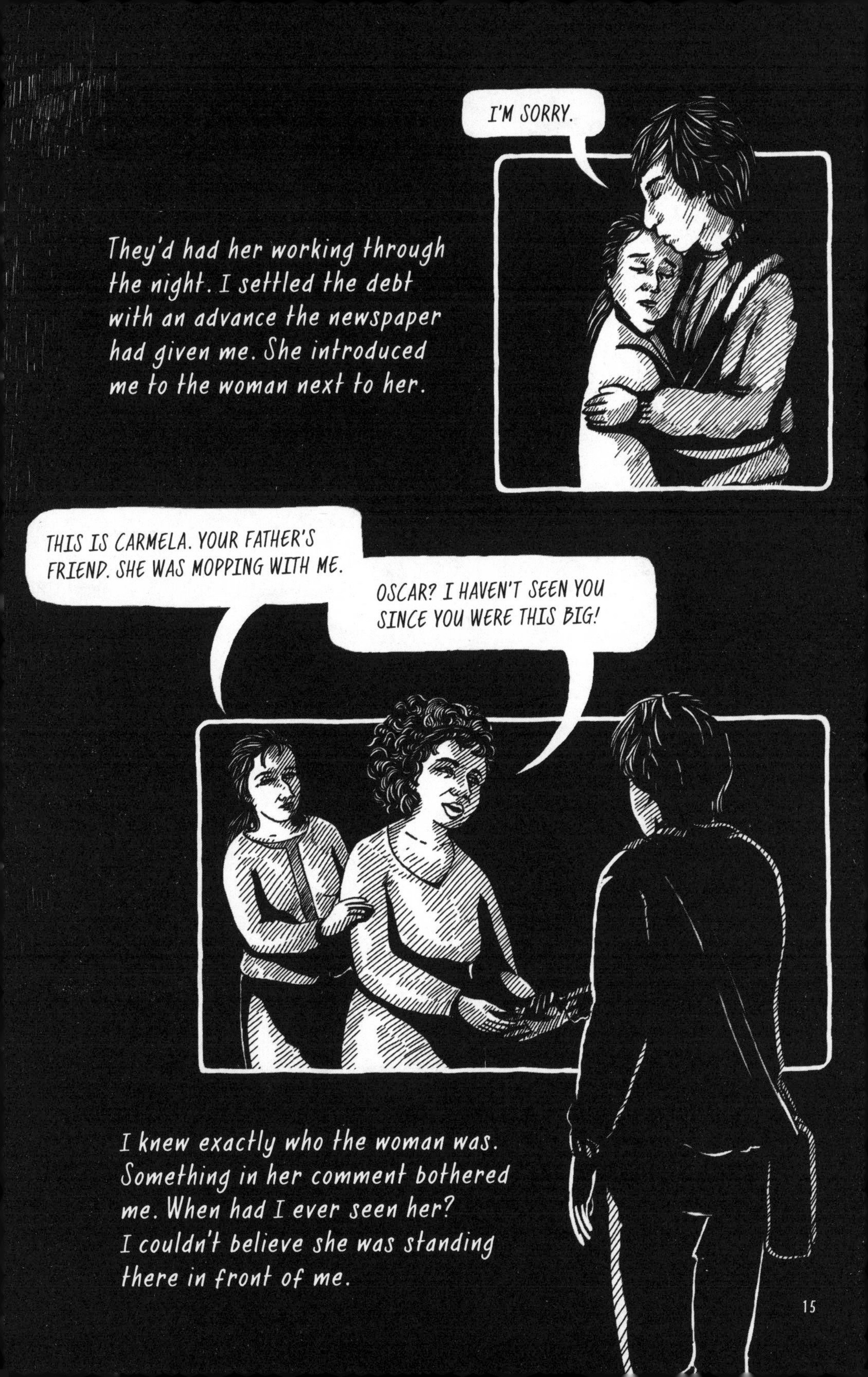
They'd had her working through the night. I settled the debt with an advance the newspaper had given me. She introduced me to the woman next to her.
I'M SORRY.
THIS IS CARMELA. YOUR FATHER'S FRIEND. SHE WAS MOPPING WITH ME.
OSCAR? I HAVEN'T SEEN YOU SINCE YOU WERE THIS BIG!
I knew exactly who the woman was. Something in her comment bothered me. When had I ever seen her? I couldn't believe she was standing there in front of me.

Carmela had been my father's lover, then his common-law wife. She was prettier than I had imagined. At the velorio, my mother and Carmela cried and consoled each other.

I met Carmela's three sons. They were my brothers, that much was clear. We all had an air of Don Hugo.

For twelve years I had insulated myself from my old man's other life—since he left us, right after my fourteenth birthday. No one had foreseen the illness that brought him down.

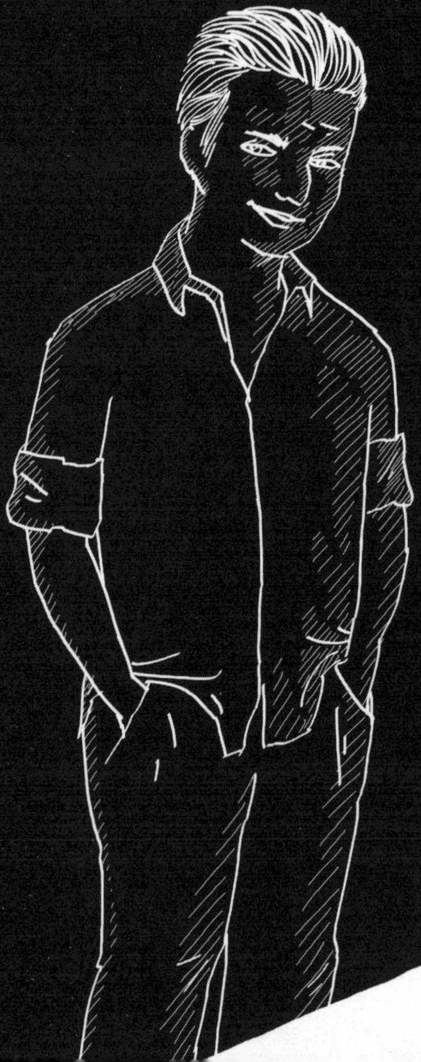

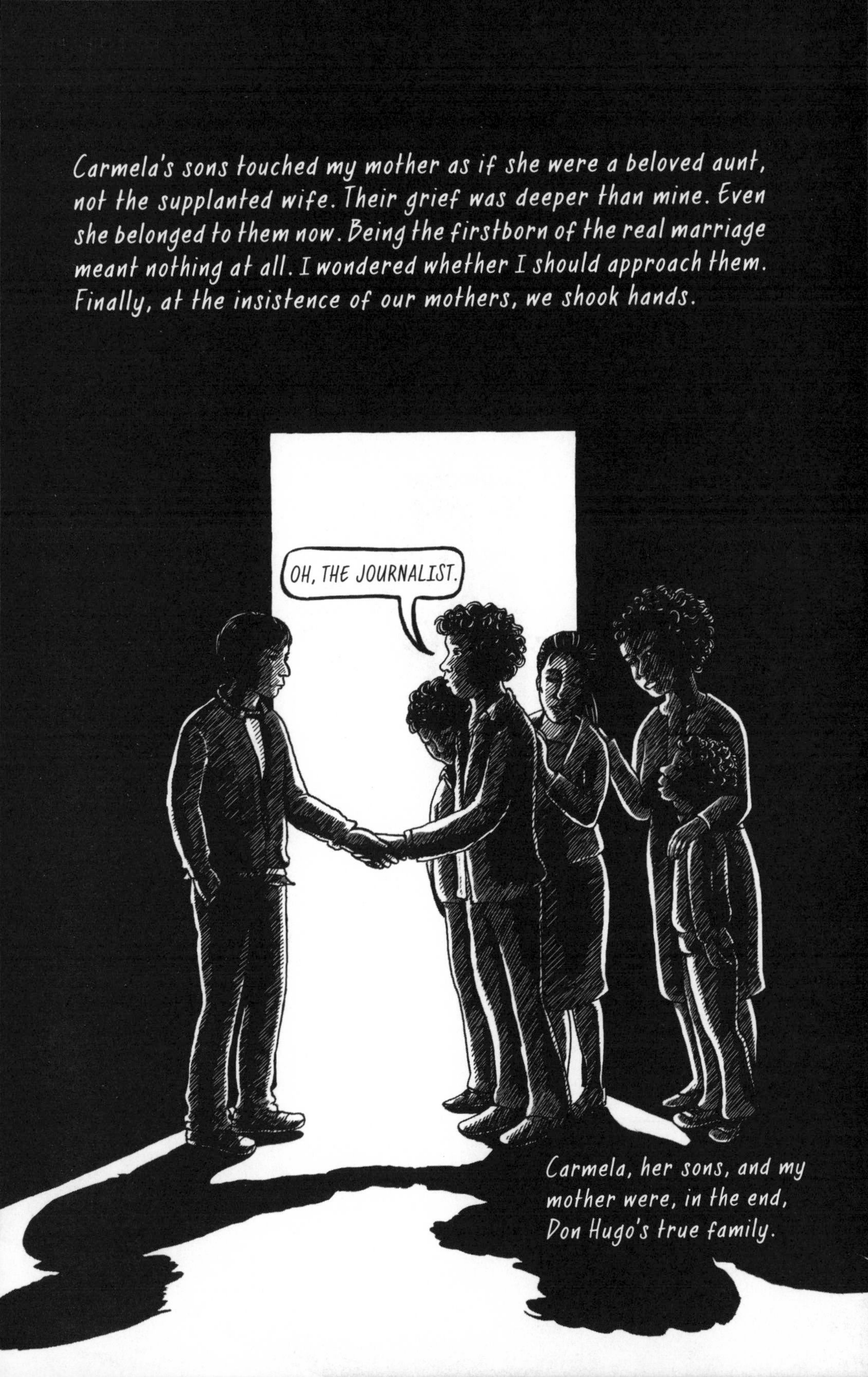
Carmela's sons touched my mother as if she were a beloved aunt, not the supplanted wife. Their grief was deeper than mine. Even she belonged to them now. Being the firstborn of the real marriage meant nothing at all. I wondered whether I should approach them. Finally, at the insistence of our mothers, we shook hands.
OH, THE JOURNALIST.
Carmela, her sons, and my mother were, in the end, Don Hugo's true family.

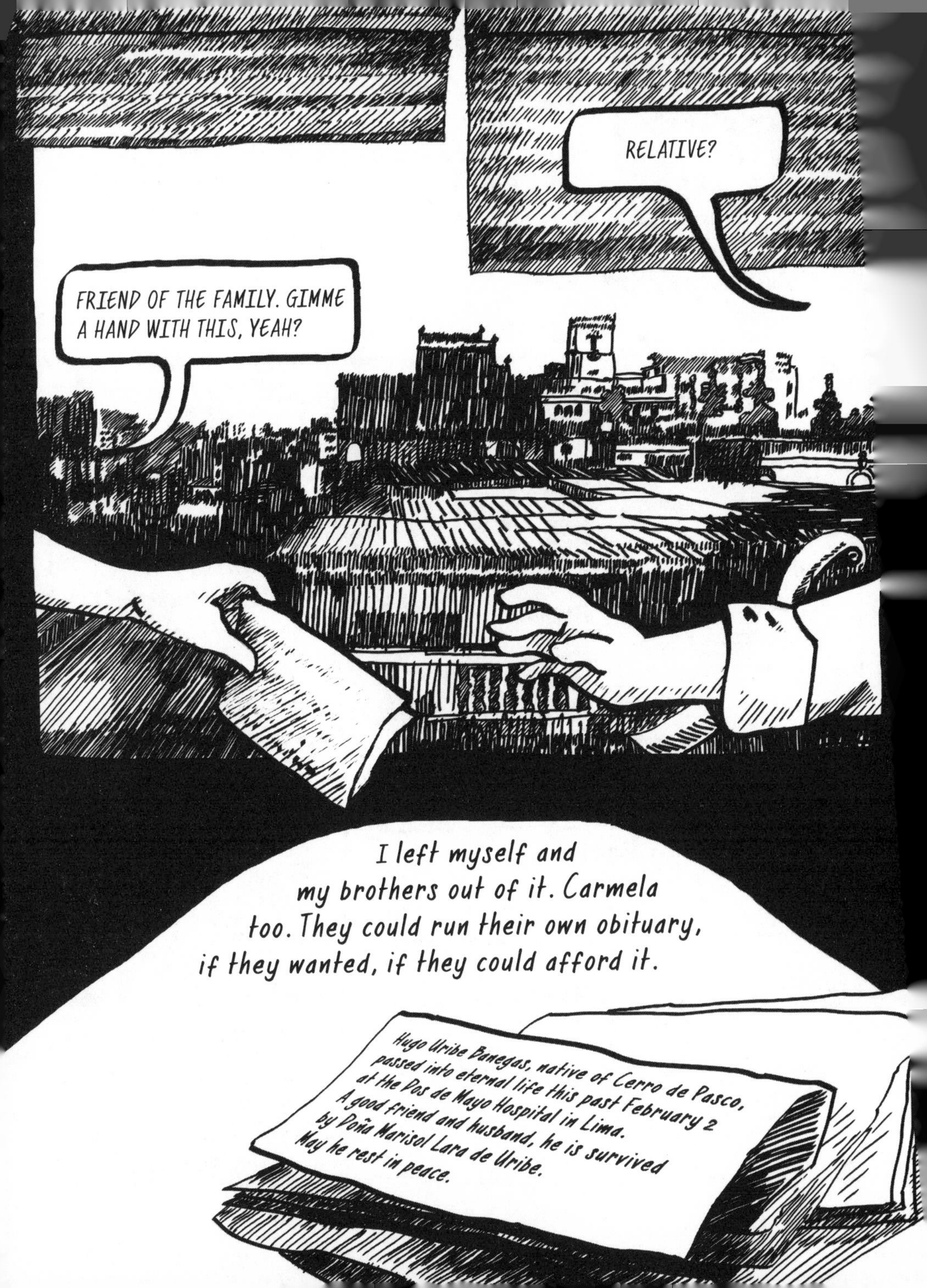
RELATIVE?
FRIEND OF THE FAMILY. GIMME A HAND WITH THIS, YEAH?
I left myself and my brothers out of it. Carmela too. They could run their own obituary, if they wanted, if they could afford it.
Hugo Uribe Banegas, native of Cerro de Pasco, passed into eternal life this past February 2 at the Dos de Mayo Hospital in Lima. A good friend and husband, he is survived by Doña Marisol Lara de Uribe. May he rest in peace.

iN LiMA

Those who die in phantasmagoric fashion, violently, spectacularly, are celebrated in the fifty-cent papers beneath gory headlines.

I don't work at that kind of newspaper, but if I did, I would write those headlines too. Like my father, I never refuse work.

I've covered drug busts, double homicides, fires at discos and markets, traffic accidents, bombs in shopping centers.

DYiNG iS

I've profiled corrupt politicians, drunken has-been soccer players, artists who hate the world.

But I've never covered the unexpected death of a middle-aged worker in a public hospital.

Mourned by his wife. His child. His other wife. Her children. My father's dying was not news.

THE LOCAL SPORT

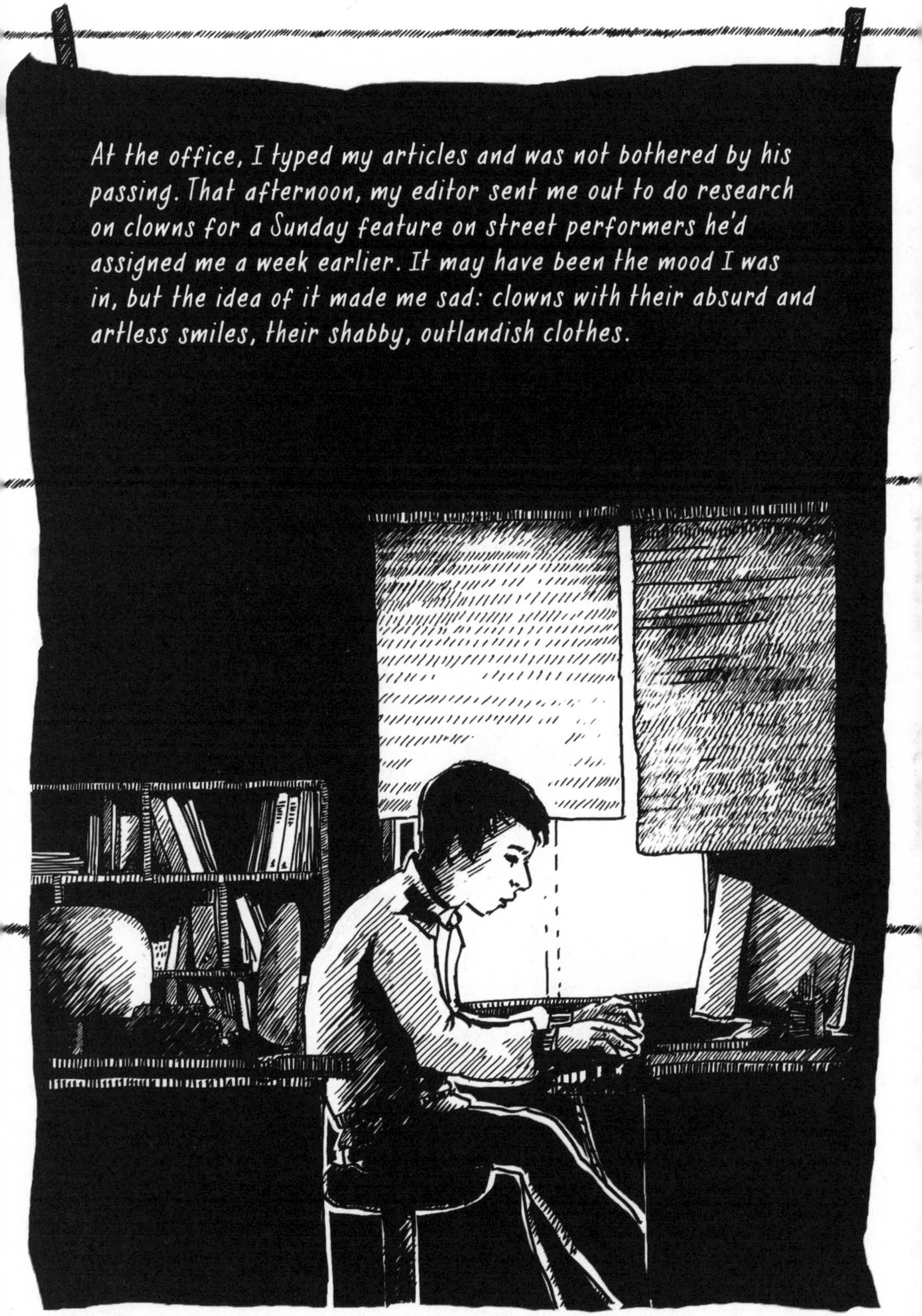
At the office, I typed my articles and was not bothered by his passing. That afternoon, my editor sent me out to do research on clowns for a Sunday feature on street performers he'd assigned me a week earlier. It may have been the mood I was in, but the idea of it made me sad: clowns with their absurd and artless smiles, their shabby, outlandish clothes.

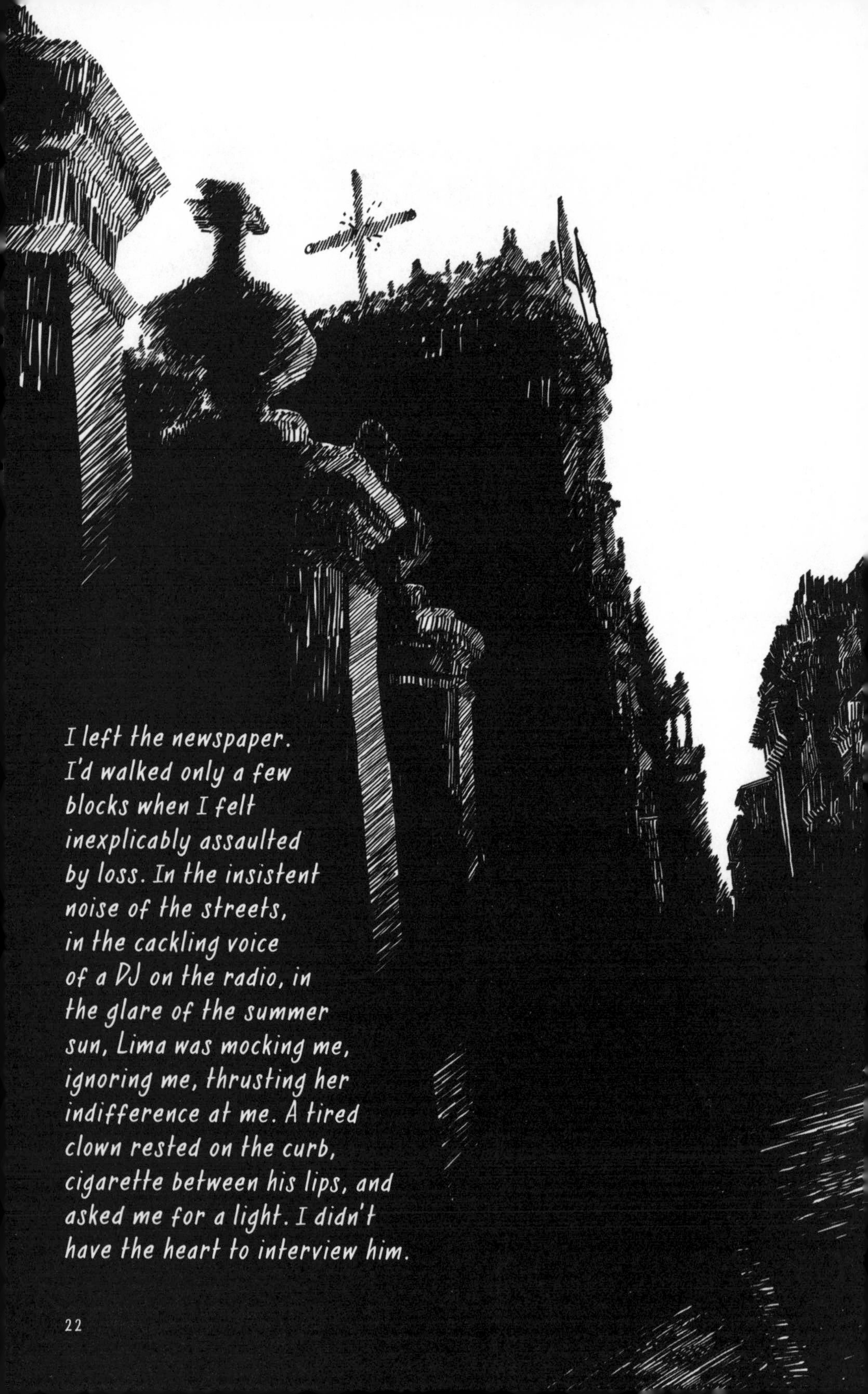
I left the newspaper. I'd walked only a few blocks when I felt inexplicably assaulted by loss. In the insistent noise of the streets, in the cackling voice of a DJ on the radio, in the glare of the summer sun, Lima was mocking me, ignoring me, thrusting her indifference at me. A tired clown rested on the curb, cigarette between his lips, and asked me for a light. I didn't have the heart to interview him.

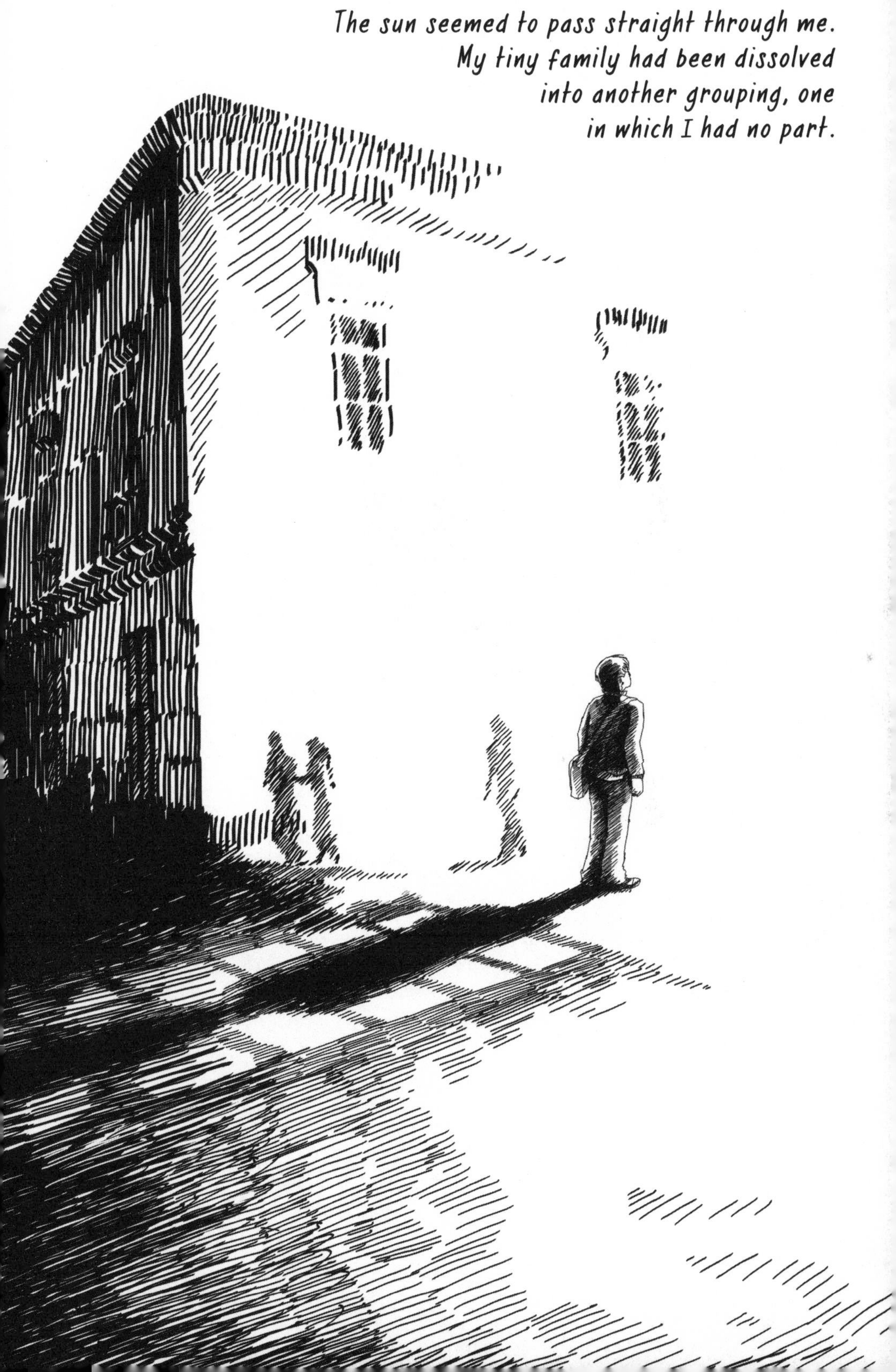
The sun seemed to pass straight through me. My tiny family had been dissolved into another grouping, one in which I had no part.

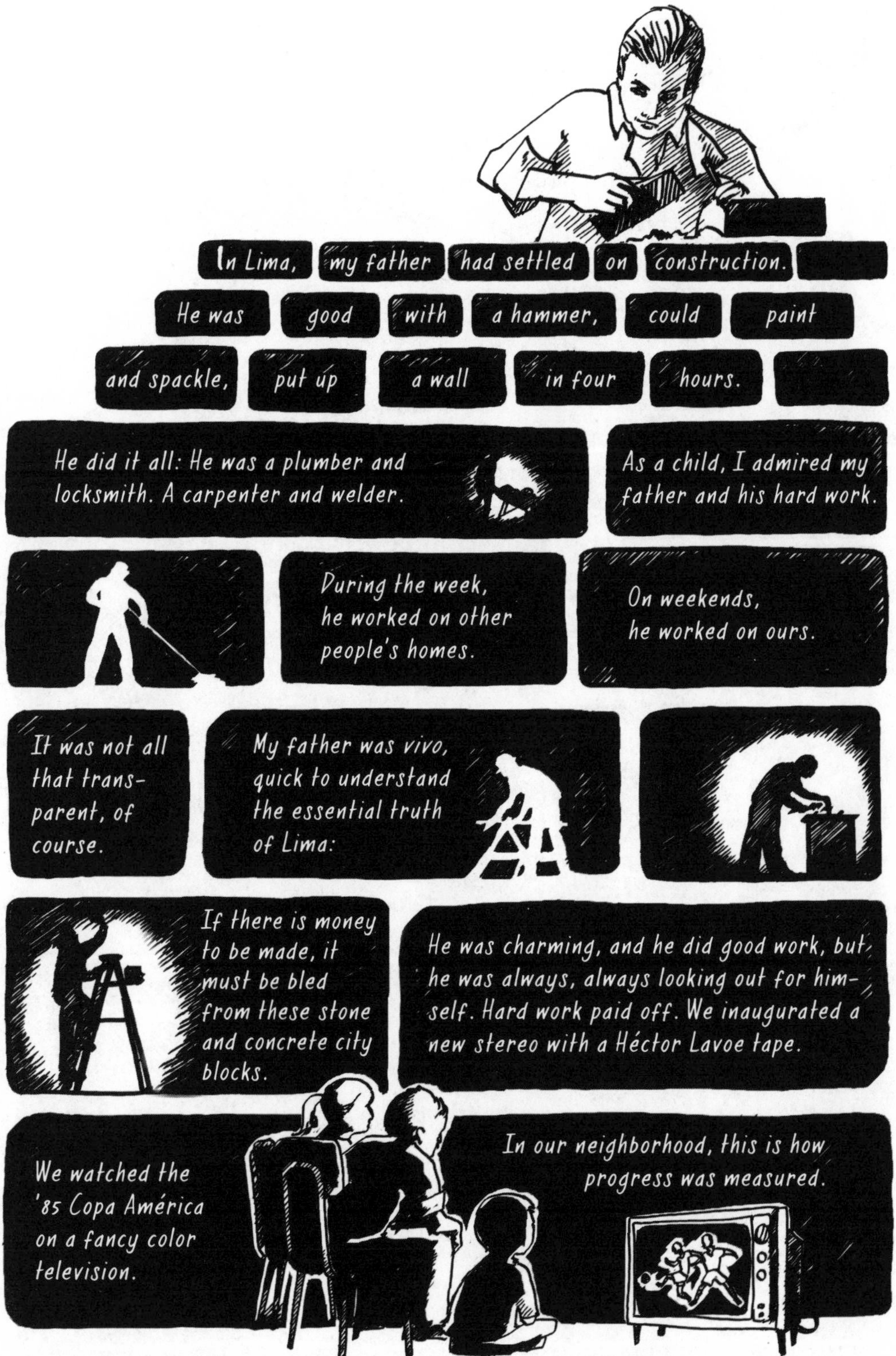
In Lima, my father had settled on construction.
He was good with a hammer, could paint
and spackle, put up a wall in four hours.
He did it all: He was a plumber and locksmith. A carpenter and welder.
As a child, I admired my father and his hard work.
During the week, he worked on other people's homes.
On weekends, he worked on ours.
It was not all that trans-parent, of course.
My father was vivo, quick to understand the essential truth of Lima:
If there is money to be made, it must be bled from these stone and concrete city blocks.
He was charming, and he did good work, but he was always, always looking out for him-self. Hard work paid off. We inaugurated a new stereo with a Héctor Lavoe tape.
We watched the '85 Copa América on a fancy color television.
In our neighborhood, this is how progress was measured.

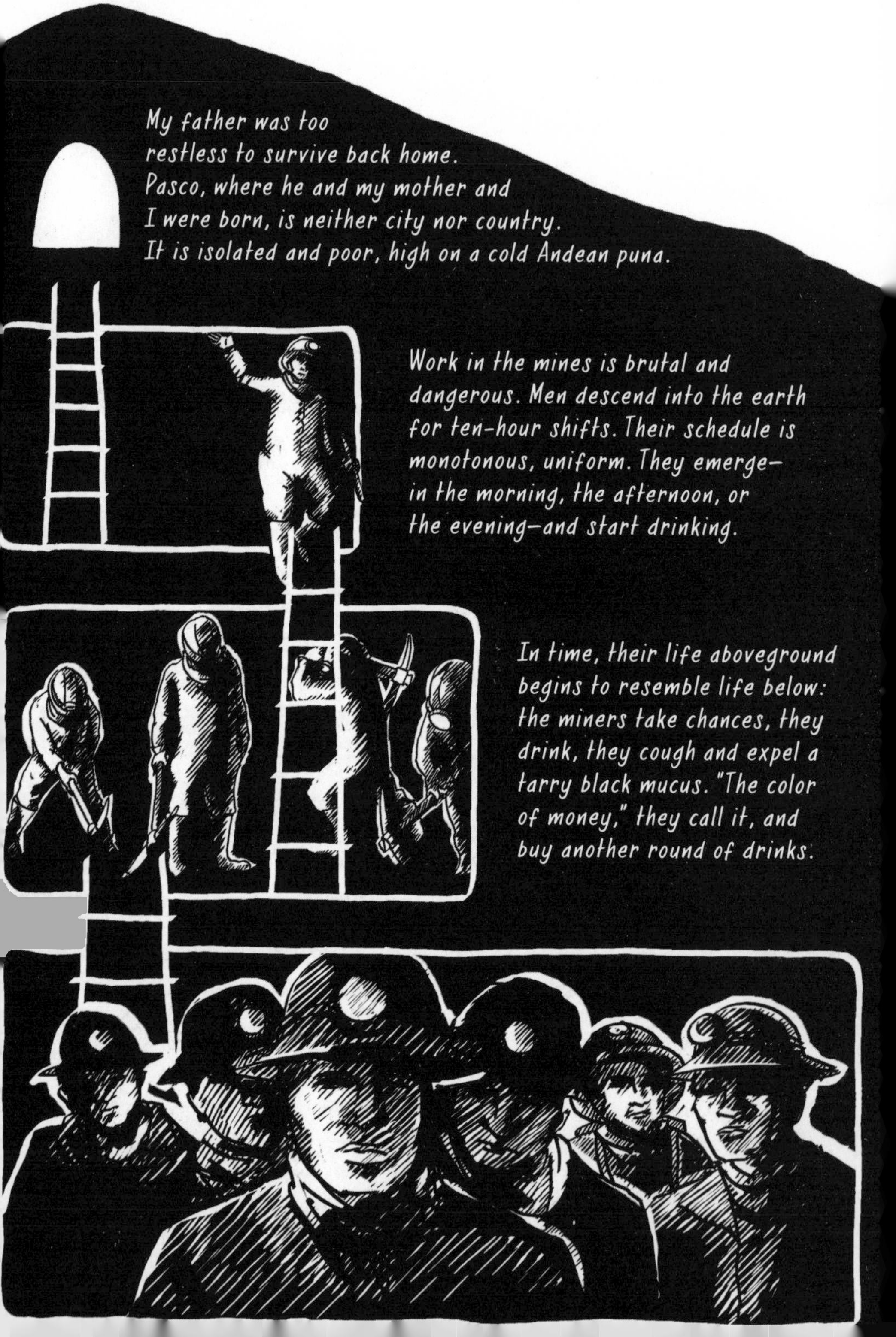
My father was too
restless to survive back home.
Pasco, where he and my mother and
I were born, is neither city nor country.
It is isolated and poor, high on a cold Andean puna.
Work in the mines is brutal and
dangerous. Men descend into the earth
for ten-hour shifts. Their schedule is
monotonous, uniform. They emerge—
in the morning, the afternoon, or
the evening—and start drinking.
In time, their life aboveground
begins to resemble life below:
the miners take chances, they
drink, they cough and expel a
tarry black mucus. "The color
of money," they call it, and
buy another round of drinks.

My old man wasn't suited to those rituals.
There was no future in Pasco, so he came to Lima to find it.

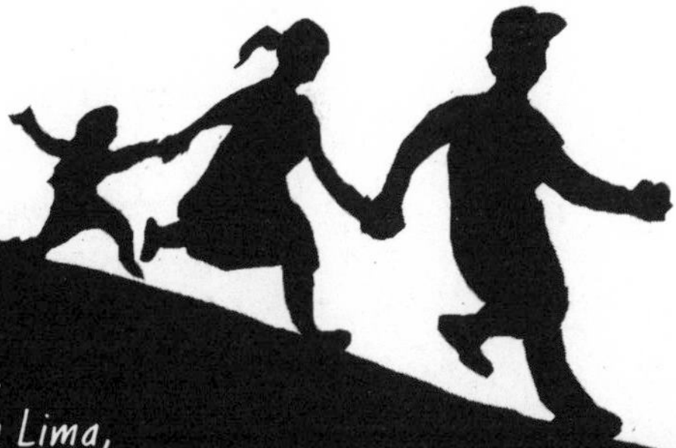

He started driving trucks to the coast and into the city. He was twenty-nine when he married my mother, nearly a decade older than his young wife. He'd spent most of his twenties working in Lima, coming back only once every three or four months. Somehow a romance blossomed on his trips home. By the time they married, they'd been a couple for five years already. I was born six months after the wedding. He went on coming and going for years, making a home for himself in the city, in the district of San Juan de Lurigancho. When my mother would no longer tolerate being left alone, he brought us here too. I was eight years old. I think moving us to the city was the only good thing he ever did for us.

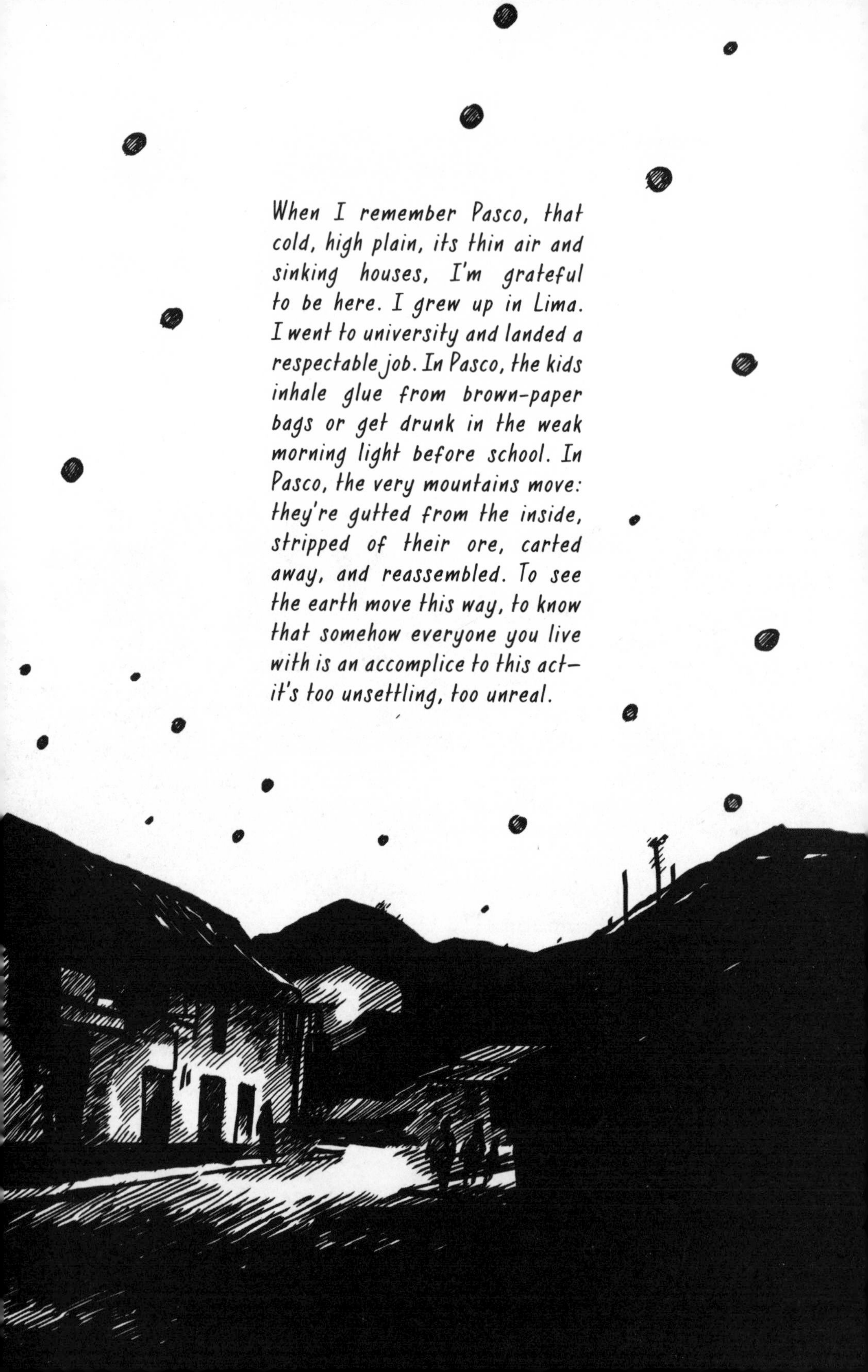
When I remember Pasco, that cold, high plain, its thin air and sinking houses, I'm grateful to be here. I grew up in Lima. I went to university and landed a respectable job. In Pasco, the kids inhale glue from brown-paper bags or get drunk in the weak morning light before school. In Pasco, the very mountains move: they're gutted from the inside, stripped of their ore, carted away, and reassembled. To see the earth move this way, to know that somehow everyone you live with is an accomplice to this act—it's too unsettling, too unreal.

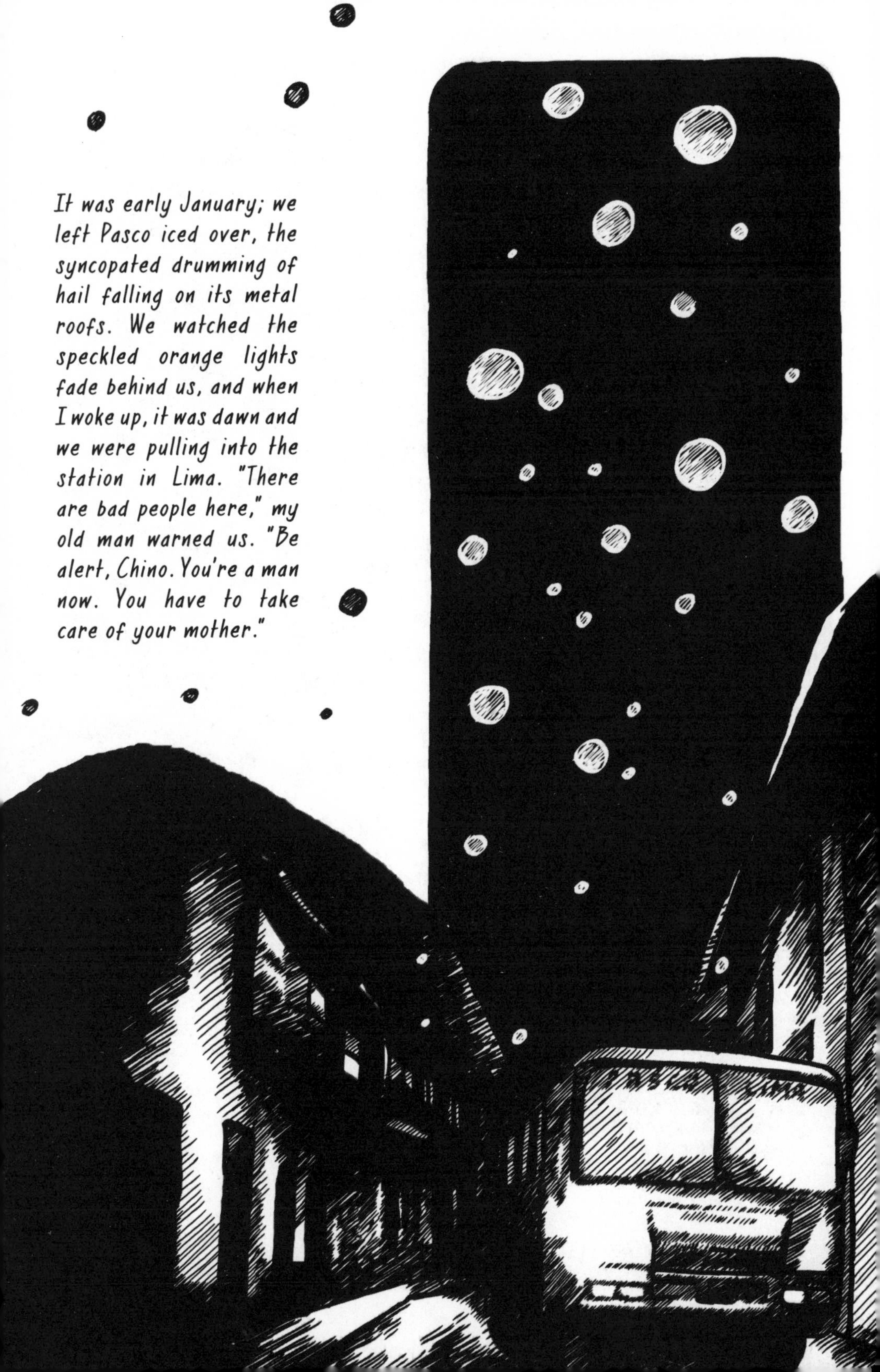
It was early January; we left Pasco iced over, the syncopated drumming of hail falling on its metal roofs. We watched the speckled orange lights fade behind us, and when I woke up, it was dawn and we were pulling into the station in Lima. "There are bad people here," my old man warned us. "Be alert, Chino. You're a man now. You have to take care of your mother."
PASCO
LIMA

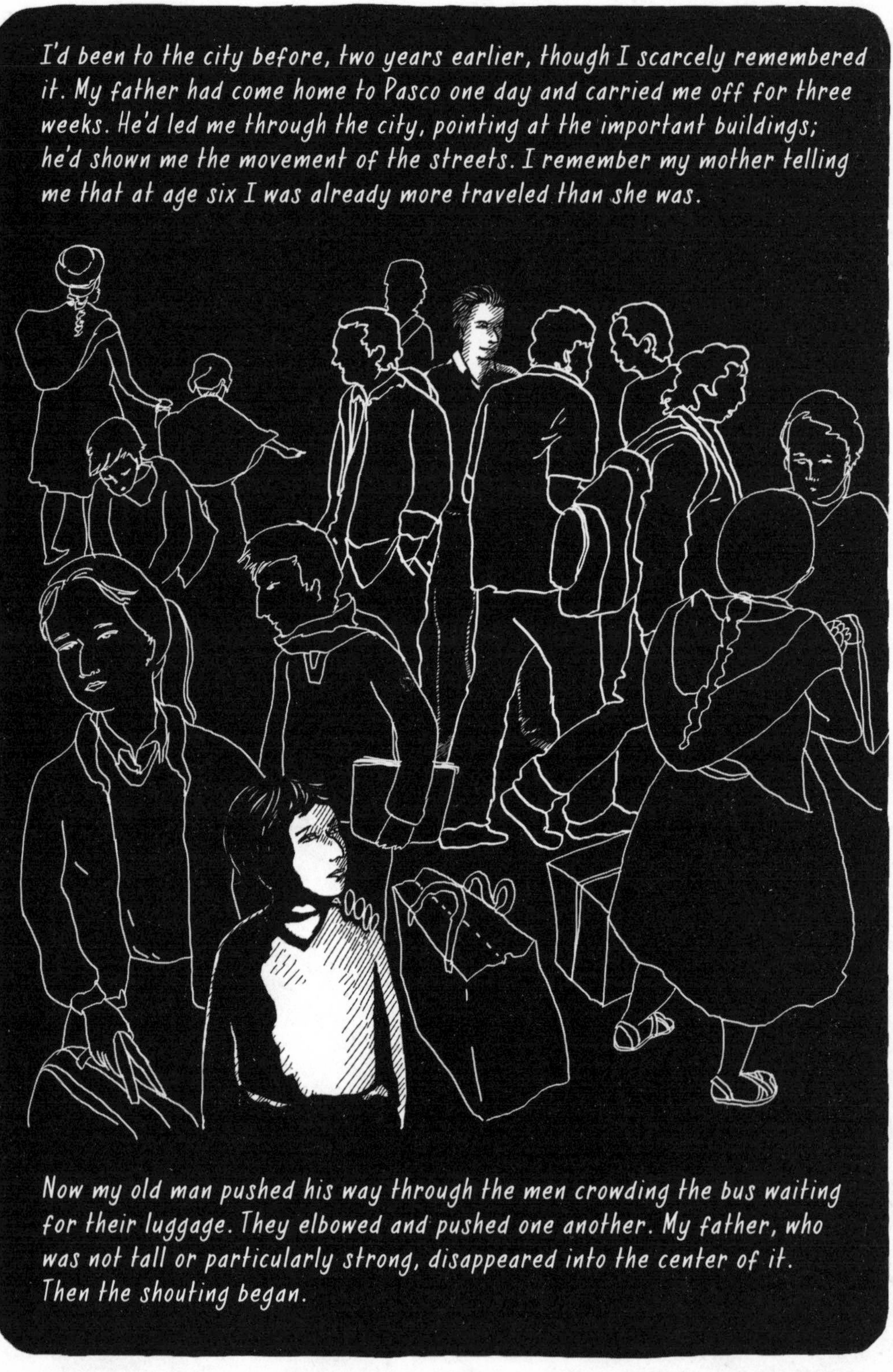
I'd been to the city before, two years earlier, though I scarcely remembered it. My father had come home to Pasco one day and carried me off for three weeks. He'd led me through the city, pointing at the important buildings; he'd shown me the movement of the streets. I remember my mother telling me that at age six I was already more traveled than she was.
Now my old man pushed his way through the men crowding the bus waiting for their luggage. They elbowed and pushed one another. My father, who was not tall or particularly strong, disappeared into the center of it. Then the shouting began.

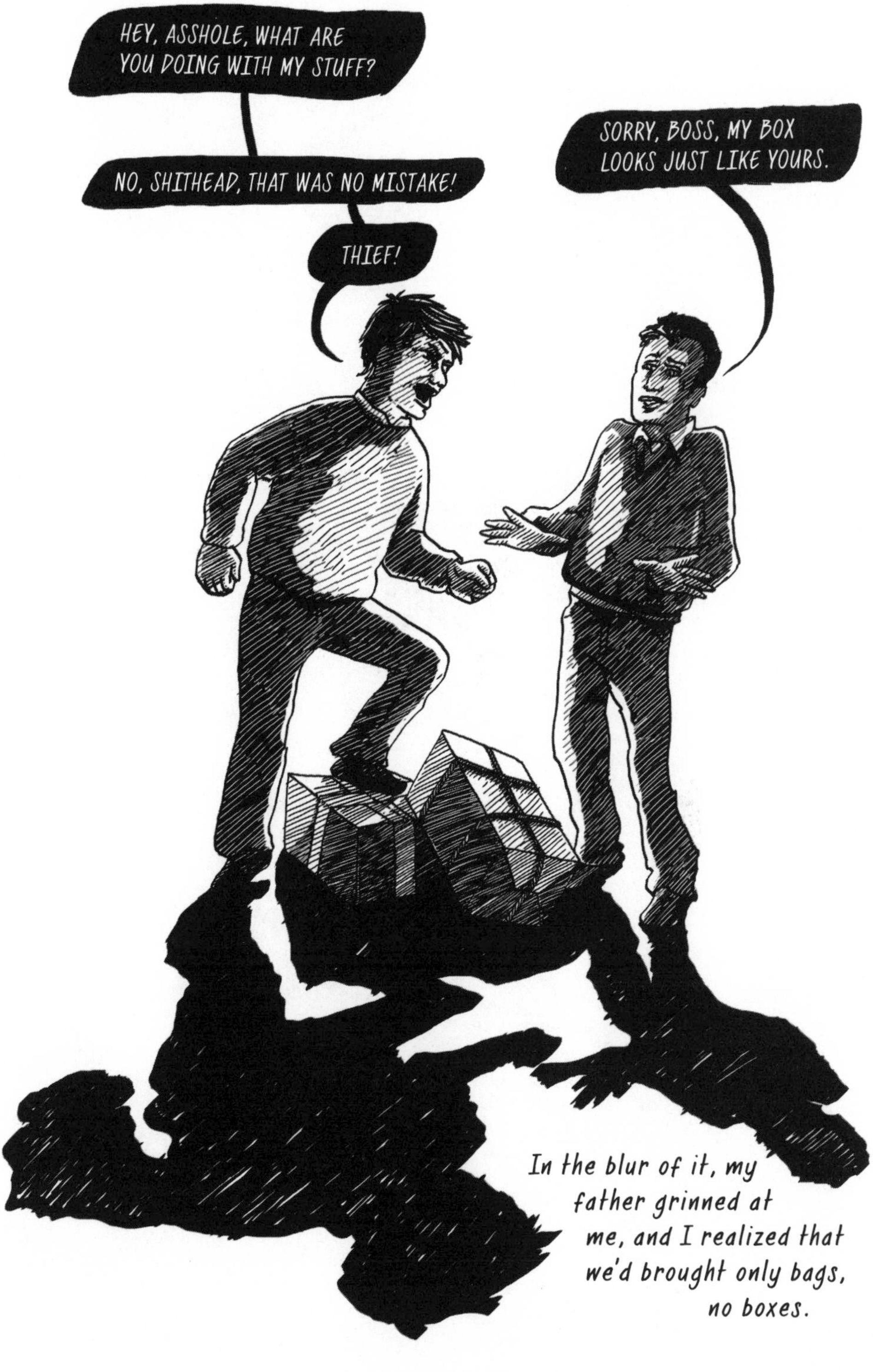
HEY, ASSHOLE, WHAT ARE YOU DOING WITH MY STUFF?
NO, SHITHEAD, THAT WAS NO MISTAKE!
THIEF!
SORRY, BOSS, MY BOX LOOKS JUST LIKE YOURS.
In the blur of it, my father grinned at me, and I realized that we'd brought only bags, no boxes.

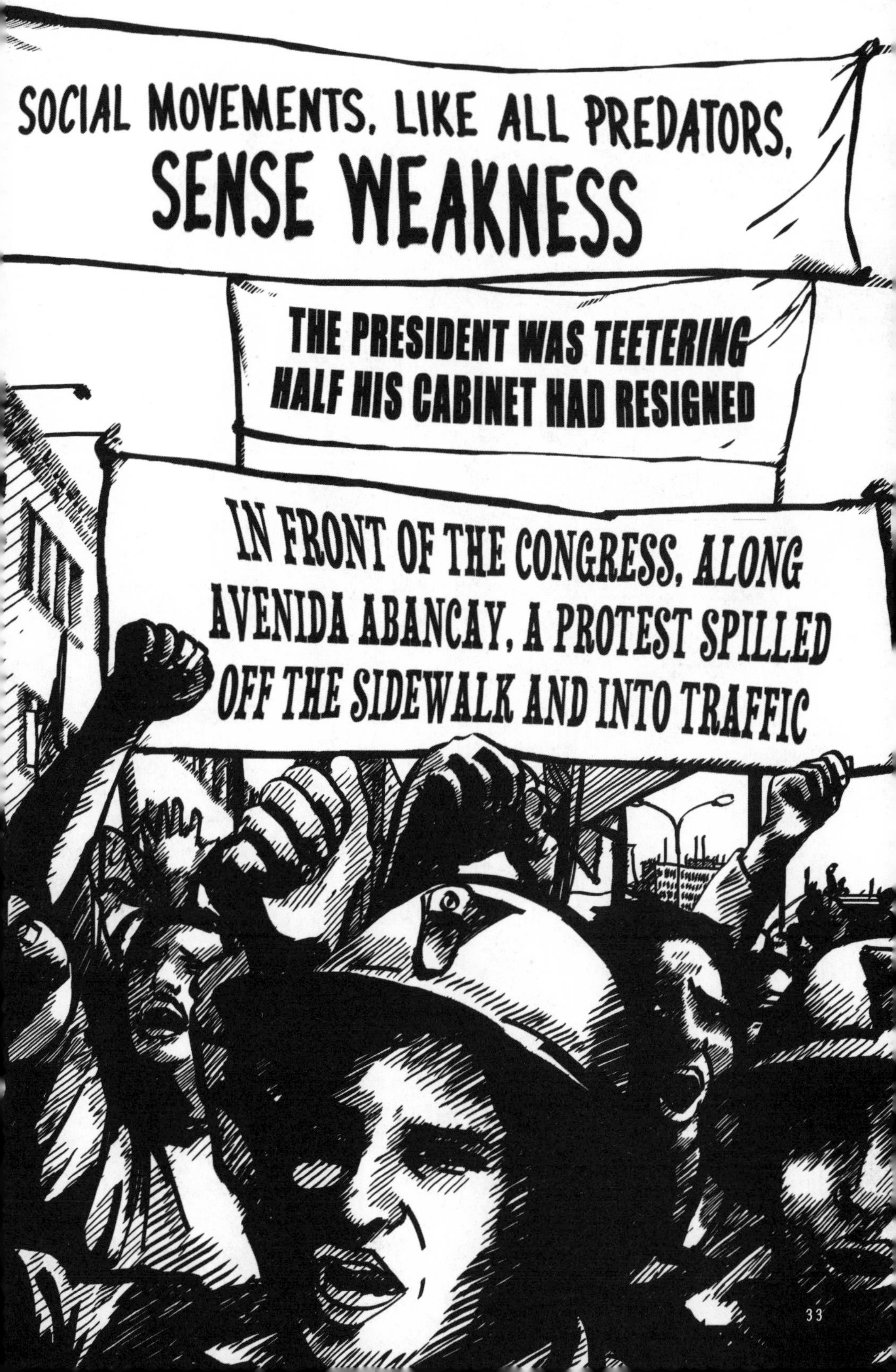
SOCIAL MOVEMENTS, LIKE ALL PREDATORS, SENSE WEAKNESS
THE PRESIDENT WAS TEETERING
HALF HIS CABINET HAD RESIGNED
IN FRONT OF THE CONGRESS, ALONG AVENIDA ABANCAY, A PROTEST SPILLED OFF THE SIDEWALK AND INTO TRAFFIC

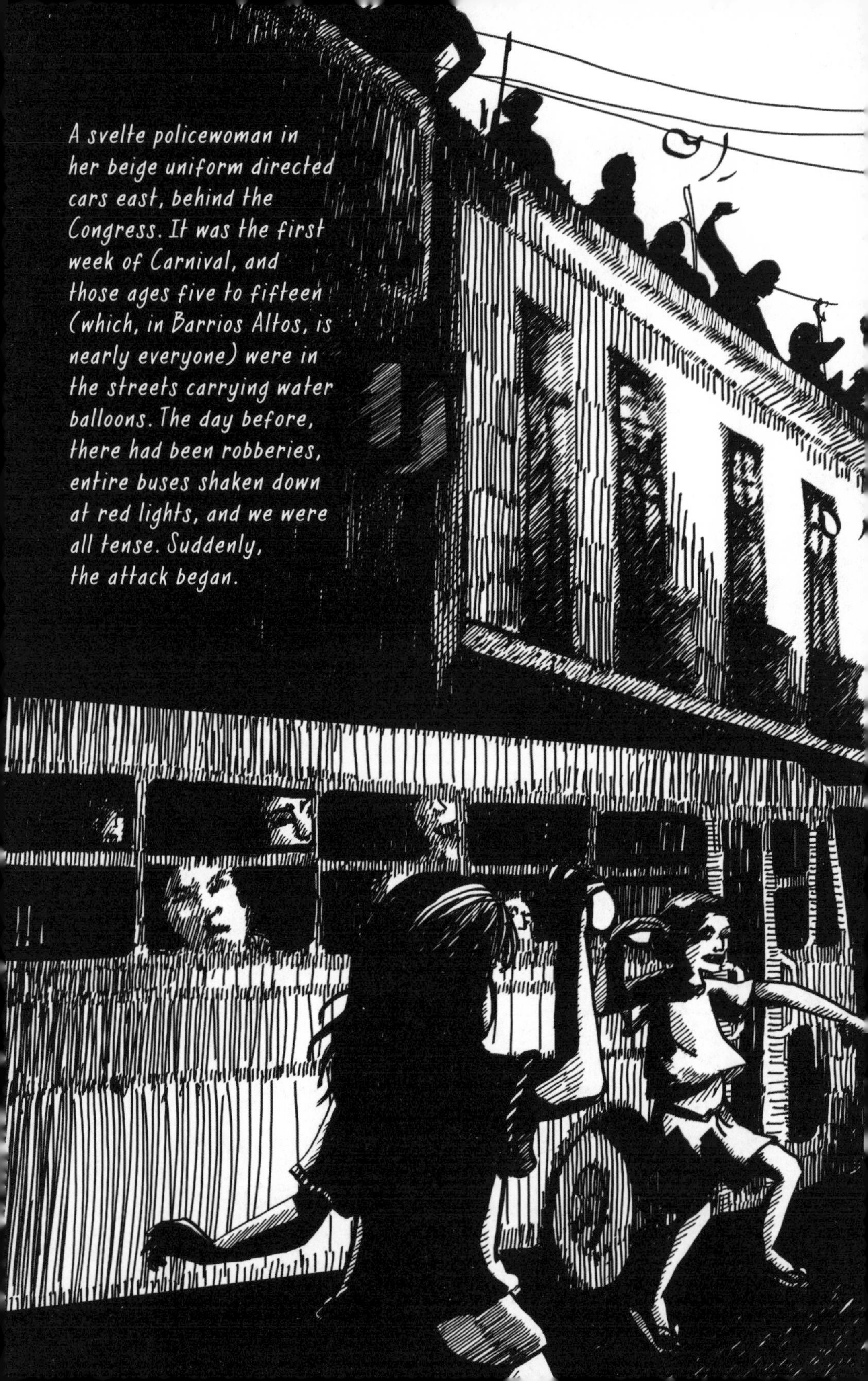
A svelte policewoman in her beige uniform directed cars east, behind the Congress. It was the first week of Carnival, and those ages five to fifteen (which, in Barrios Altos, is nearly everyone) were in the streets carrying water balloons. The day before, there had been robberies, entire buses shaken down at red lights, and we were all tense. Suddenly, the attack began.

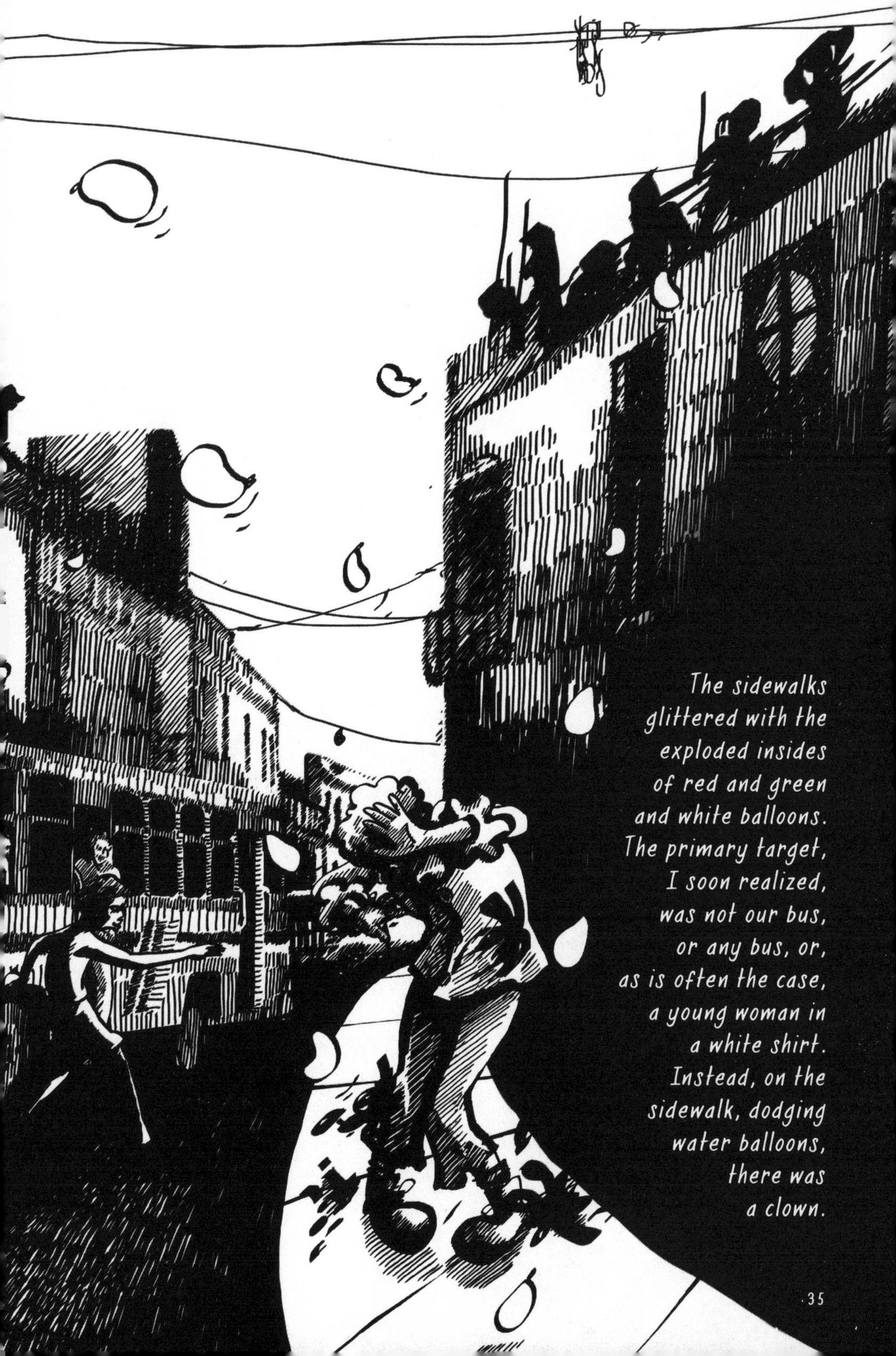
The sidewalks glittered with the exploded insides of red and green and white balloons. The primary target, I soon realized, was not our bus, or any bus, or, as is often the case, a young woman in a white shirt. Instead, on the sidewalk, dodging water balloons, there was a clown.

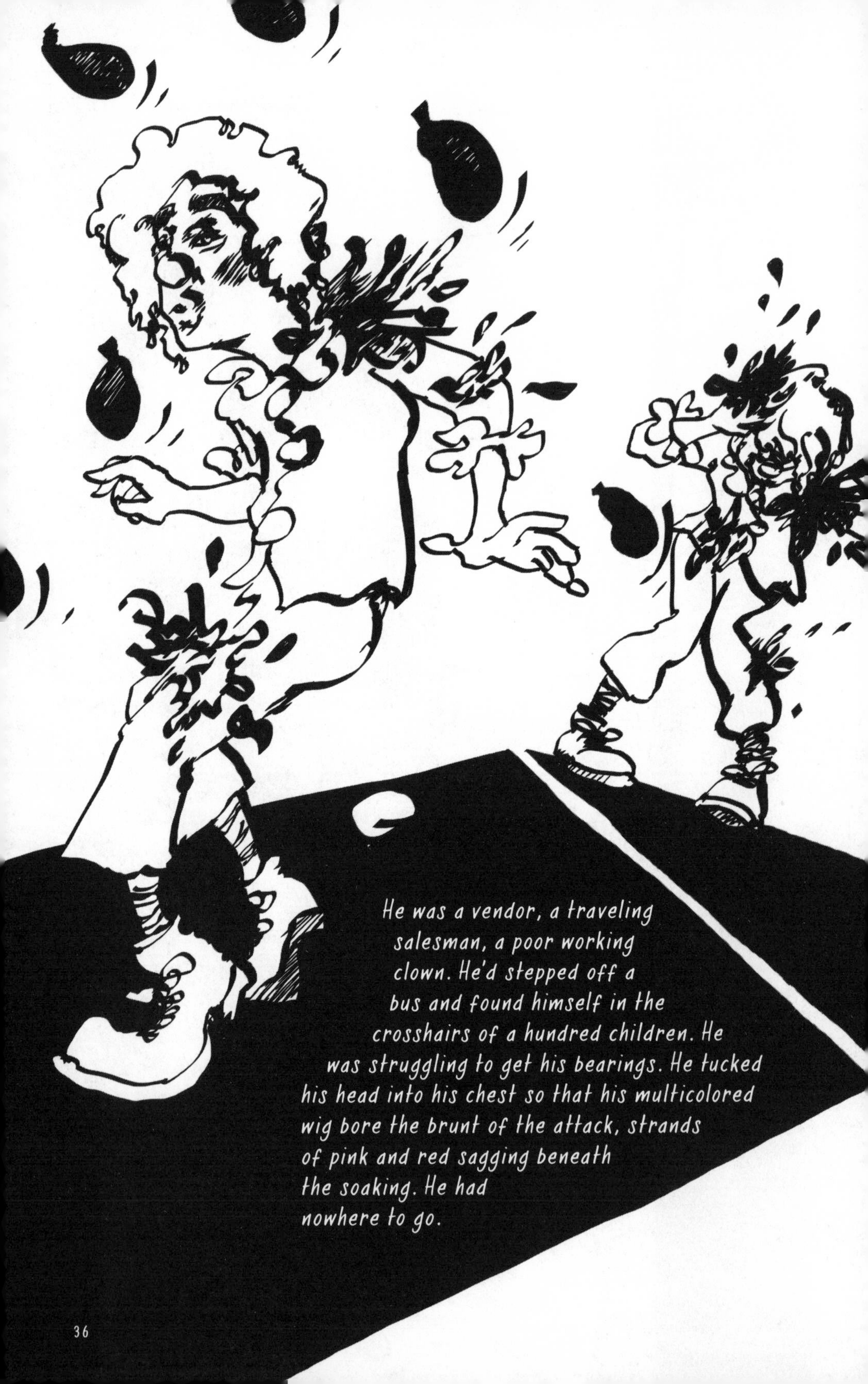
He was a vendor, a traveling salesman, a poor working clown. He'd stepped off a bus and found himself in the crosshairs of a hundred children. He was struggling to get his bearings. He tucked his head into his chest so that his multicolored wig bore the brunt of the attack, strands of pink and red sagging beneath the soaking. He had nowhere to go.

The ticket collector, moved by pity, opened the door and pulled the clown in.

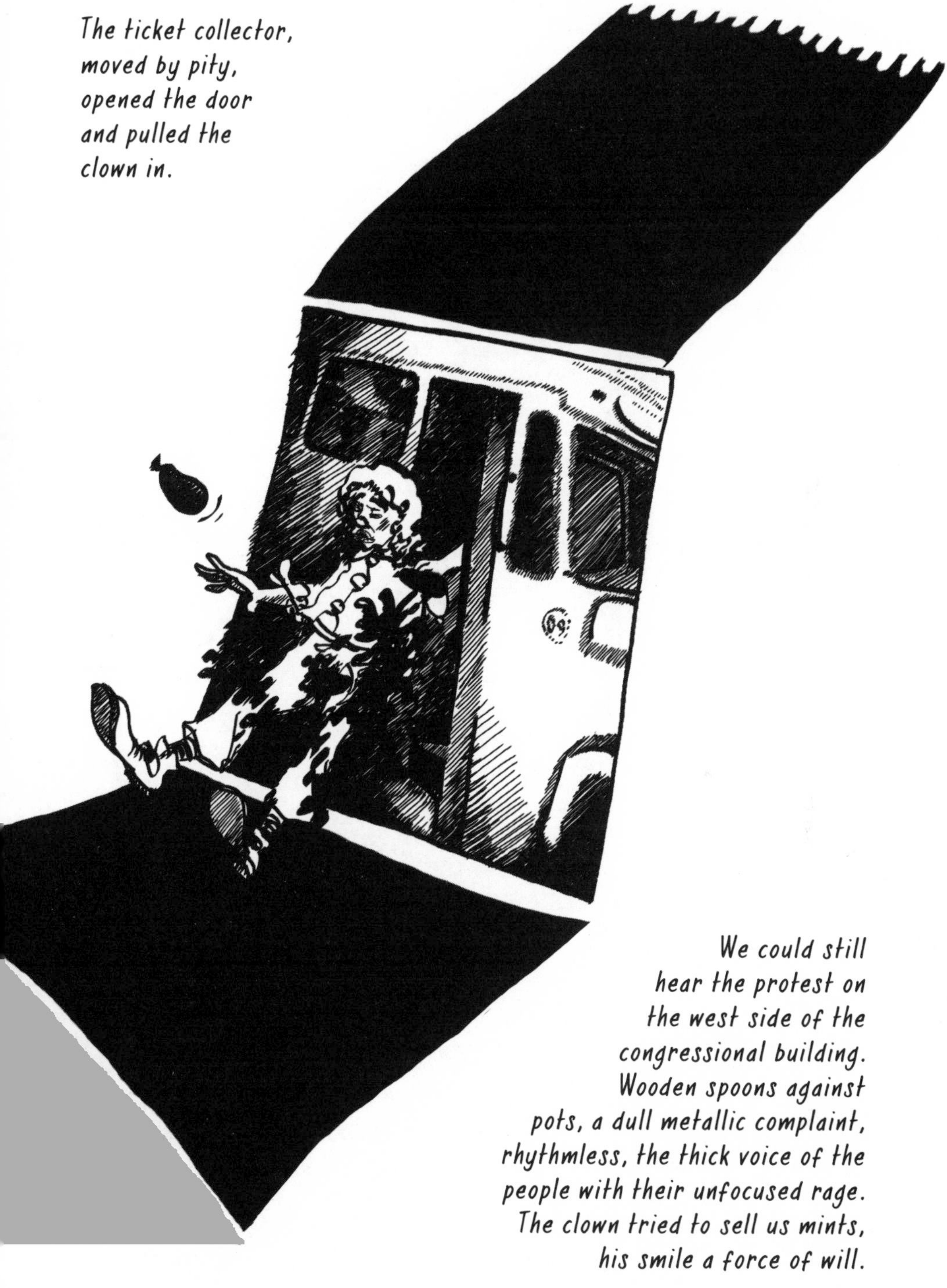

We could still hear the protest on the west side of the congressional building. Wooden spoons against pots, a dull metallic complaint, rhythmless, the thick voice of the people with their unfocused rage. The clown tried to sell us mints, his smile a force of will.

The newsroom swarmed with activity; a presidential pronouncement on the economy had set everyone to work. There were rumors: a cabinet member had fled the country. I didn't pay much attention. I left the office early and went to San Juan to see my mother.

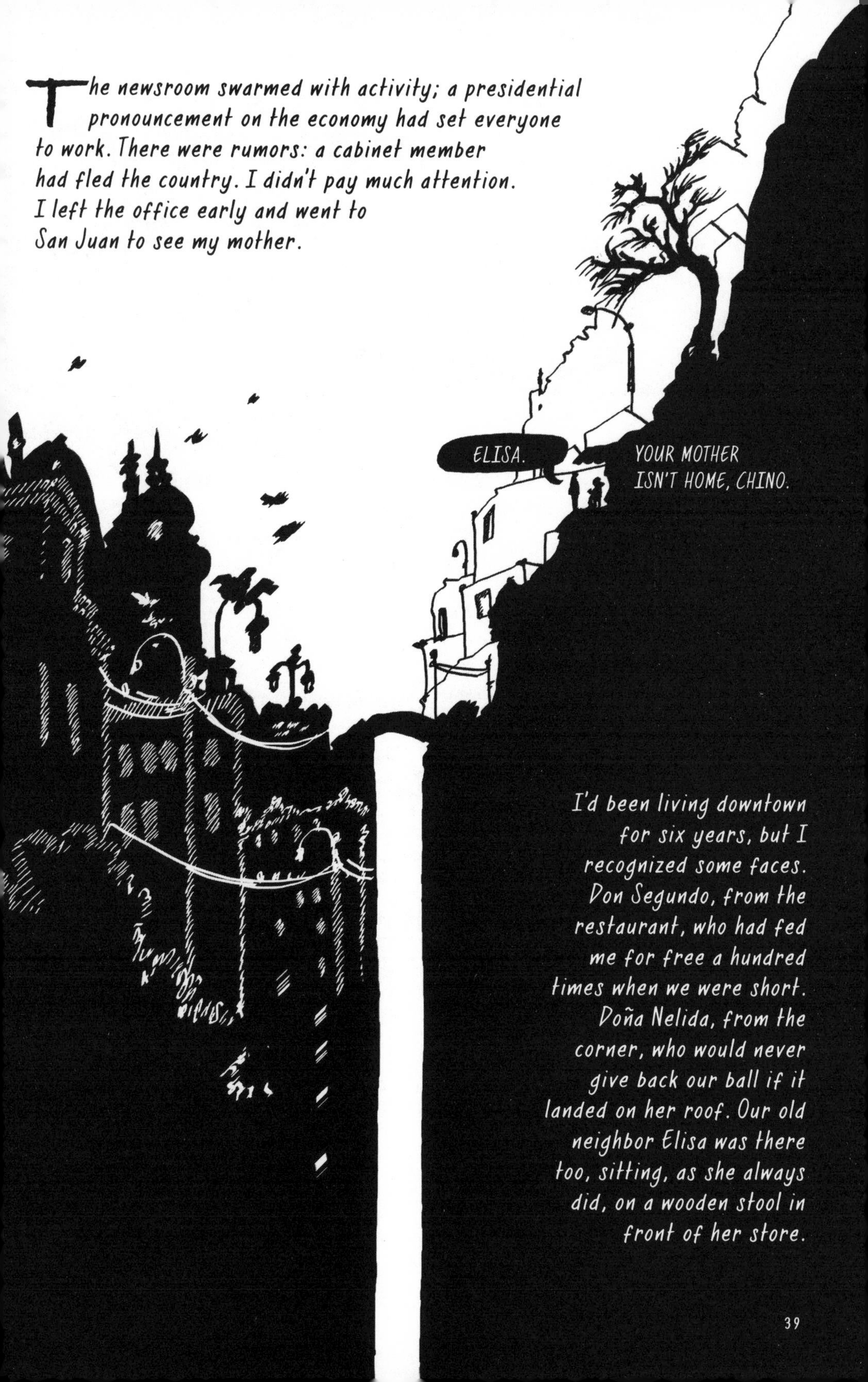
ELISA.
YOUR MOTHER ISN'T HOME, CHINO.
I'd been living downtown for six years, but I recognized some faces. Don Segundo, from the restaurant, who had fed me for free a hundred times when we were short. Doña Nelida, from the corner, who would never give back our ball if it landed on her roof. Our old neighbor Elisa was there too, sitting, as she always did, on a wooden stool in front of her store.

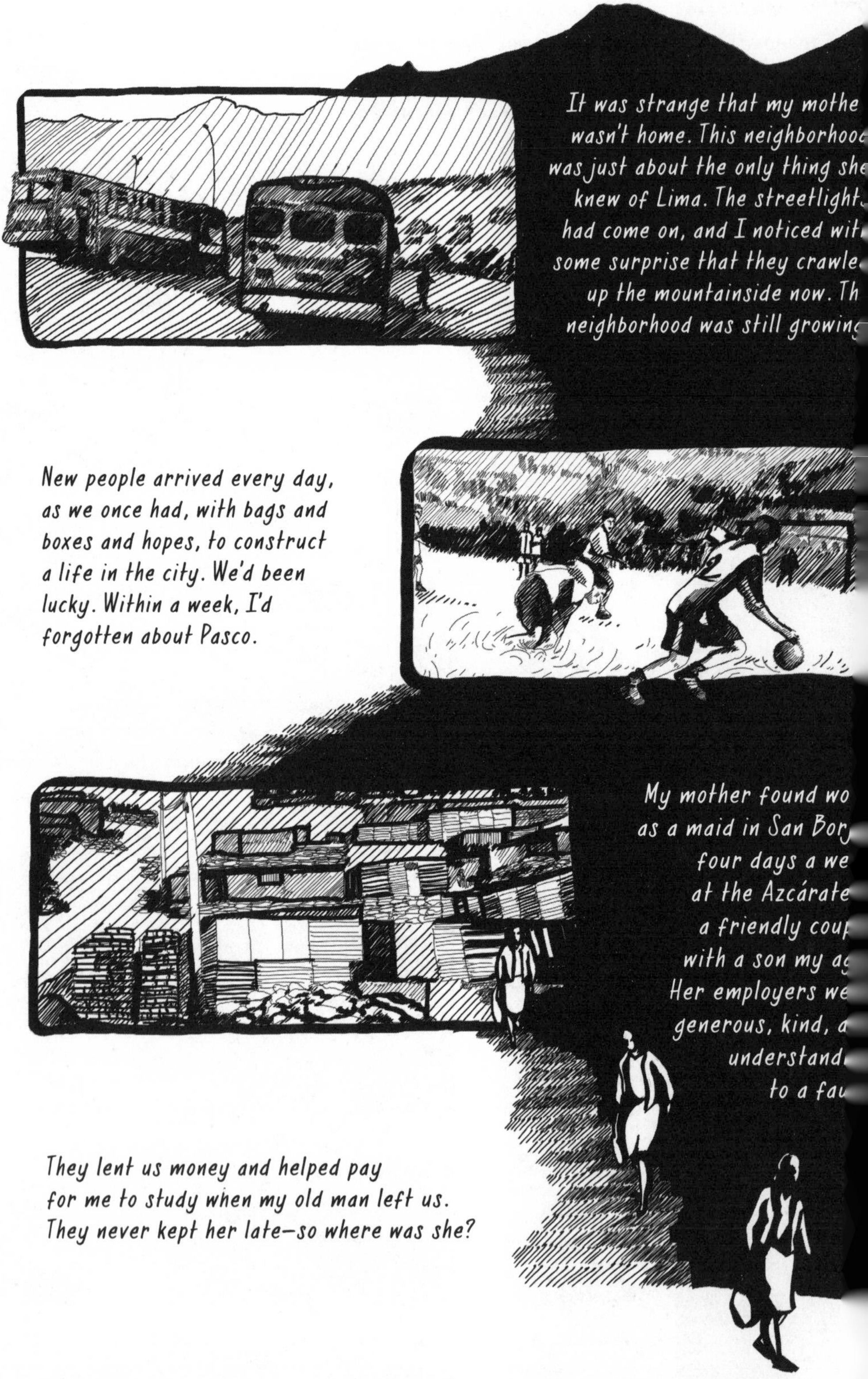
It was strange that my mothe
wasn't home. This neighborhoo
was just about the only thing she
knew of Lima. The streetlights
had come on, and I noticed wit
some surprise that they crawle
up the mountainside now. Th
neighborhood was still growing
New people arrived every day,
as we once had, with bags and
boxes and hopes, to construct
a life in the city. We'd been
lucky. Within a week, I'd
forgotten about Pasco.
My mother found wo
as a maid in San Bor
four days a we
at the Azcárate
a friendly coup
with a son my ag
Her employers we
generous, kind, a
understand
to a fa
They lent us money and helped pay
for me to study when my old man left us.
They never kept her late—so where was she?

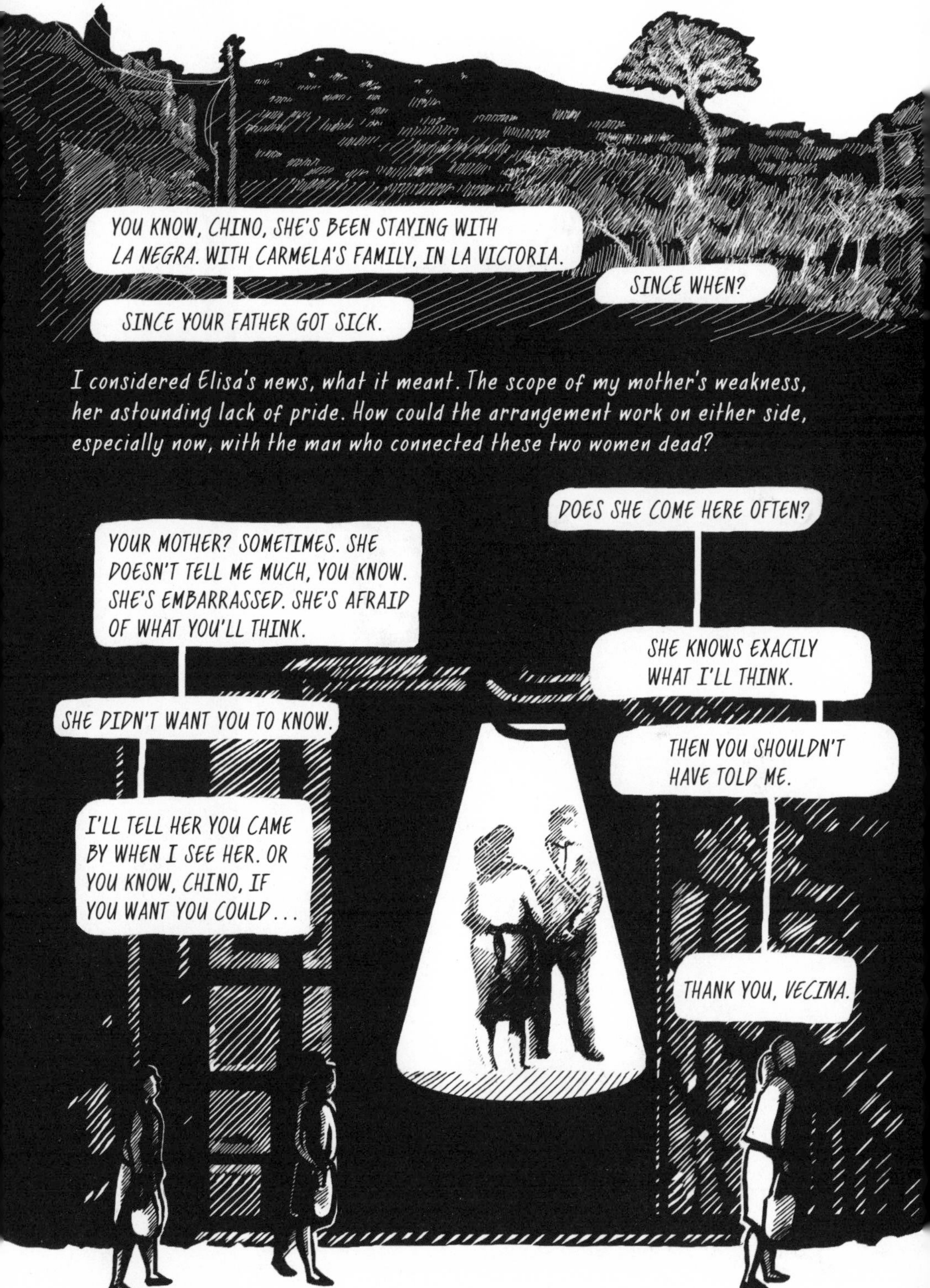
YOU KNOW, CHINO, SHE'S BEEN STAYING WITH LA NEGRA. WITH CARMELA'S FAMILY, IN LA VICTORIA.
SINCE WHEN?
SINCE YOUR FATHER GOT SICK.
I considered Elisa's news, what it meant. The scope of my mother's weakness, her astounding lack of pride. How could the arrangement work on either side, especially now, with the man who connected these two women dead?
DOES SHE COME HERE OFTEN?
YOUR MOTHER? SOMETIMES. SHE DOESN'T TELL ME MUCH, YOU KNOW. SHE'S EMBARRASSED. SHE'S AFRAID OF WHAT YOU'LL THINK.
SHE KNOWS EXACTLY WHAT I'LL THINK.
SHE DIDN'T WANT YOU TO KNOW.
THEN YOU SHOULDN'T HAVE TOLD ME.
I'LL TELL HER YOU CAME BY WHEN I SEE HER. OR YOU KNOW, CHINO, IF YOU WANT YOU COULD . . .
THANK YOU, VECINA.

I tried to picture my mother in her new home, sleeping on the guest bed or on a cot that she put away each morning.

My mother had capitulated. It made me dizzy to think of it.

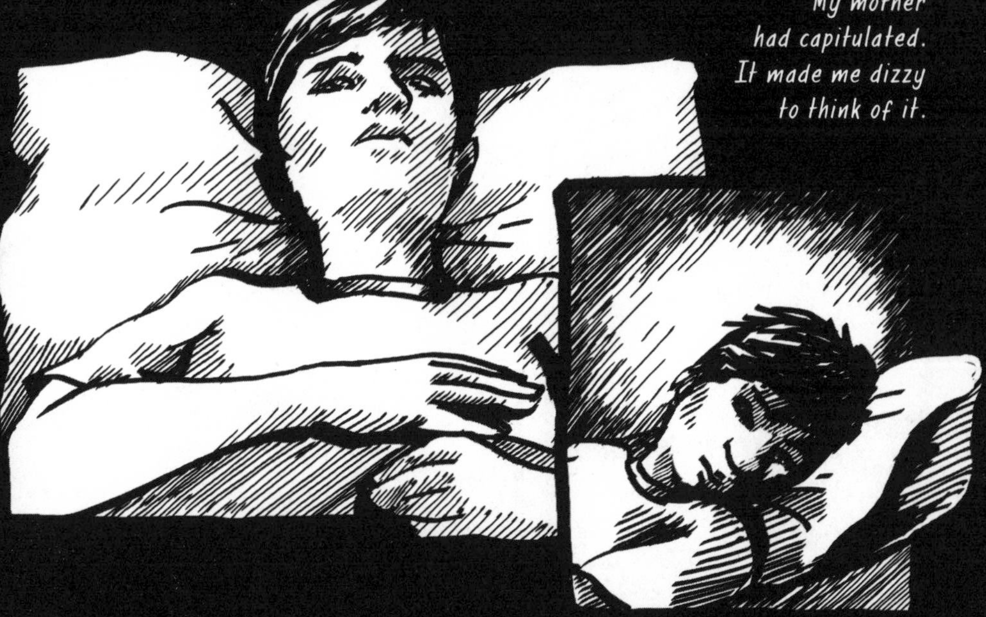

She and Carmela, sharing stories and tears, forgiving the old man in a nostalgic widows' duet. What could they have in common?

What could Carmela and my mother share besides a battleground?

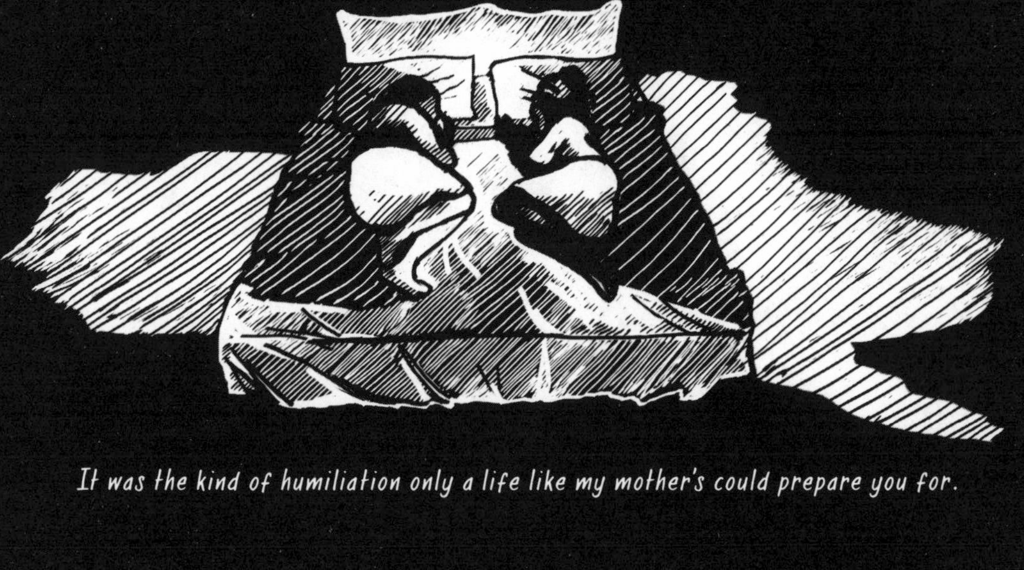

It was the kind of humiliation only a life like my mother's could prepare you for.

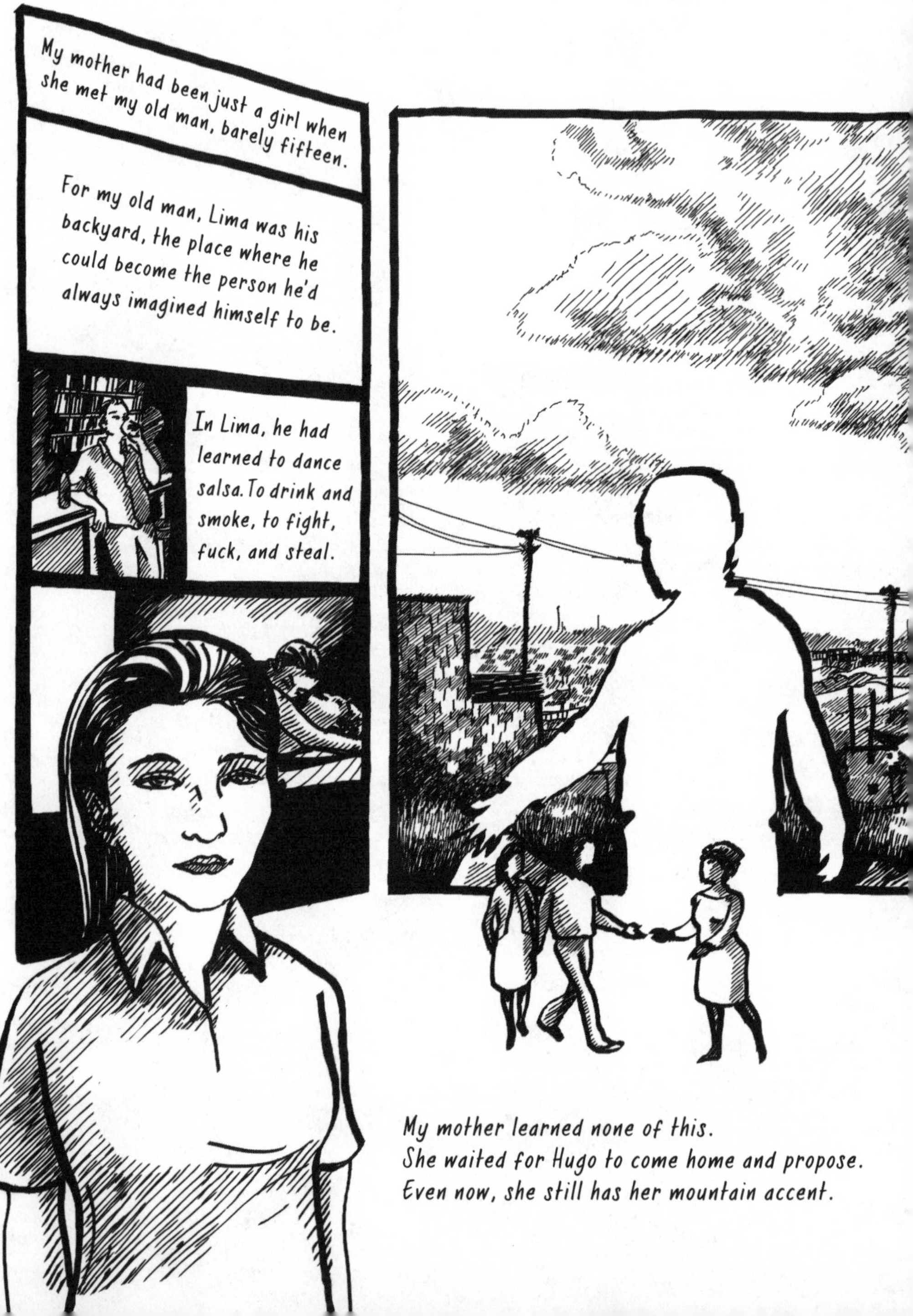
My mother had been just a girl when she met my old man, barely fifteen.
For my old man, Lima was his backyard, the place where he could become the person he'd always imagined himself to be.
In Lima, he had learned to dance salsa. To drink and smoke, to fight, fuck, and steal.
My mother learned none of this.
She waited for Hugo to come home and propose.
Even now, she still has her mountain accent.

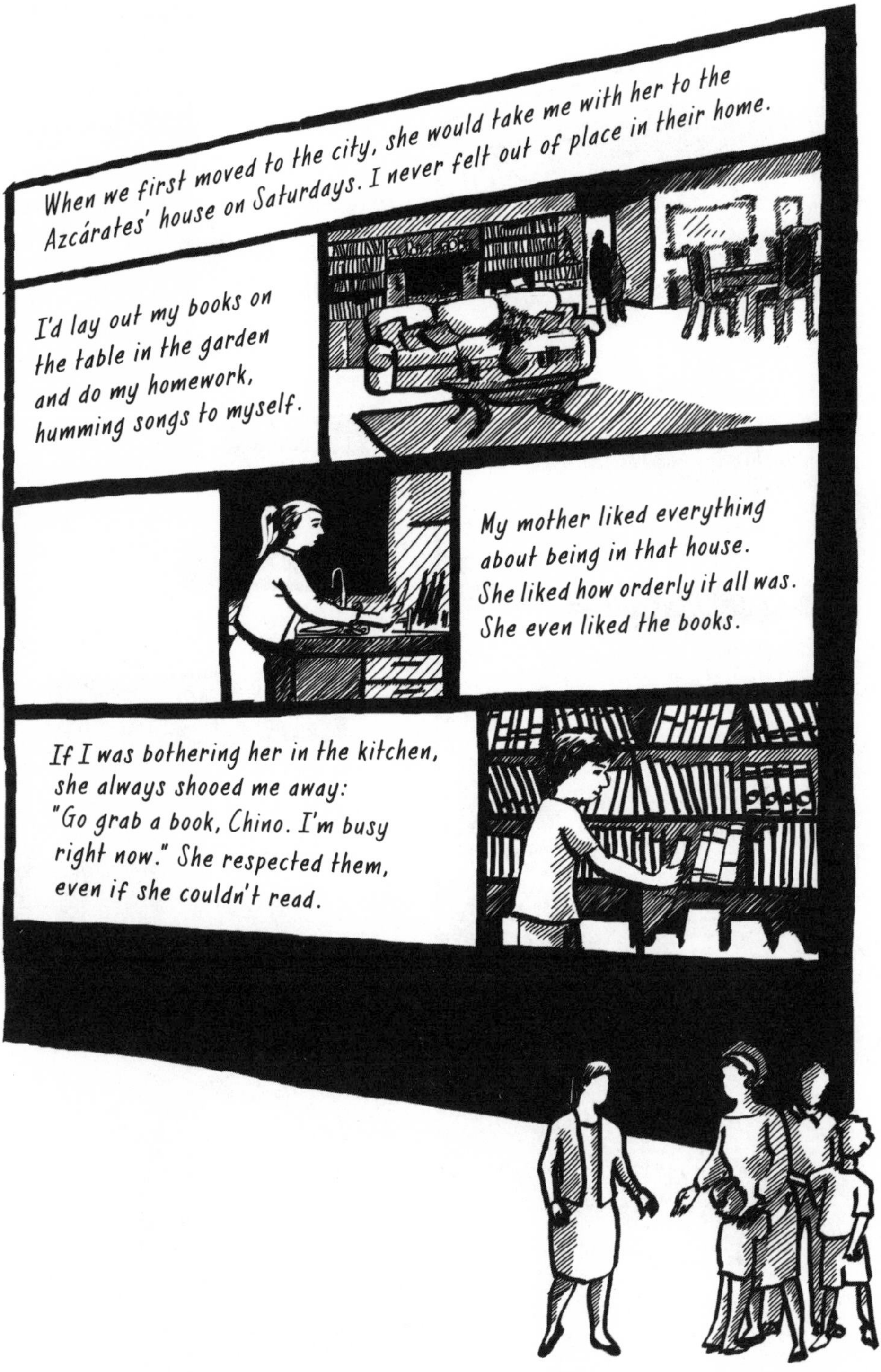
When we first moved to the city, she would take me with her to the Azcárates' house on Saturdays. I never felt out of place in their home.
I'd lay out my books on the table in the garden and do my homework, humming songs to myself.
My mother liked everything about being in that house. She liked how orderly it all was. She even liked the books.
If I was bothering her in the kitchen, she always shooed me away: "Go grab a book, Chino. I'm busy right now." She respected them, even if she couldn't read.

The way my mother sometimes spoke of Pasco, one might imagine an Andean paradise instead of the poor and violent mining town it really was. Lima frightened her. She felt safe in exactly two places: our house and the Azcárates' house. One day I asked her why we had moved.

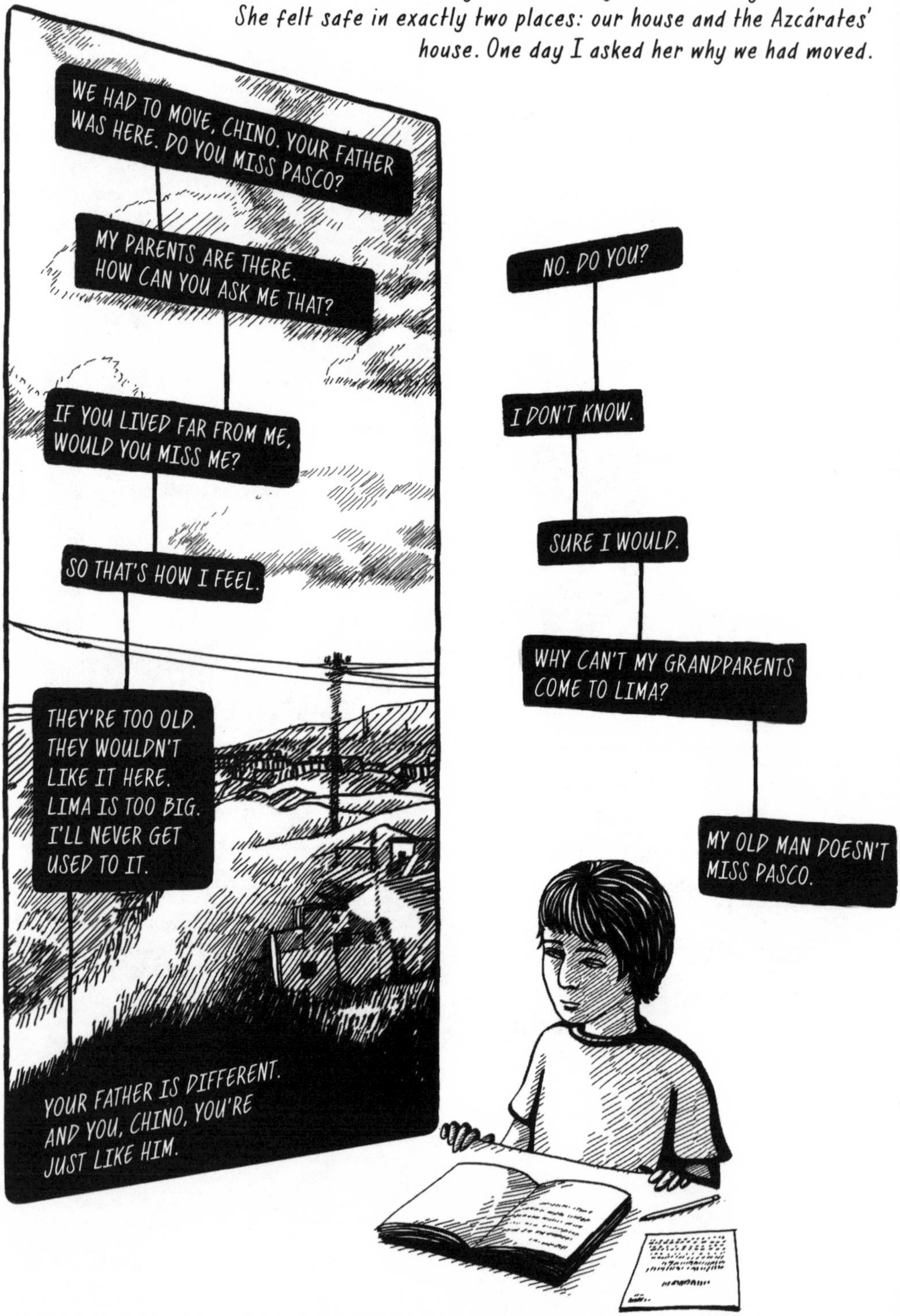
WE HAD TO MOVE, CHINO. YOUR FATHER WAS HERE. DO YOU MISS PASCO?
NO. DO YOU?
MY PARENTS ARE THERE. HOW CAN YOU ASK ME THAT?
I DON'T KNOW.
IF YOU LIVED FAR FROM ME, WOULD YOU MISS ME?
SURE I WOULD.
SO THAT'S HOW I FEEL.
WHY CAN'T MY GRANDPARENTS COME TO LIMA?
THEY'RE TOO OLD. THEY WOULDN'T LIKE IT HERE. LIMA IS TOO BIG. I'LL NEVER GET USED TO IT.
MY OLD MAN DOESN'T MISS PASCO.
YOUR FATHER IS DIFFERENT. AND YOU, CHINO, YOU'RE JUST LIKE HIM.

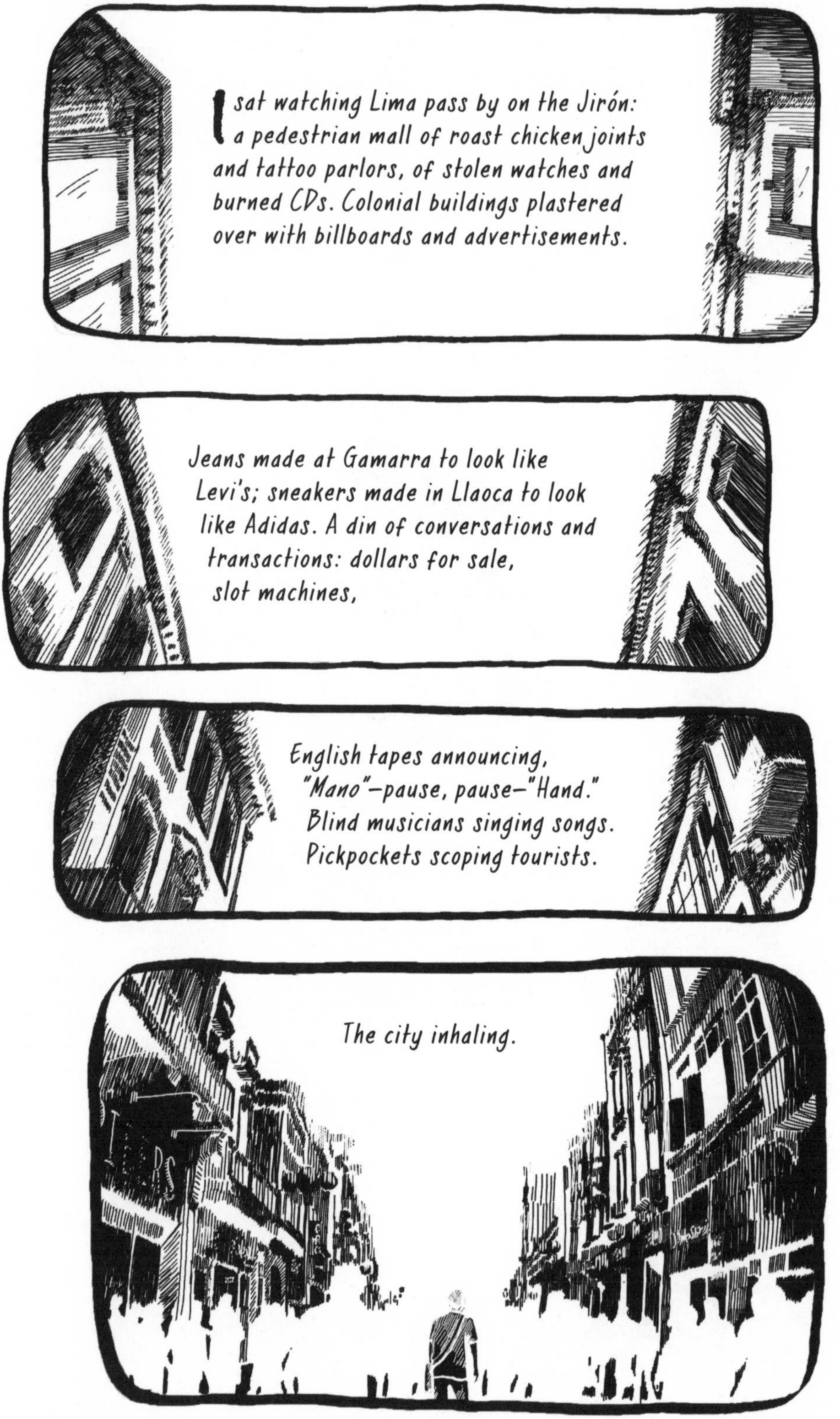
I sat watching Lima pass by on the Jirón: a pedestrian mall of roast chicken joints and tattoo parlors, of stolen watches and burned CDs. Colonial buildings plastered over with billboards and advertisements.
Jeans made at Gamarra to look like Levi's; sneakers made in Llaoca to look like Adidas. A din of conversations and transactions: dollars for sale, slot machines,
English tapes announcing, "Mano"—pause, pause—"Hand." Blind musicians singing songs. Pickpockets scoping tourists.
The city inhaling.

I'd read my father's short obituary over and over, read it against the other news of the day, looking for connections, for overlaps, for sense.

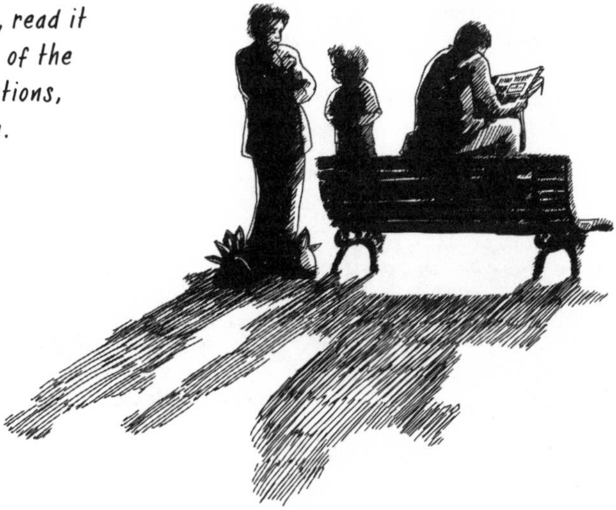

The president seemed dazed and disoriented before the press. Ministers disappeared on midnight charters to Florida. Life moved.

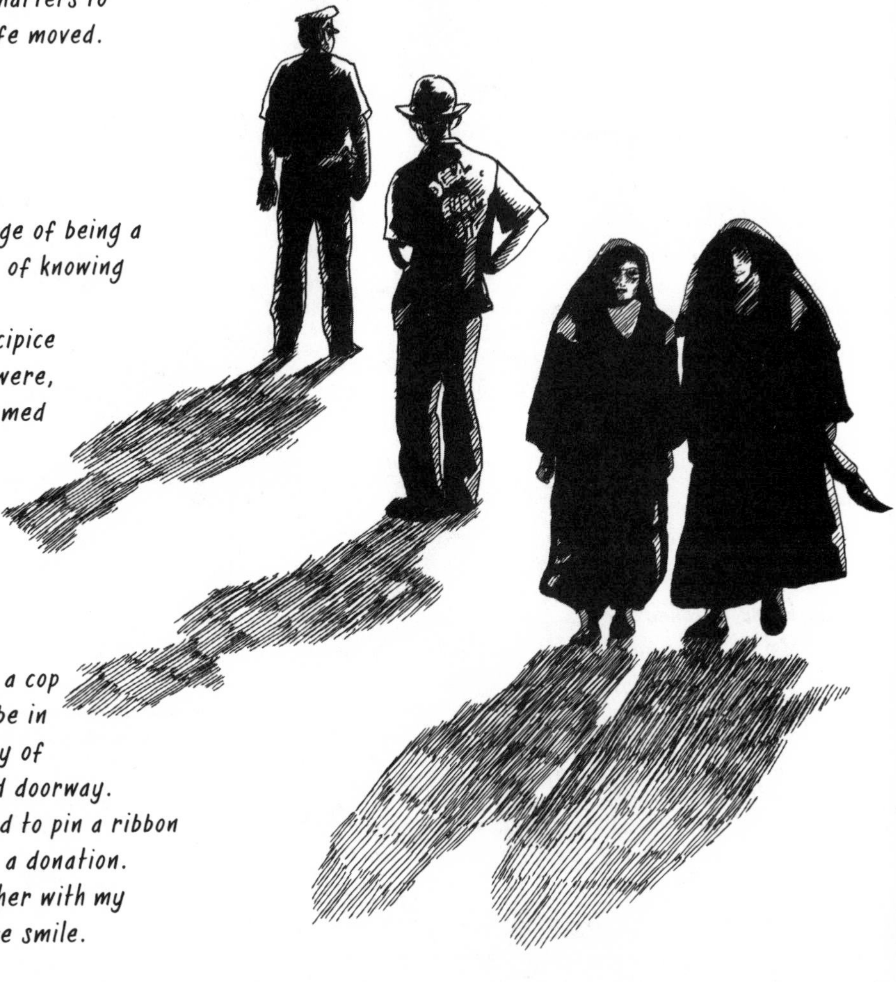

The privilege of being a journalist, of knowing how close to the precipice we really were, hardly seemed worth it at times.

I watched a cop take a bribe in the privacy of a recessed doorway. A nun tried to pin a ribbon on me for a donation. I dodged her with my most polite smile.

Then, from the Plaza San Martín, the whole world was running toward me, and past me, on to the Plaza Mayor. Metal gates closed with clangs and crashes all along the Jirón. The cop disappeared.

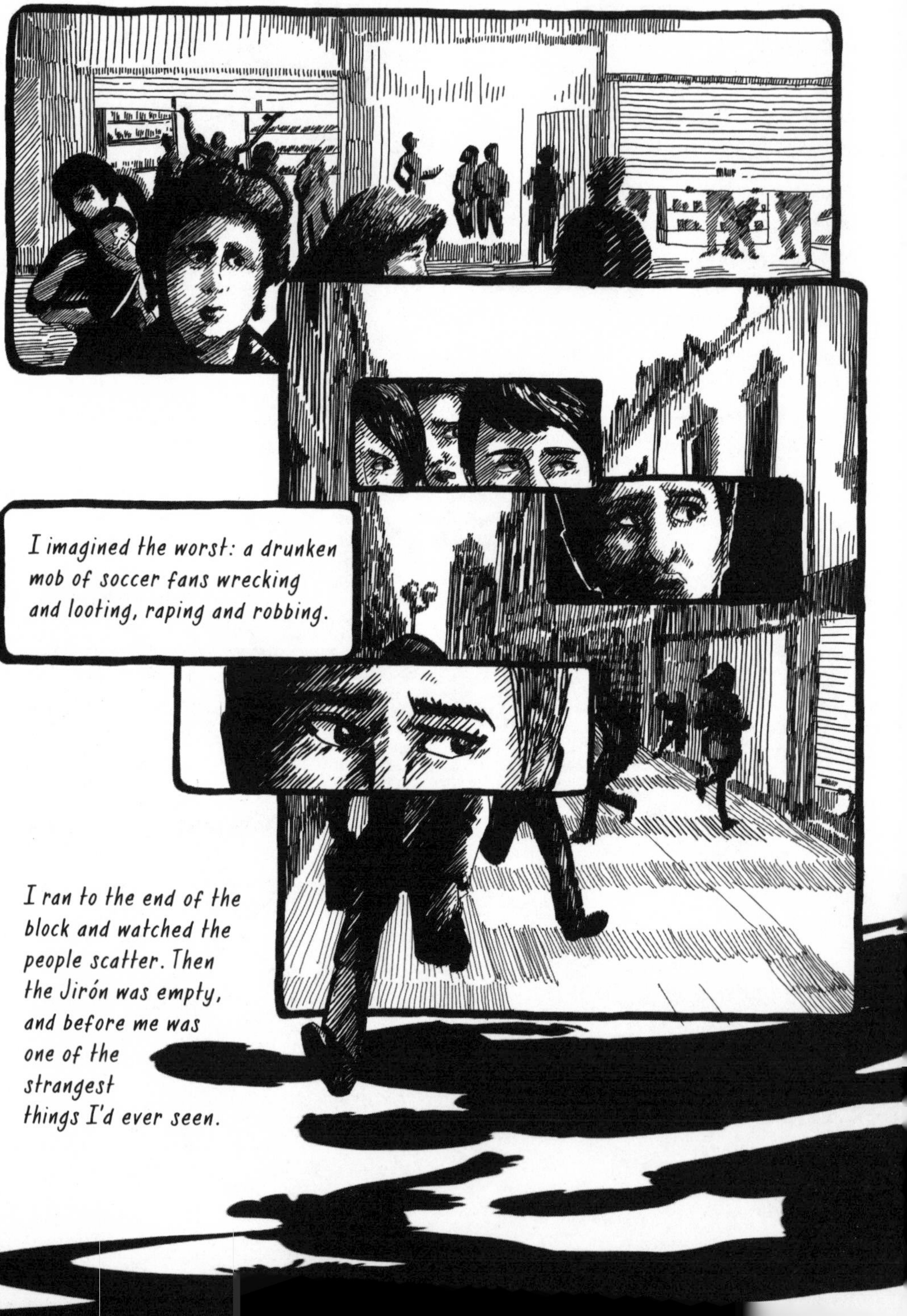
I imagined the worst: a drunken mob of soccer fans wrecking and looting, raping and robbing.
I ran to the end of the block and watched the people scatter. Then the Jirón was empty, and before me was one of the strangest things I'd ever seen.

Fifteen shoeshine boys walked in rows of three, dressed in secondhand clothes, sneakers worn at the heels, donated shirts with American logos. Some were so young they were dwarfed by their kits. One dragged his wooden box behind him, unconcerned as it bumped and bounced along the cobblestones. All were skinny, fragile, and smiling.

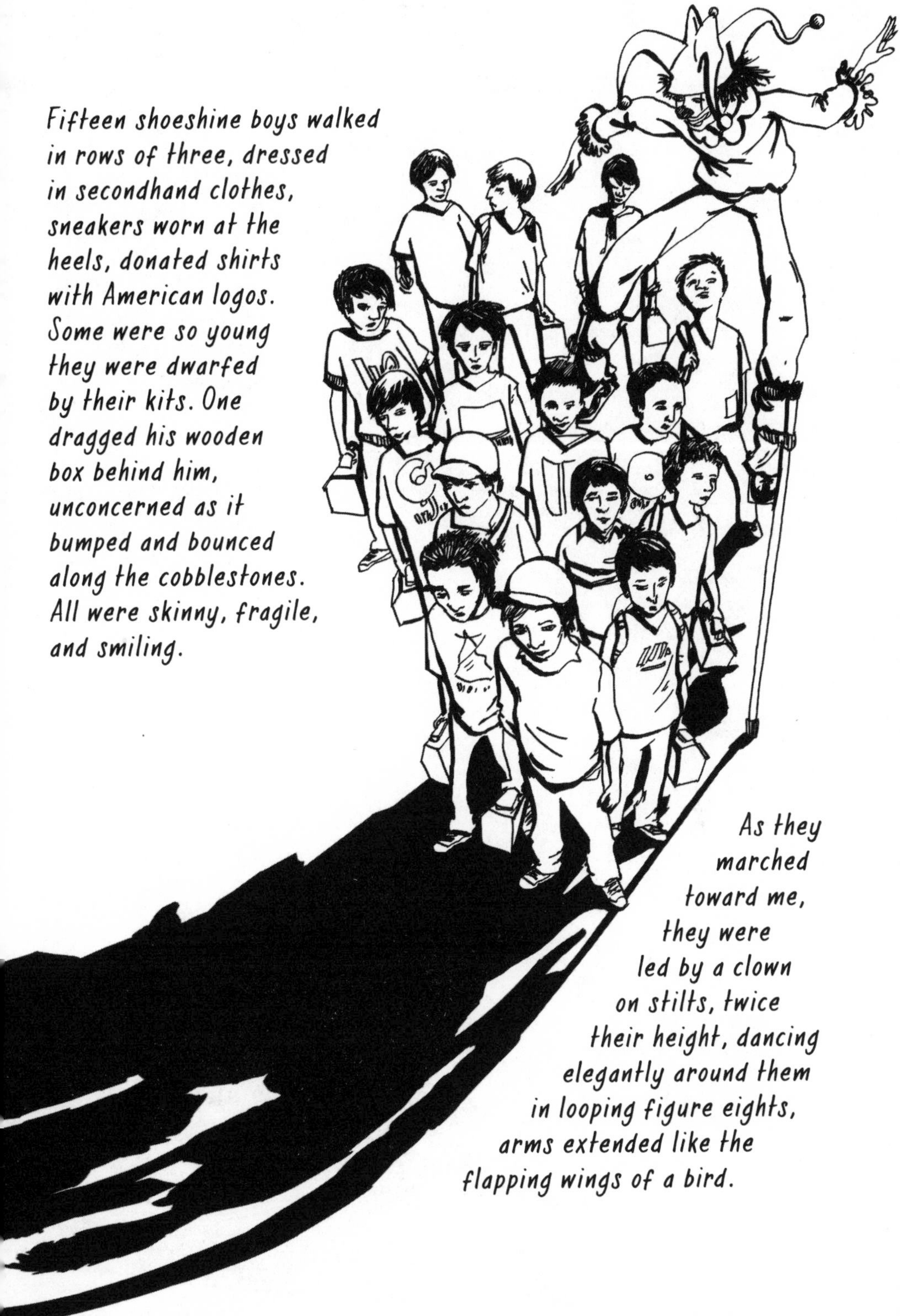

As they marched toward me, they were led by a clown on stilts, twice their height, dancing elegantly around them in looping figure eights, arms extended like the flapping wings of a bird.

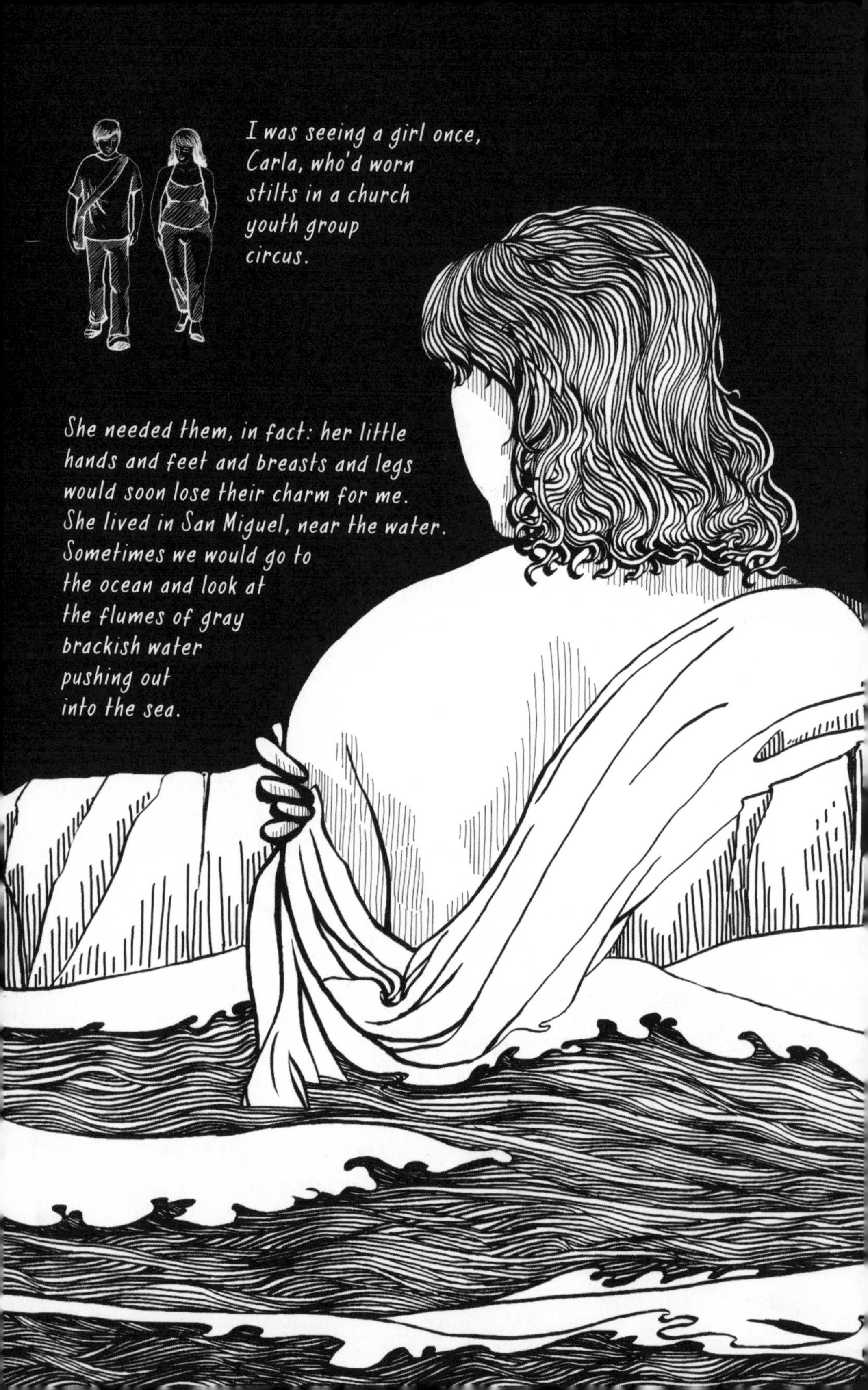
I was seeing a girl once, Carla, who'd worn stilts in a church youth group circus.
She needed them, in fact: her little hands and feet and breasts and legs would soon lose their charm for me. She lived in San Miguel, near the water. Sometimes we would go to the ocean and look at the flumes of gray brackish water pushing out into the sea.

Once she brought along her stilts, which
she claimed not to have used in years.
I helped her up on them, and
suddenly she was imposing,
half a body above me.

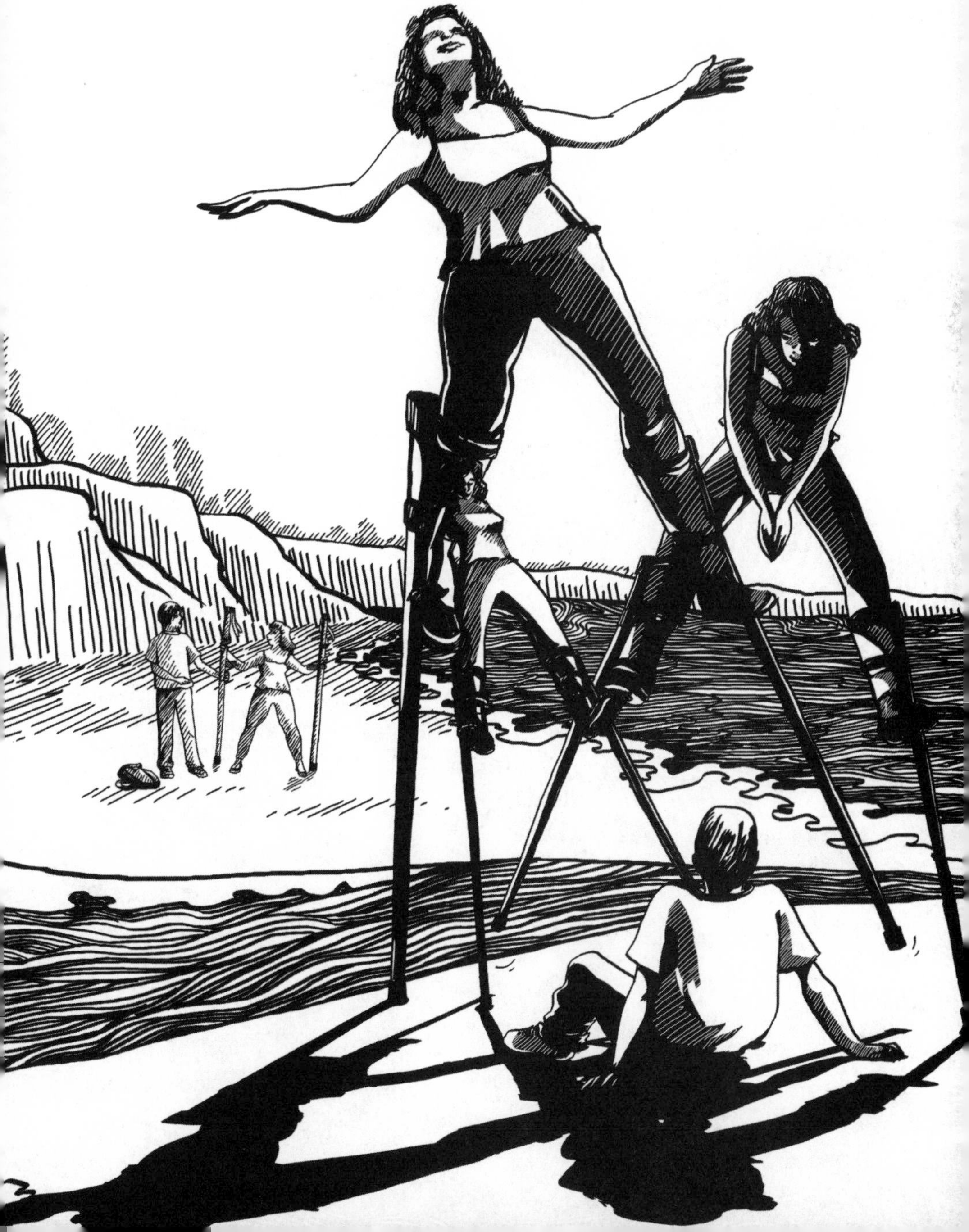

Gone was the timid and cautious girl I knew. Everything about her seemed larger, fuller. She waltzed along the gravel, patting me on the head, and I was a child again.

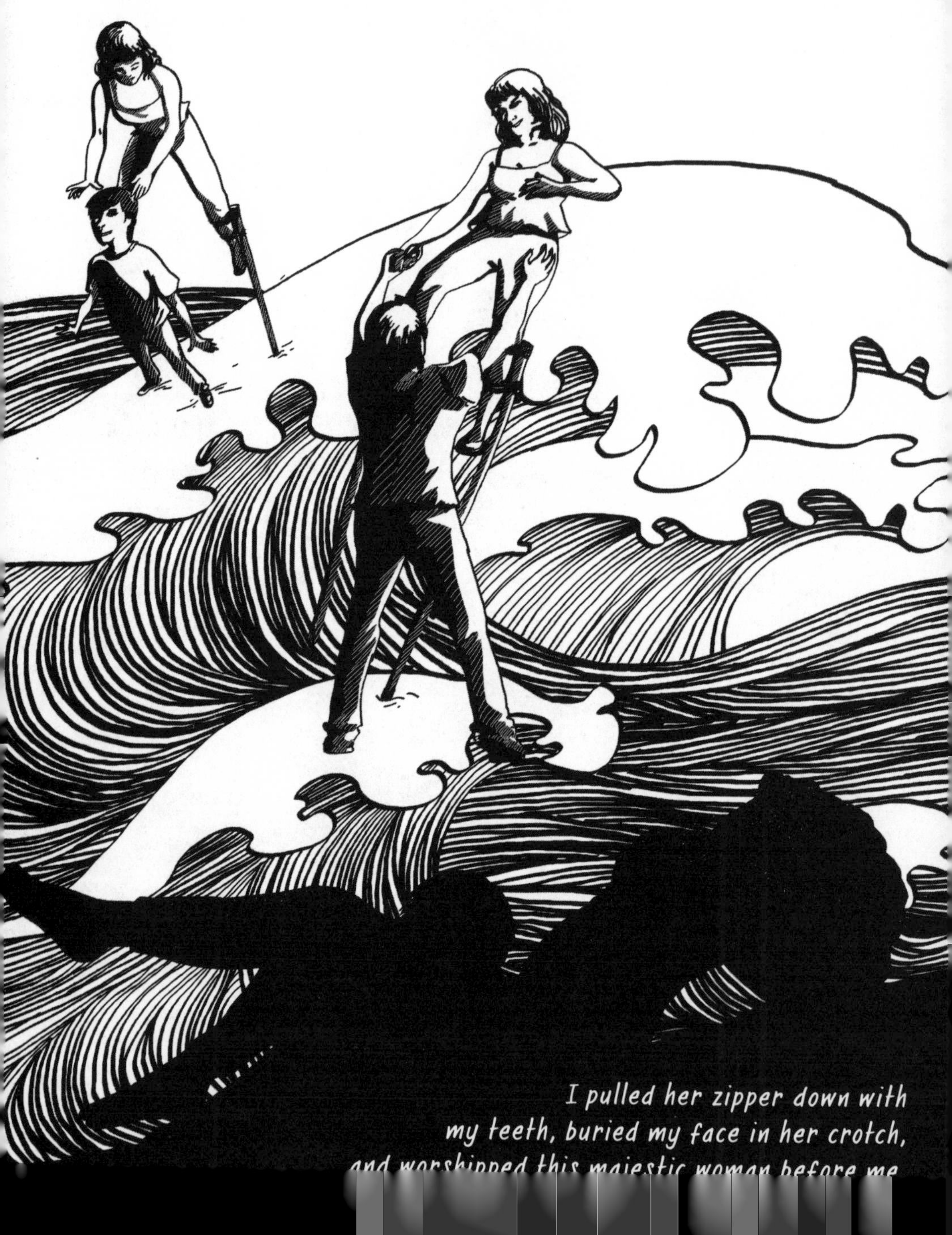
I pulled her zipper down with
my teeth, buried my face in her crotch,
and worshipped this majestic woman before me.

Now I watched in amazement as the protest strode past me, the children whispering their demands, the panic subsiding.

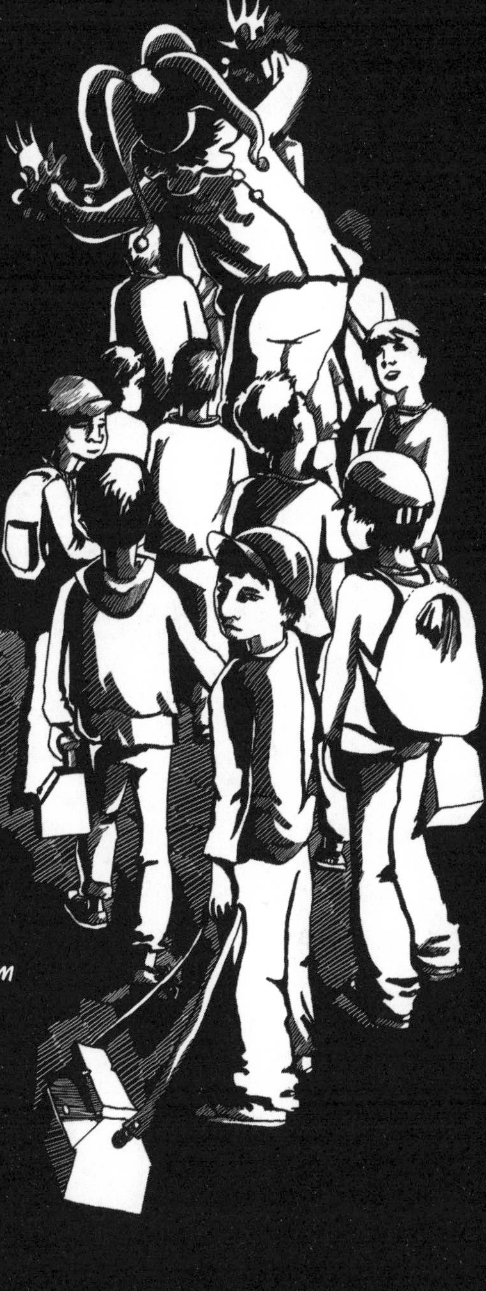

Had it been a drill? A joke of some sort? Store owners and customers emerged from their bunkers, relieved and confused. Lima was playing tricks again.

...e when I learned my old man had another angle. The scheme...
...You put in a new bathroom, or tile a kitchen, or add a third...
...in Surco or La Molina. You are a model worker, always polite...
...You don't play your music too loud. You wipe your feet and...
...ourself. All the while, you do your real work with your eyes.

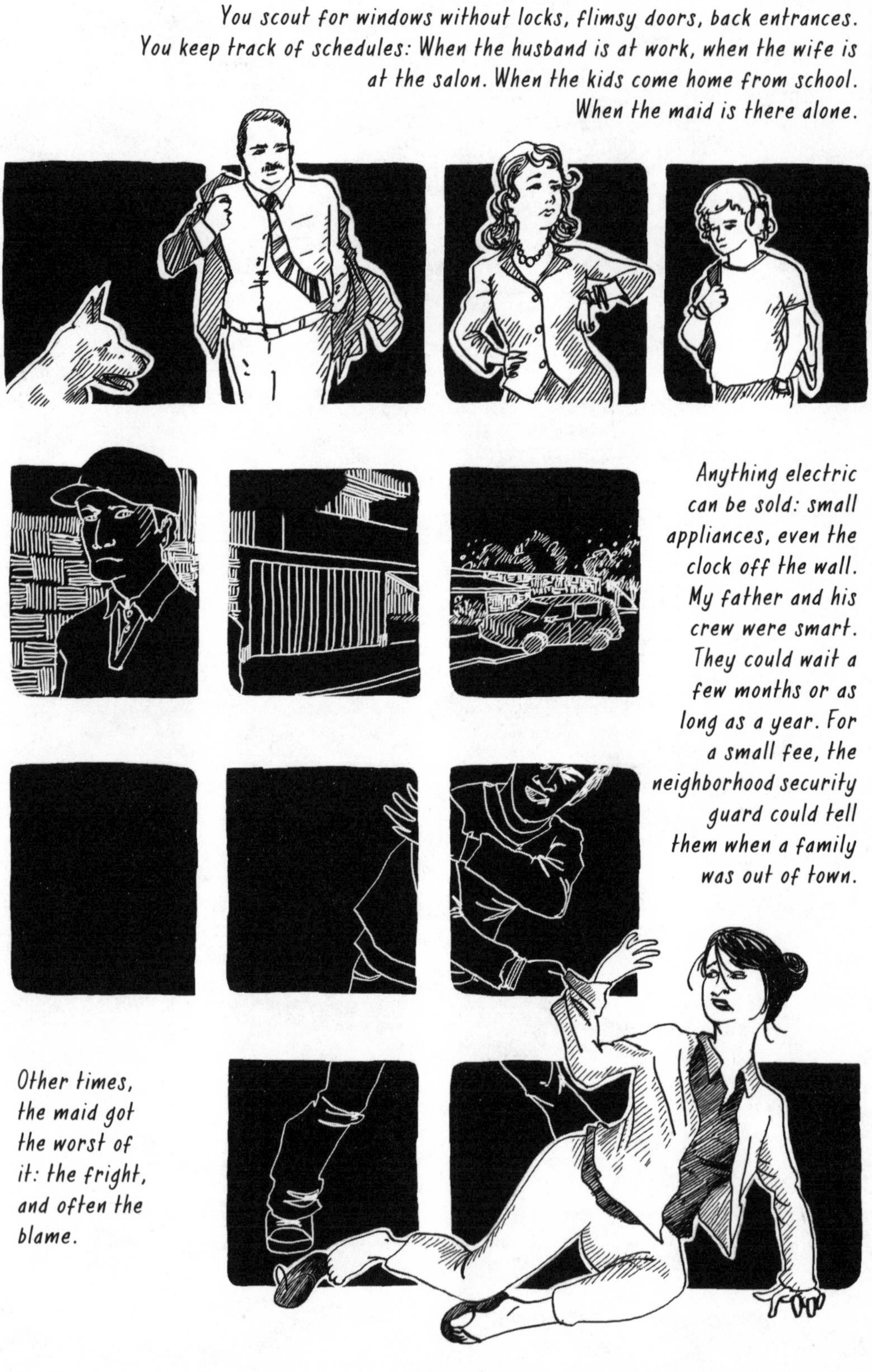
You scout for windows without locks, flimsy doors, back entrances. You keep track of schedules: When the husband is at work, when the wife is at the salon. When the kids come home from school. When the maid is there alone.
Anything electric can be sold: small appliances, even the clock off the wall. My father and his crew were smart. They could wait a few months or as long as a year. For a small fee, the neighborhood security guard could tell them when a family was out of town.
Other times, the maid got the worst of it: the fright, and often the blame.

I remember one evening at our house. They were planning, or perhaps celebrating. There were six of them, and they sat close together, talking in low voices, bubbling now and then into laughter.

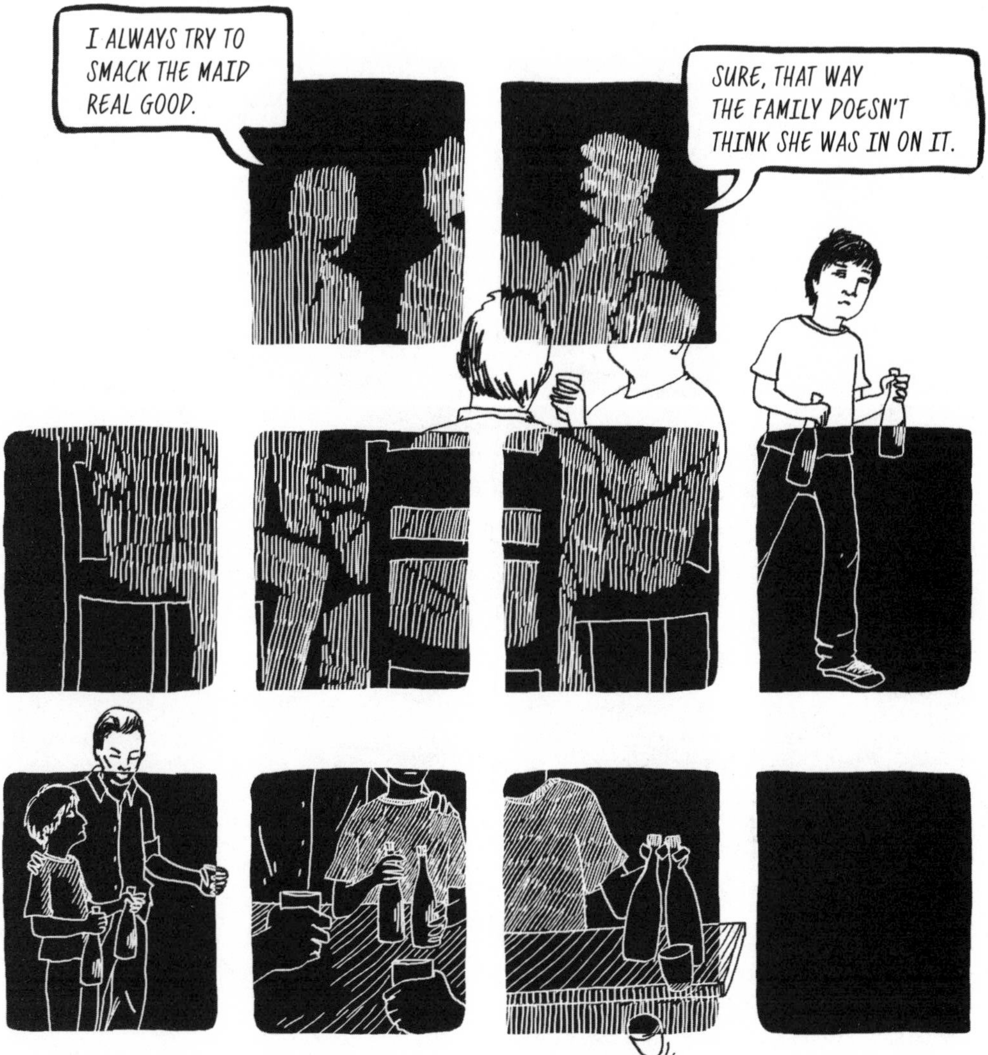
I ALWAYS TRY TO SMACK THE MAID REAL GOOD.
SURE, THAT WAY THE FAMILY DOESN'T THINK SHE WAS IN ON IT.

Everyone cheered
this perverse generosity.
My father too. I stood there,
thinking of my own mother
falling to the floor.

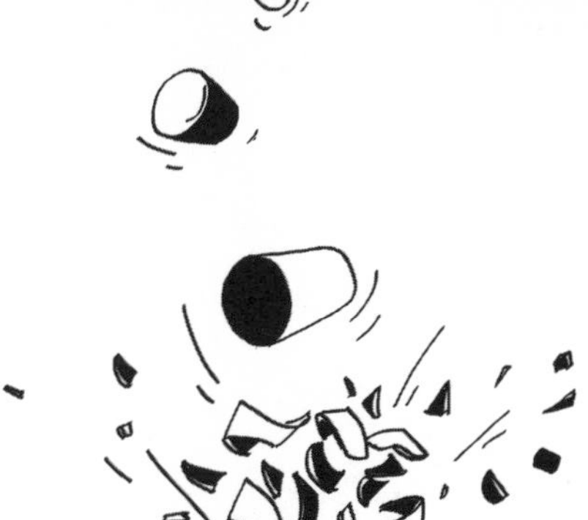

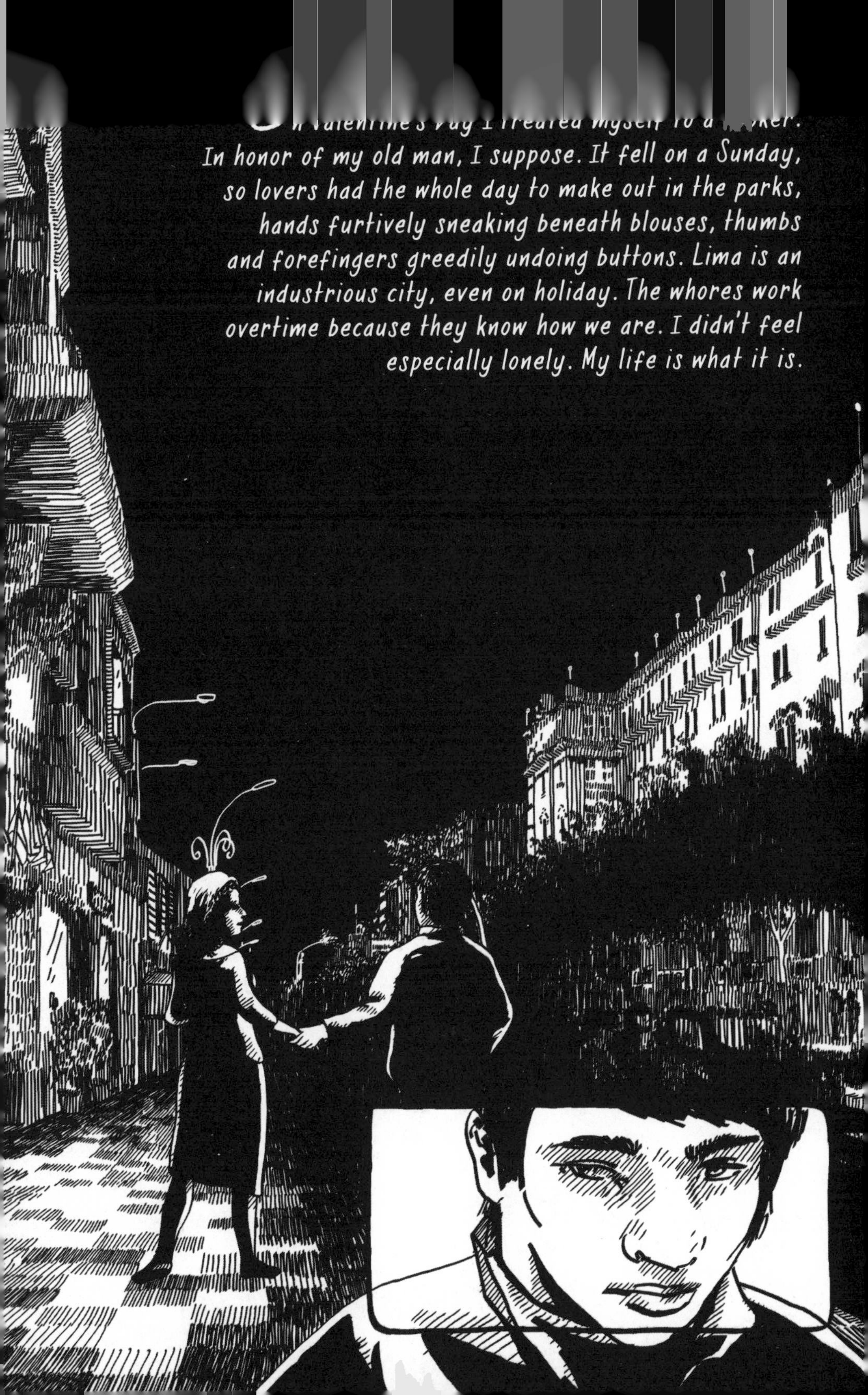
n Valentine's Day I treated myself to a ker.
In honor of my old man, I suppose. It fell on a Sunday, so lovers had the whole day to make out in the parks, hands furtively sneaking beneath blouses, thumbs and forefingers greedily undoing buttons. Lima is an industrious city, even on holiday. The whores work overtime because they know how we are. I didn't feel especially lonely. My life is what it is.

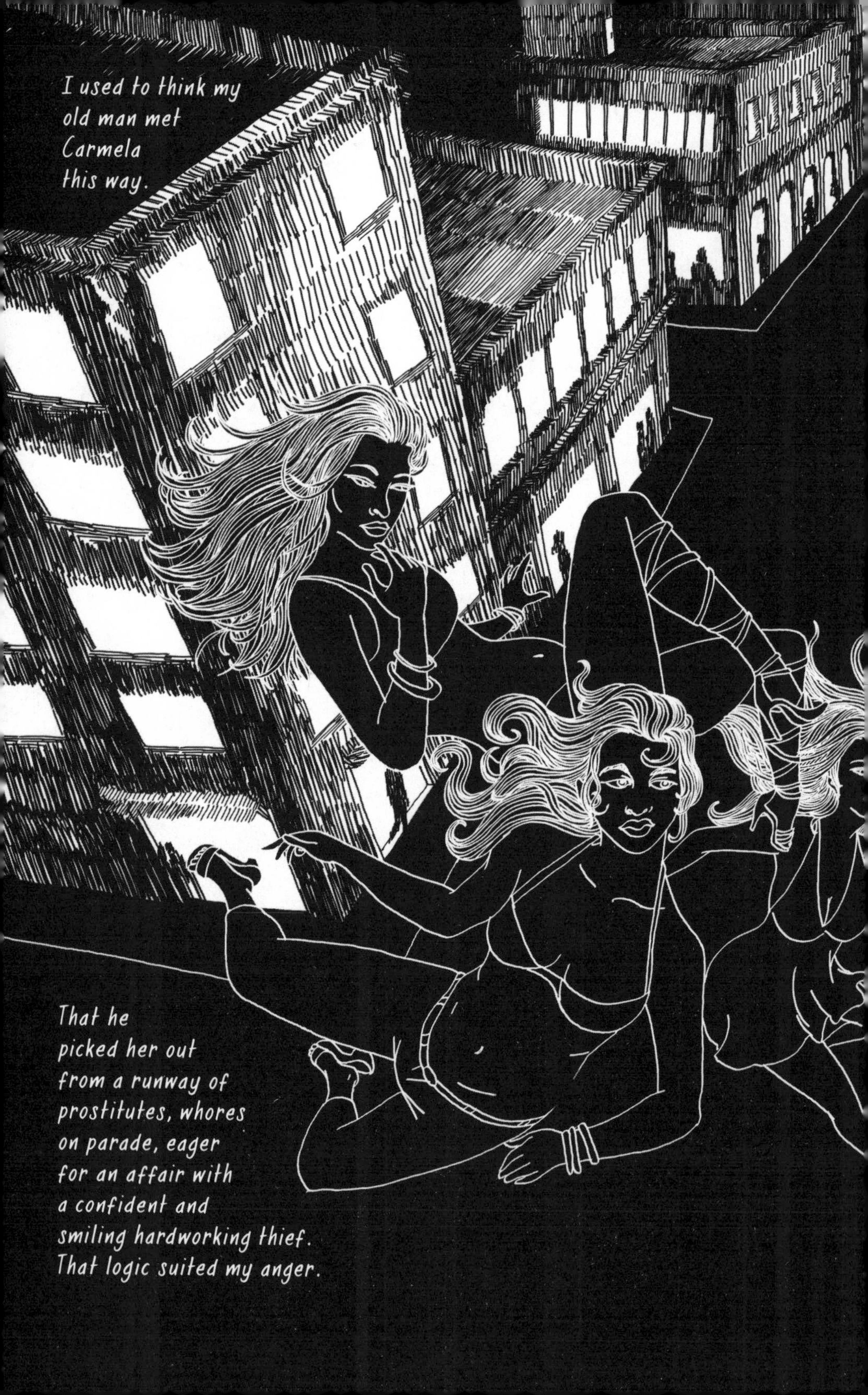
I used to think my old man met Carmela this way.
That he picked her out from a runway of prostitutes, whores on parade, eager for an affair with a confident and smiling hardworking thief. That logic suited my anger.

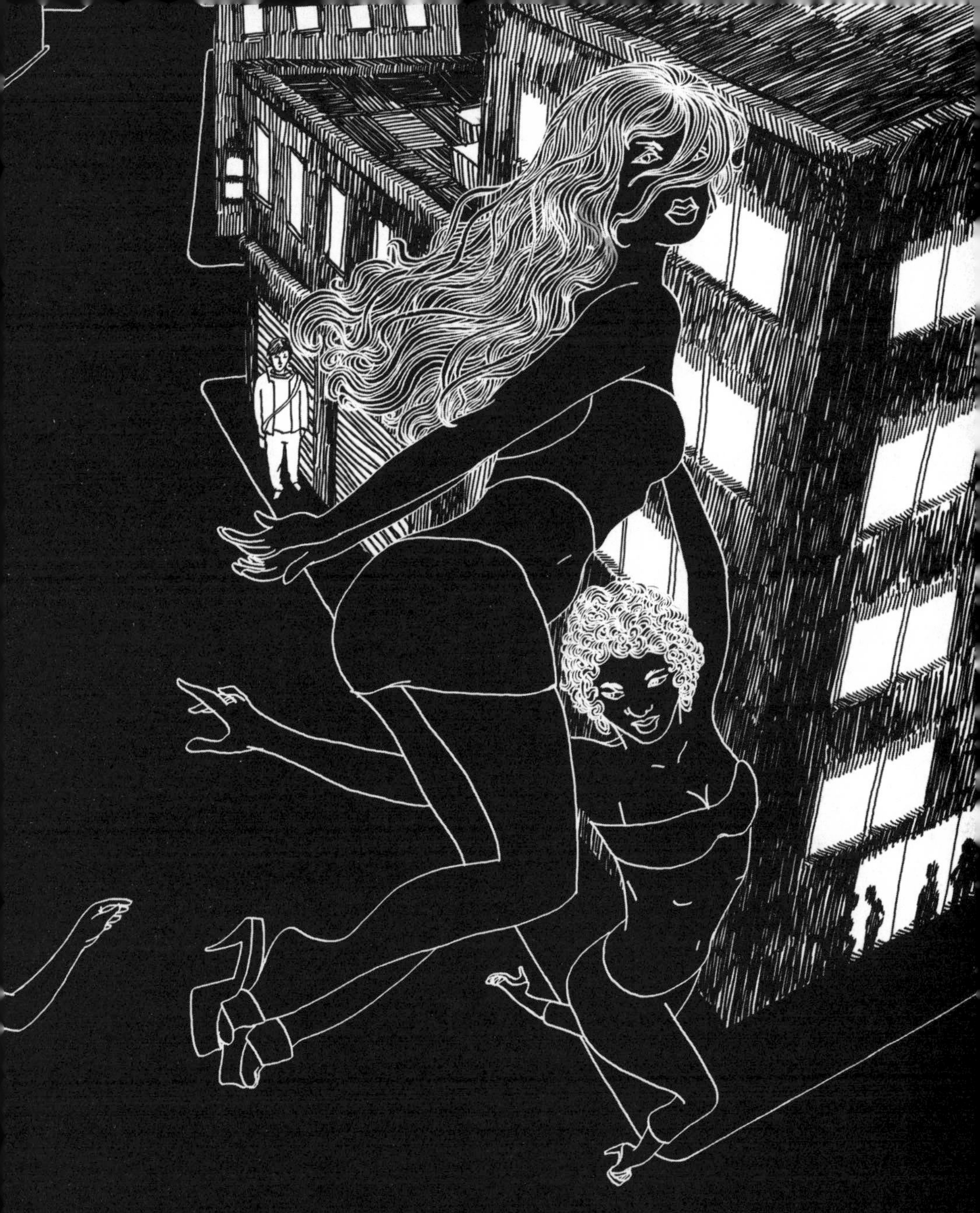

Maybe he fell in love with Carmela. Maybe she made him feel things my mother didn't. I don't care. You don't do those things. You don't let yourself be drawn into a parallel life, another marriage, another commitment. You go home to your wife. You live with the decisions you made.

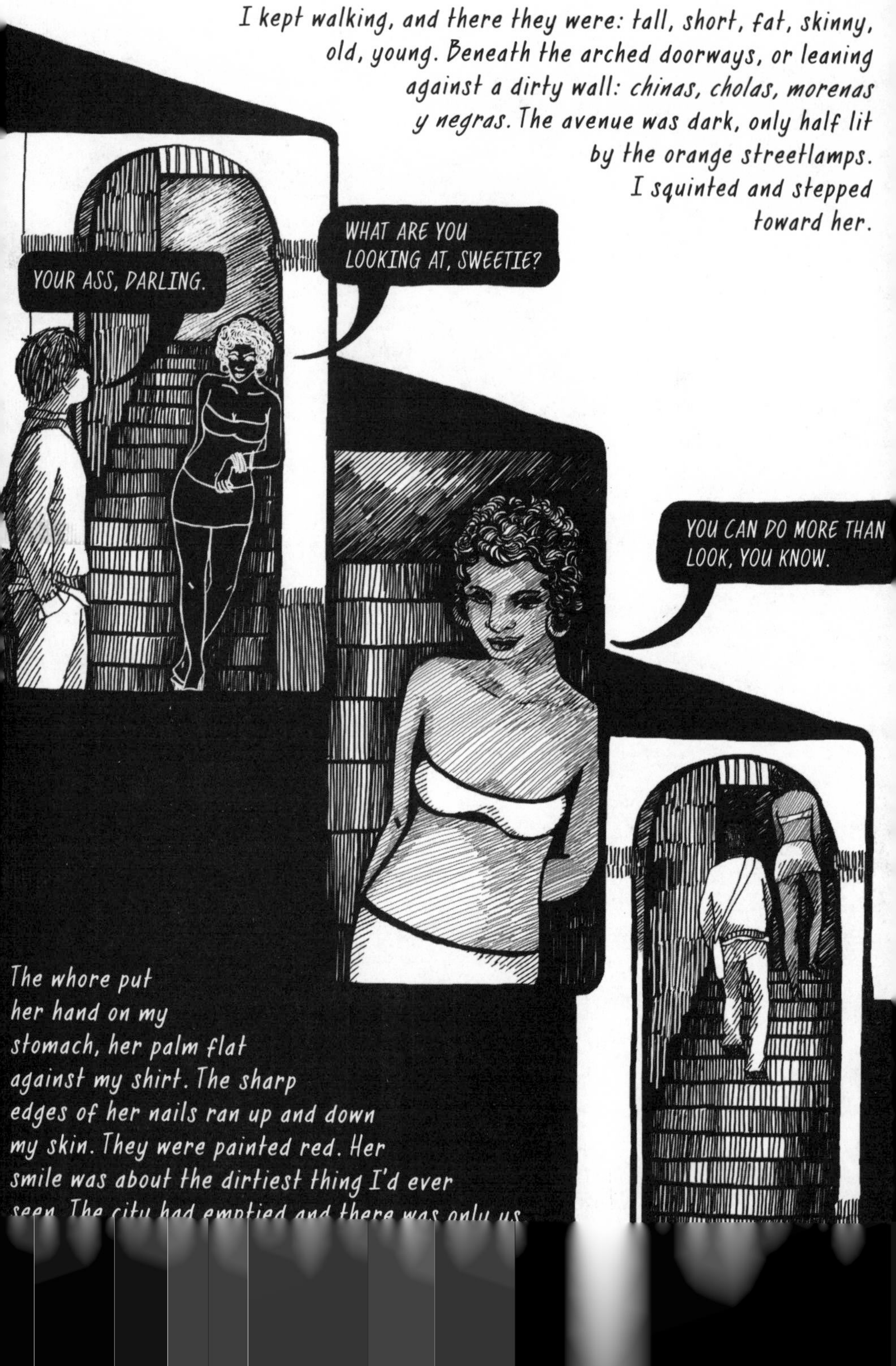
I kept walking, and there they were: tall, short, fat, skinny, old, young. Beneath the arched doorways, or leaning against a dirty wall: chinas, cholas, morenas y negras. The avenue was dark, only half lit by the orange streetlamps. I squinted and stepped toward her.
WHAT ARE YOU LOOKING AT, SWEETIE?
YOUR ASS, DARLING.
YOU CAN DO MORE THAN LOOK, YOU KNOW.
The whore put her hand on my stomach, her palm flat against my shirt. The sharp edges of her nails ran up and down my skin. They were painted red. Her smile was about the dirtiest thing I'd ever seen. The city had emptied and there was only us.

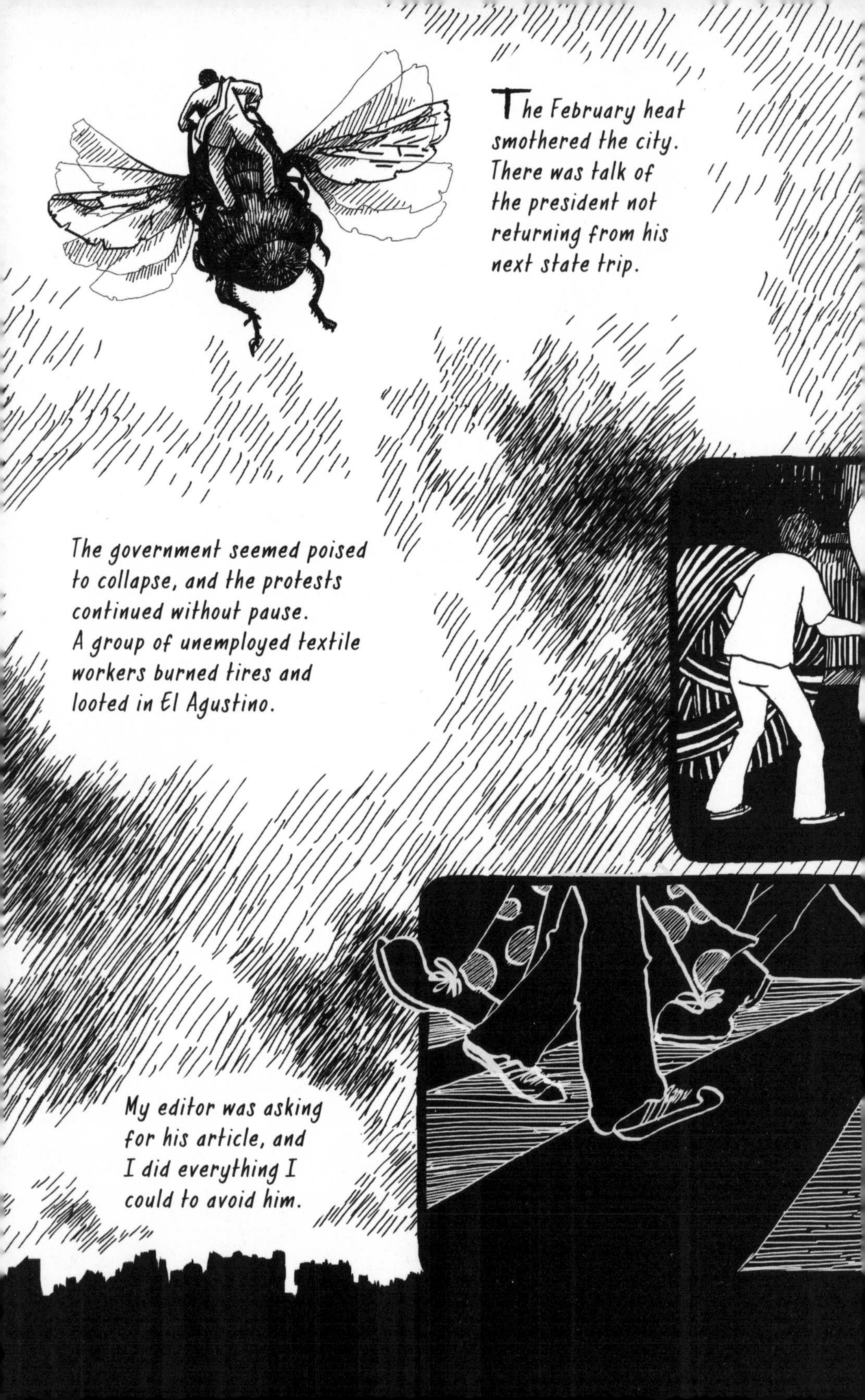
The February heat smothered the city. There was talk of the president not returning from his next state trip.
The government seemed poised to collapse, and the protests continued without pause. A group of unemployed textile workers burned tires and looted in El Agustino.
My editor was asking for his article, and I did everything I could to avoid him.

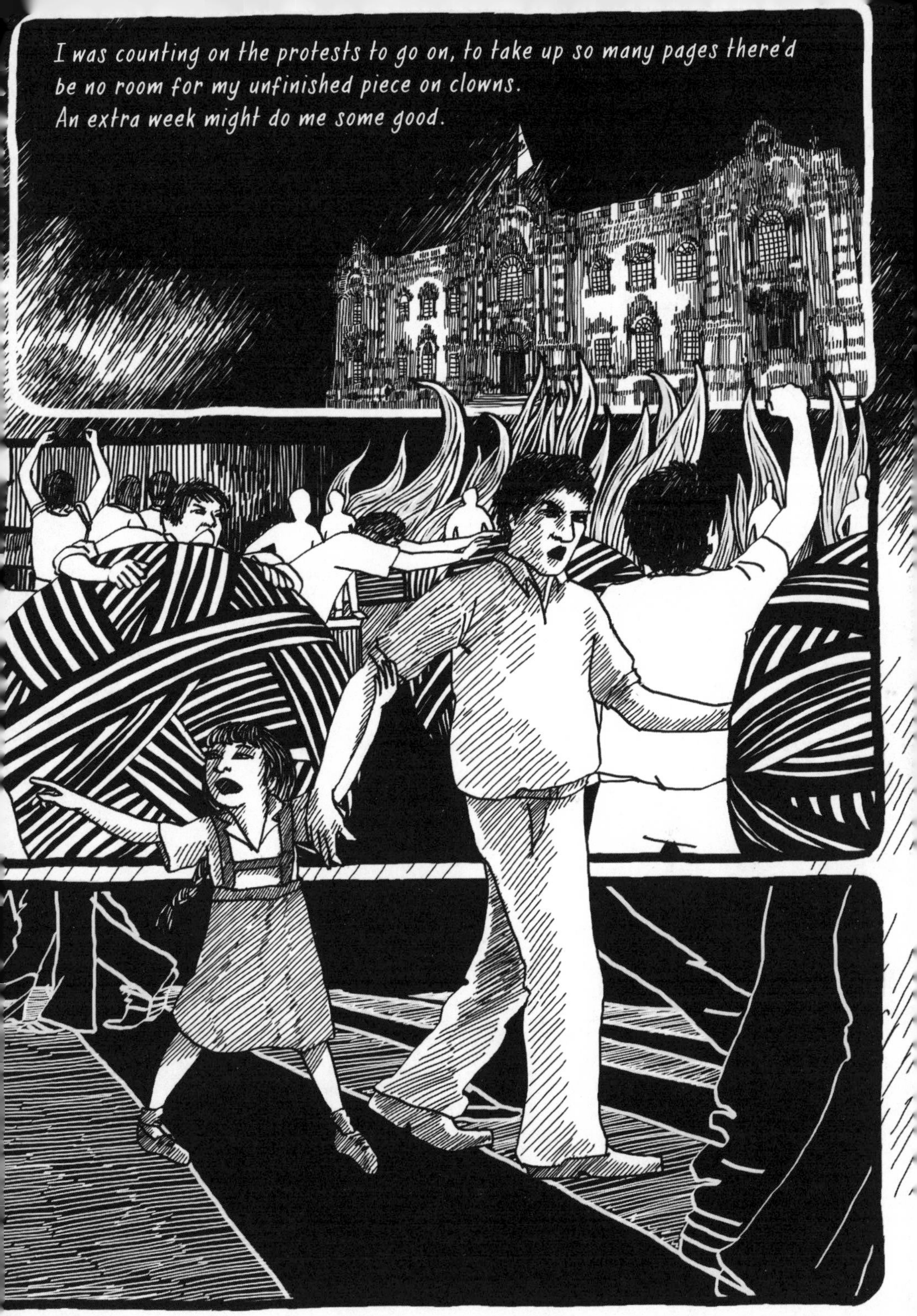
I was counting on the protests to go on, to take up so many pages there'd be no room for my unfinished piece on clowns.
An extra week might do me some good.

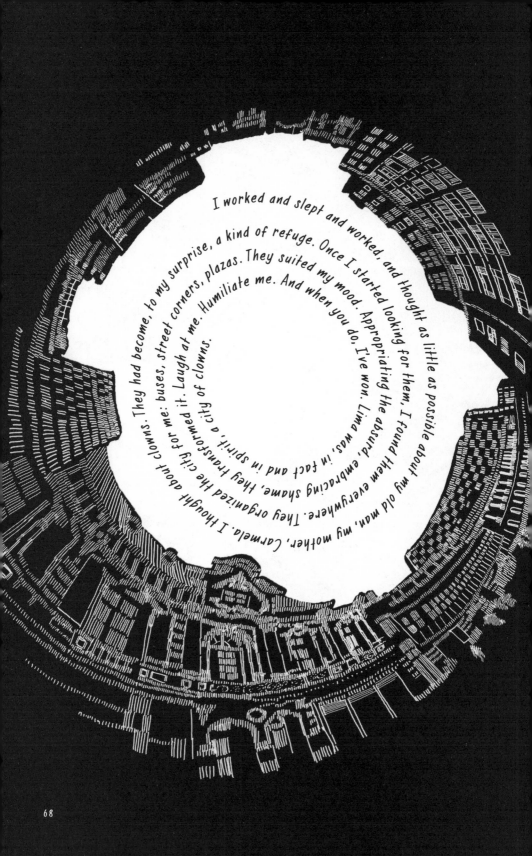

I worked and slept and worked, and thought as little as possible about my old man, my mother, Carmela. I thought about clowns. They had become, to my surprise, a kind of refuge. Once I started looking for them, I found them everywhere. They organized the city for me: buses, street corners, plazas. They suited my mood. Appropriating the absurd, embracing shame, they transformed the city, a city of clowns. Lima was, in fact and in spirit. I've won. Humiliate me. And when you do, Laugh at me. Laugh at it.

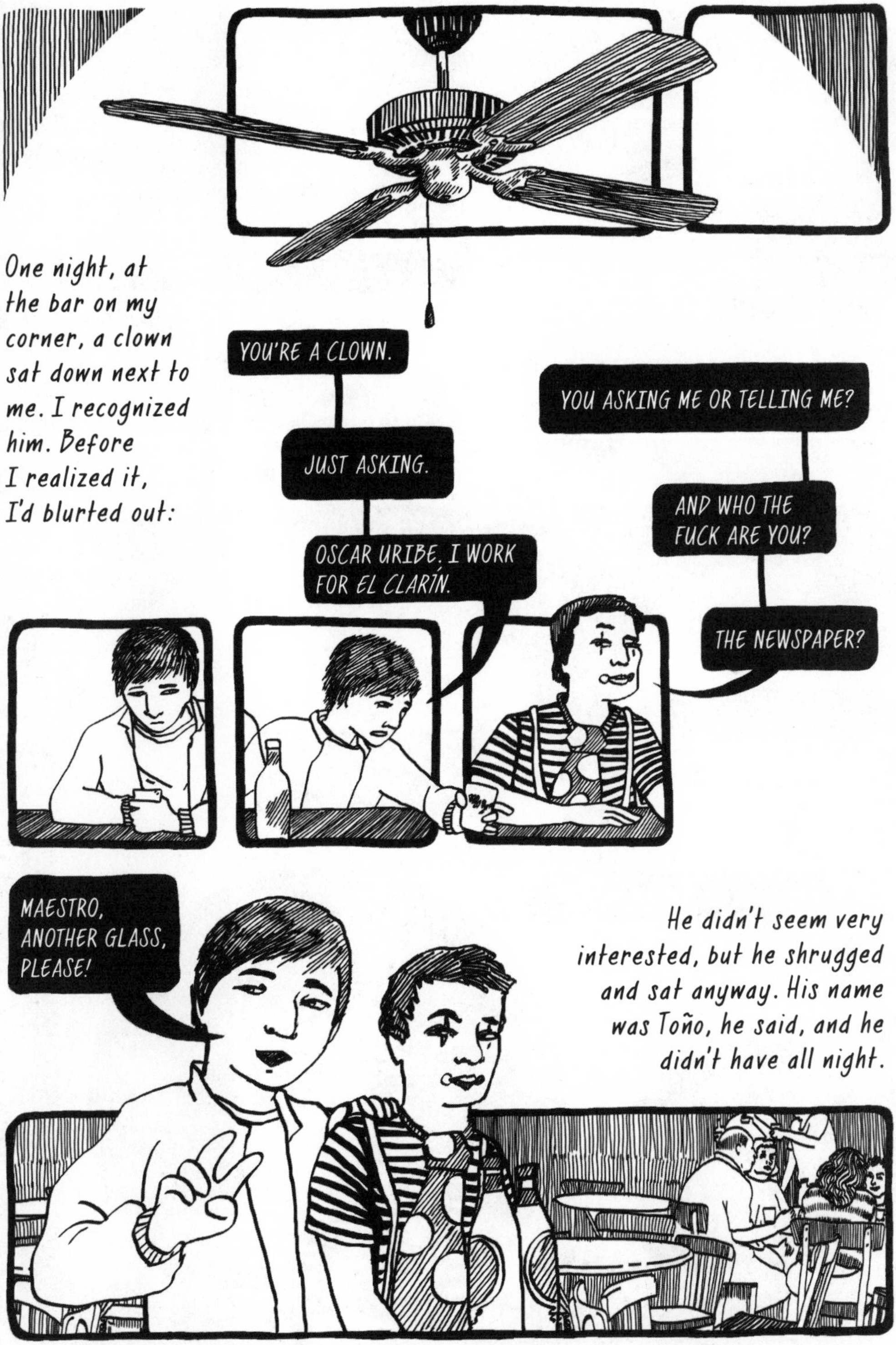
One night, at the bar on my corner, a clown sat down next to me. I recognized him. Before I realized it, I'd blurted out:
YOU'RE A CLOWN.
JUST ASKING.
OSCAR URIBE. I WORK FOR EL CLARÍN.
YOU ASKING ME OR TELLING ME?
AND WHO THE FUCK ARE YOU?
THE NEWSPAPER?
MAESTRO, ANOTHER GLASS, PLEASE!
He didn't seem very interested, but he shrugged and sat anyway. His name was Toño, he said, and he didn't have all night.

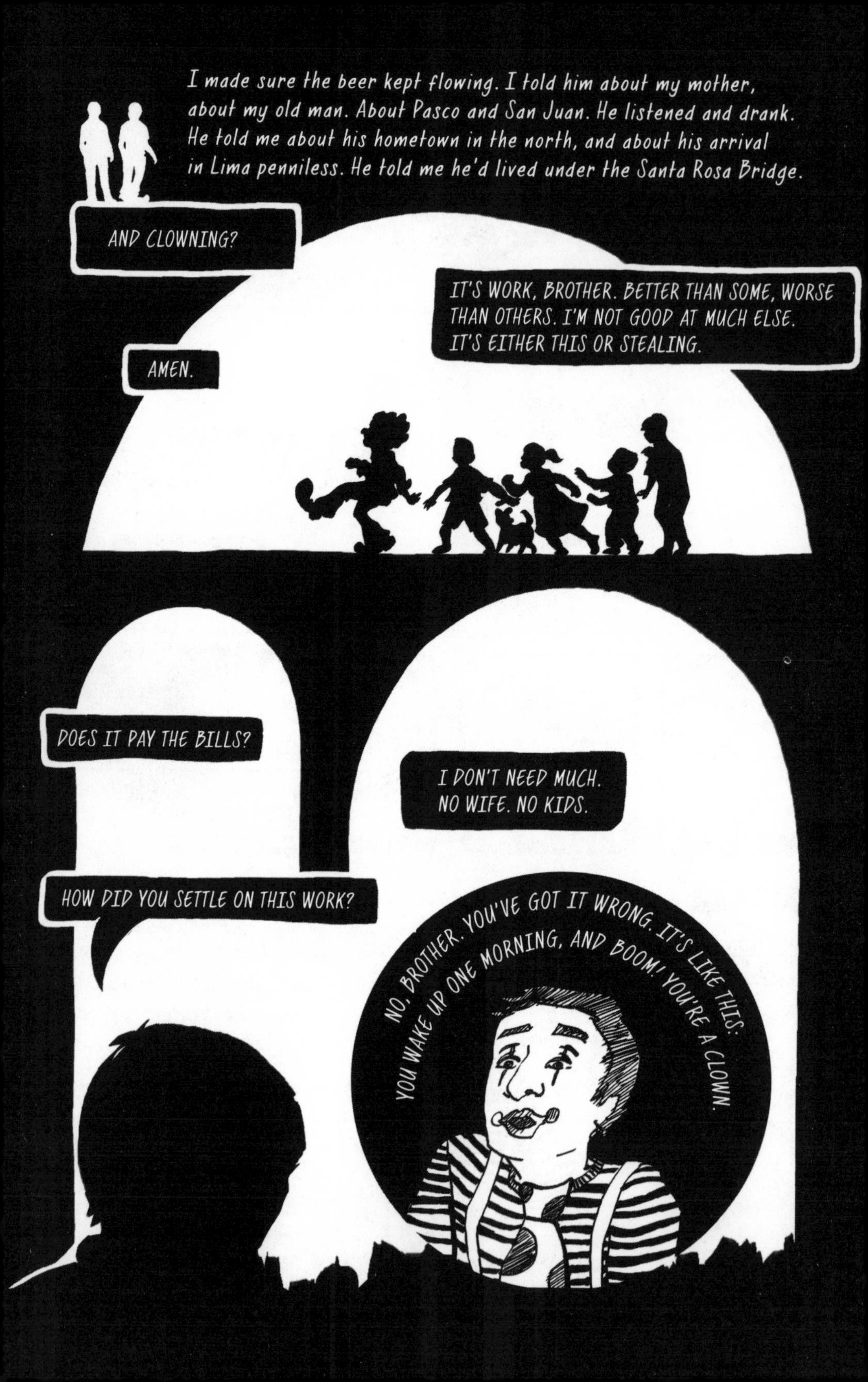

I made sure the beer kept flowing. I told him about my mother, about my old man. About Pasco and San Juan. He listened and drank. He told me about his hometown in the north, and about his arrival in Lima penniless. He told me he'd lived under the Santa Rosa Bridge.
AND CLOWNING?
IT'S WORK, BROTHER. BETTER THAN SOME, WORSE THAN OTHERS. I'M NOT GOOD AT MUCH ELSE. IT'S EITHER THIS OR STEALING.
AMEN.
DOES IT PAY THE BILLS?
I DON'T NEED MUCH. NO WIFE. NO KIDS.
HOW DID YOU SETTLE ON THIS WORK?
NO, BROTHER. YOU'VE GOT IT WRONG. IT'S LIKE THIS: YOU WAKE UP ONE MORNING, AND BOOM! YOU'RE A CLOWN.

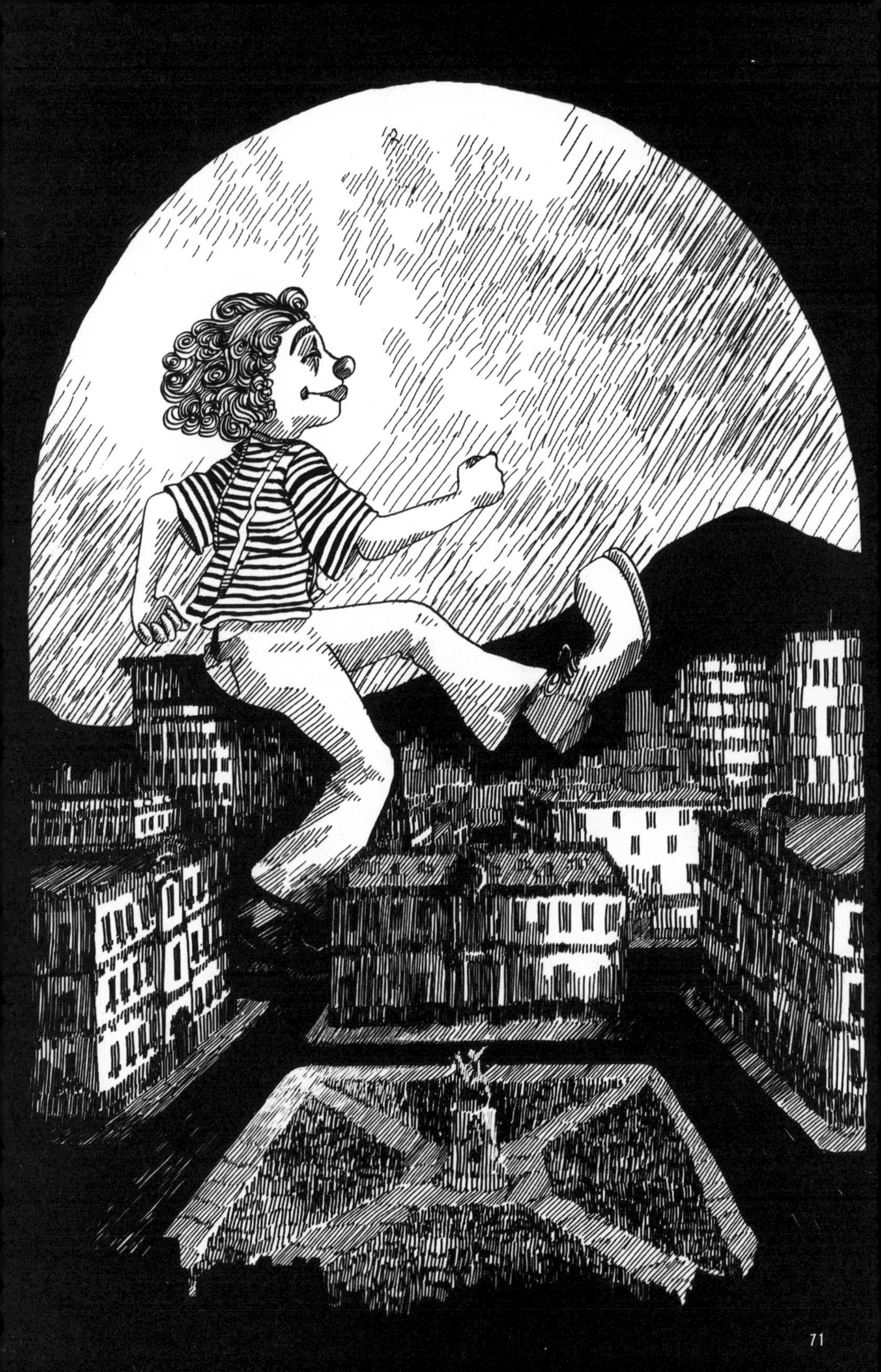

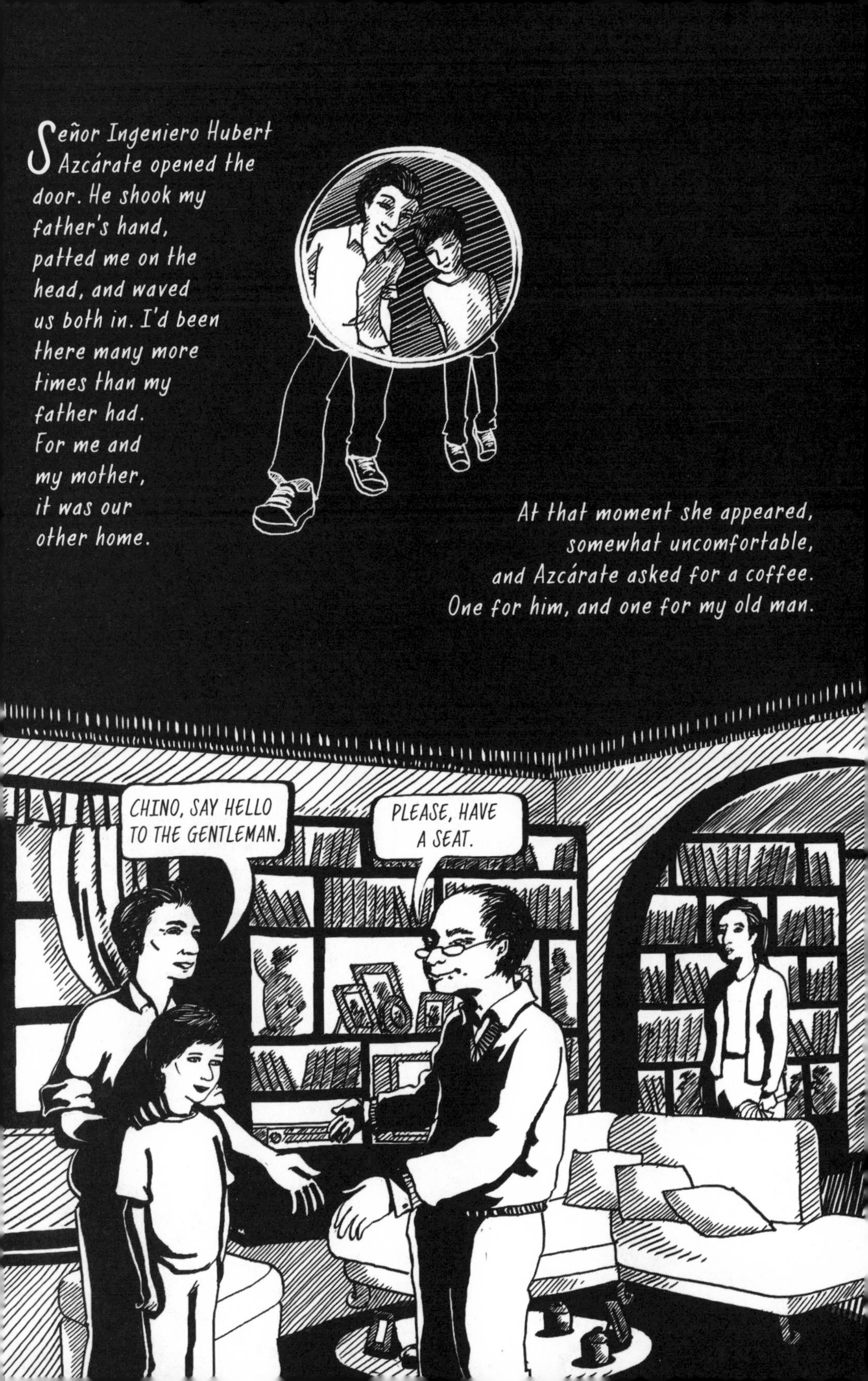
Señor Ingeniero Hubert Azcárate opened the door. He shook my father's hand, patted me on the head, and waved us both in. I'd been there many more times than my father had. For me and my mother, it was our other home.
At that moment she appeared, somewhat uncomfortable, and Azcárate asked for a coffee. One for him, and one for my old man.
CHINO, SAY HELLO TO THE GENTLEMAN.
PLEASE, HAVE A SEAT.

My father began by recounting reasons we were grateful to the Azcárate family. The generosity, the solidarity, the understanding. Señor Azcárate had arranged a scholarship so I could study at a private school in San Isidro. I knew what he was after.

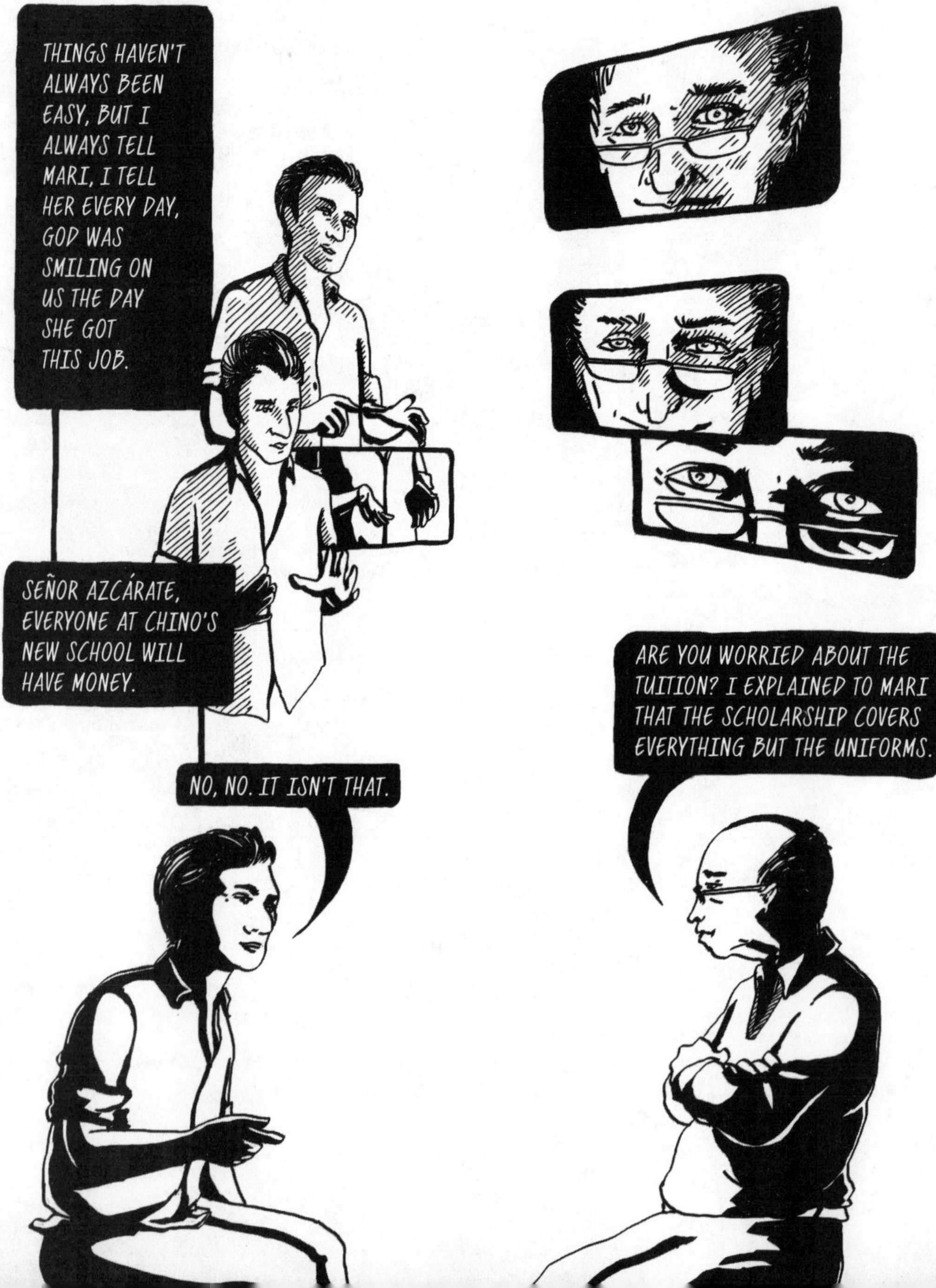
THINGS HAVEN'T ALWAYS BEEN EASY, BUT I ALWAYS TELL MARI, I TELL HER EVERY DAY, GOD WAS SMILING ON US THE DAY SHE GOT THIS JOB.
SEÑOR AZCÁRATE, EVERYONE AT CHINO'S NEW SCHOOL WILL HAVE MONEY.
ARE YOU WORRIED ABOUT THE TUITION? I EXPLAINED TO MARI THAT THE SCHOLARSHIP COVERS EVERYTHING BUT THE UNIFORMS.
NO, NO. IT ISN'T THAT.

The engineer observed with an air of patrician benevolence.

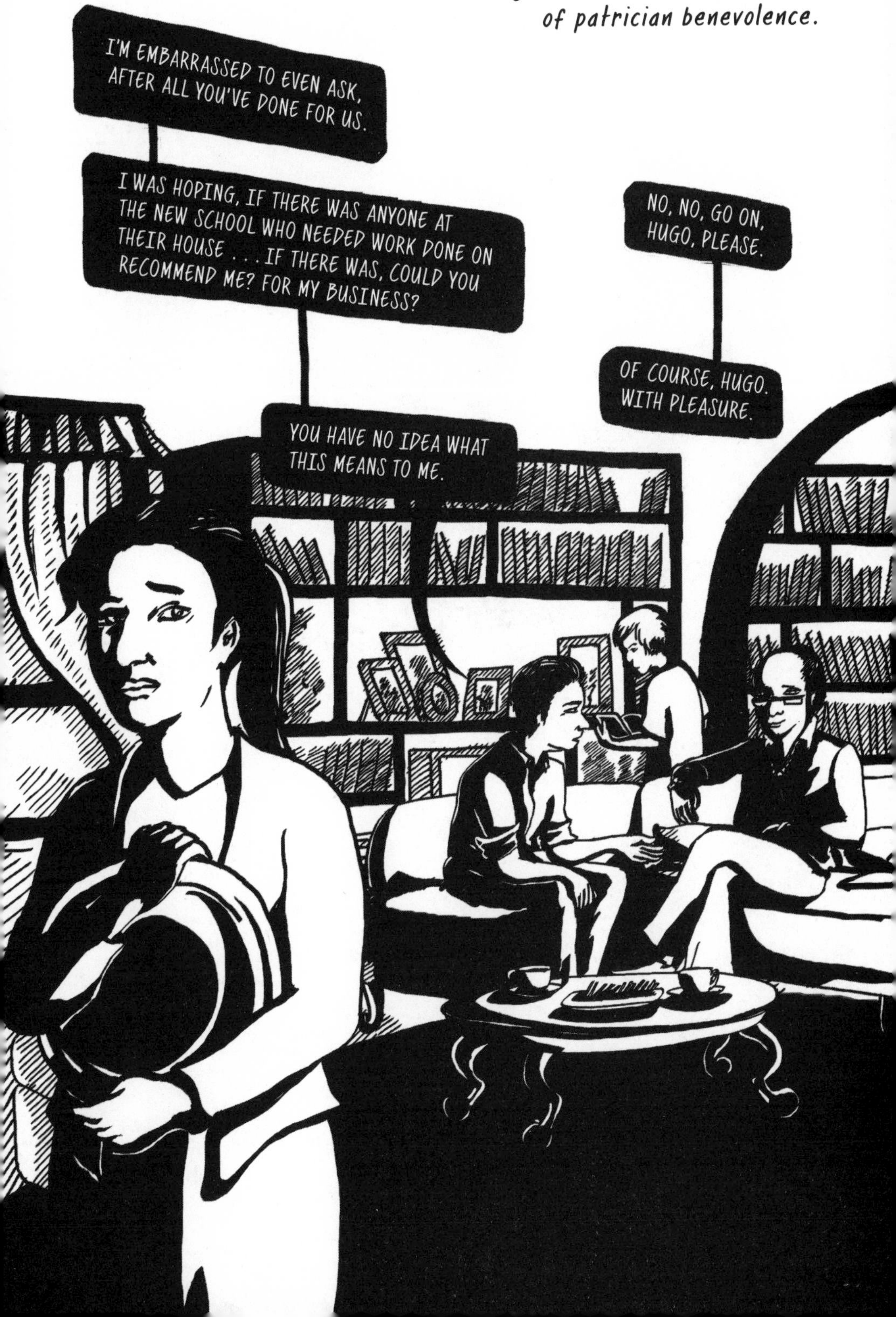
I'M EMBARRASSED TO EVEN ASK, AFTER ALL YOU'VE DONE FOR US.
I WAS HOPING, IF THERE WAS ANYONE AT THE NEW SCHOOL WHO NEEDED WORK DONE ON THEIR HOUSE . . . IF THERE WAS, COULD YOU RECOMMEND ME? FOR MY BUSINESS?
NO, NO, GO ON, HUGO, PLEASE.
OF COURSE, HUGO. WITH PLEASURE.
YOU HAVE NO IDEA WHAT THIS MEANS TO ME.

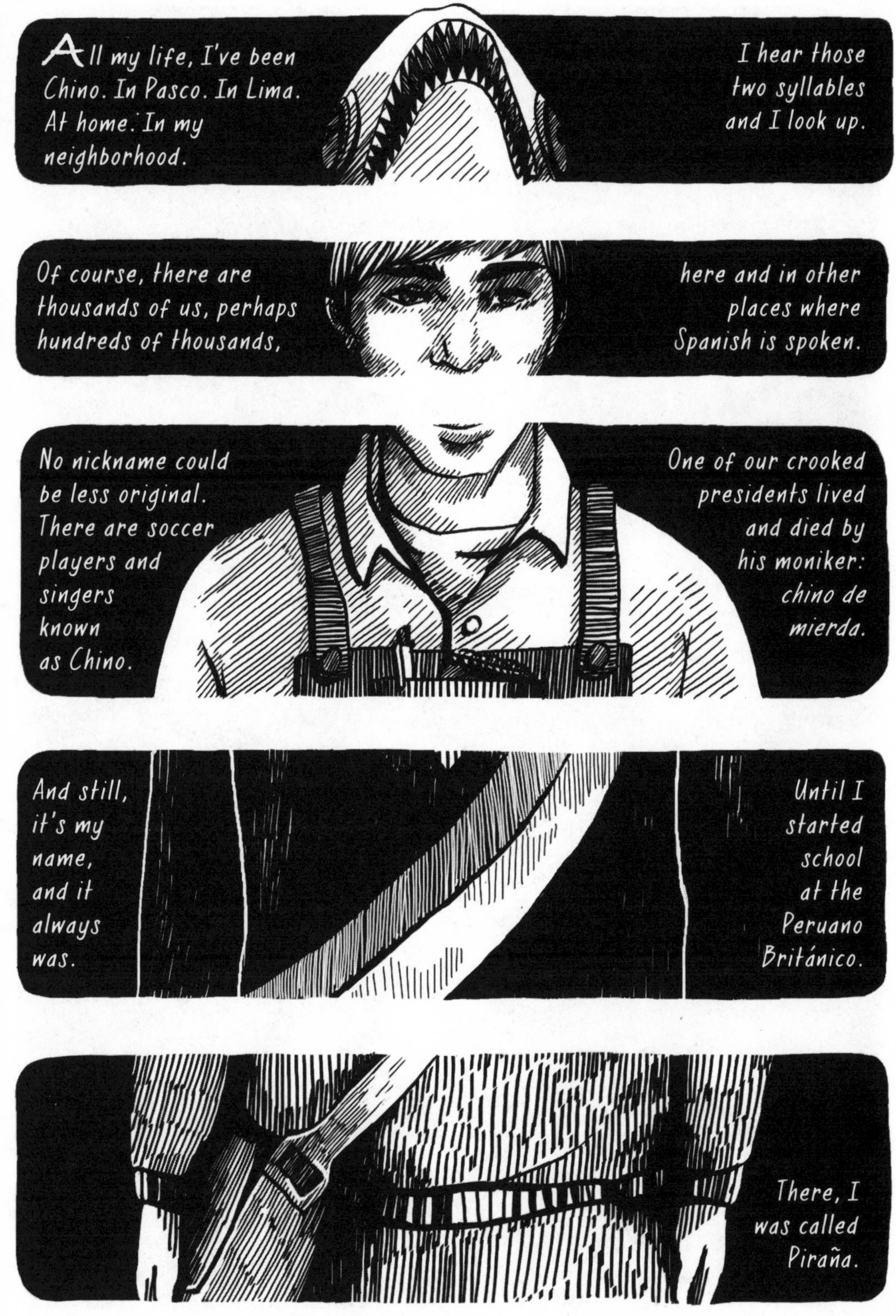
All my life, I've been Chino. In Pasco. In Lima. At home. In my neighborhood.
I hear those two syllables and I look up.
Of course, there are thousands of us, perhaps hundreds of thousands,
here and in other places where Spanish is spoken.
No nickname could be less original. There are soccer players and singers known as Chino.
One of our crooked presidents lived and died by his moniker: chino de mierda.
And still, it's my name, and it always was.
Until I started school at the Peruano Británico.
There, I was called Piraña.

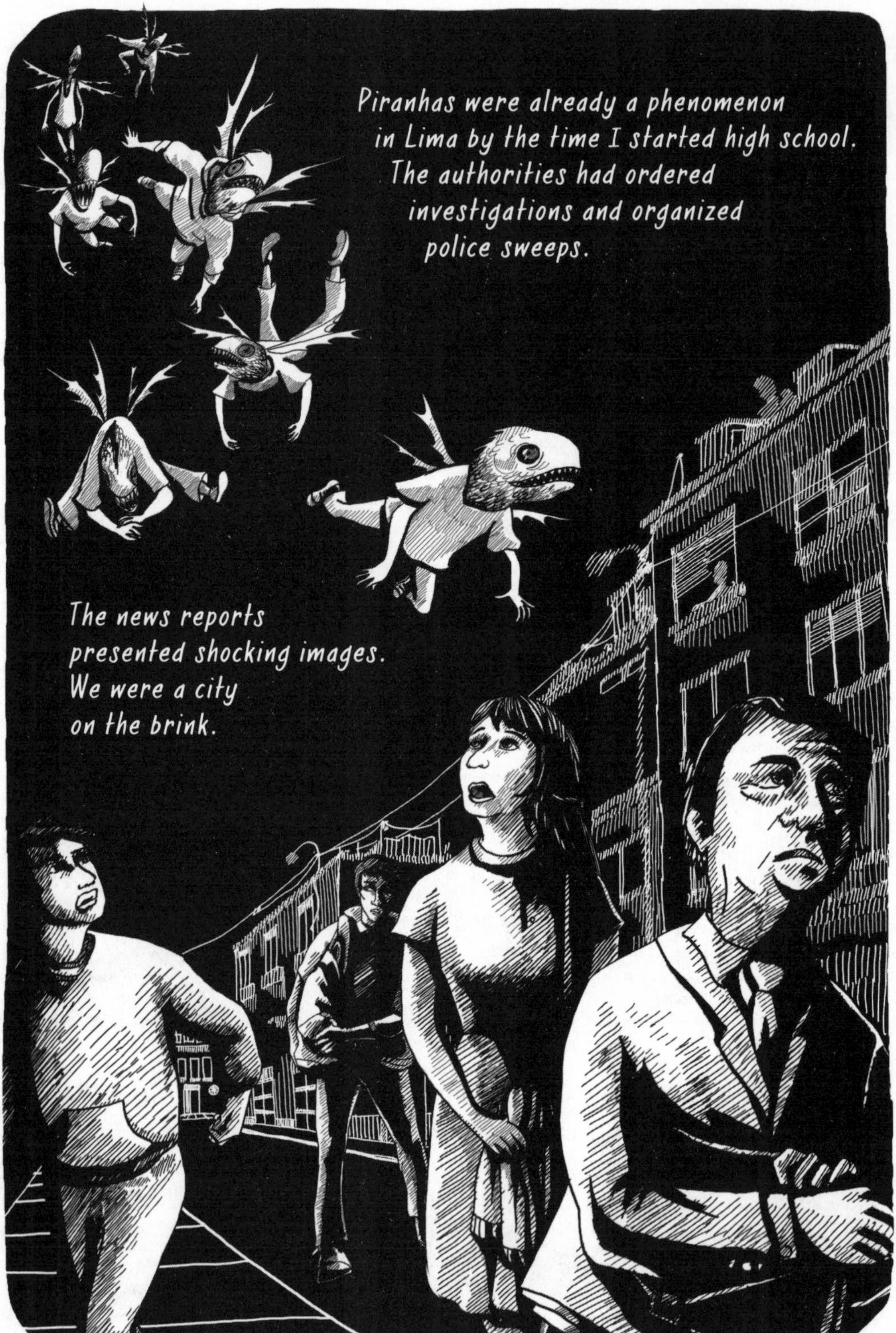
Piranhas were already a phenomenon in Lima by the time I started high school. The authorities had ordered investigations and organized police sweeps.
The news reports presented shocking images. We were a city on the brink.

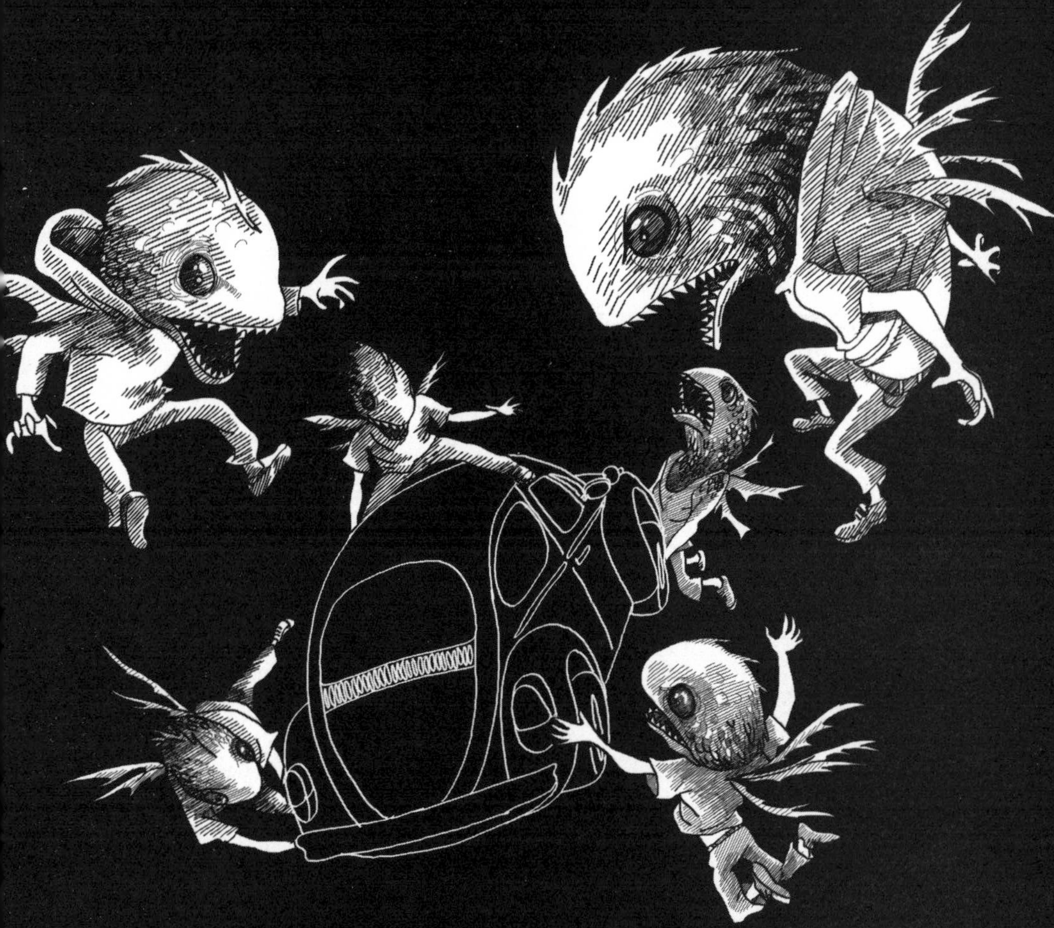

In packs of fifteen or twenty, they would swarm a car and swiftly, ruthlessly undress it. Hubcaps, mirrors, lights. More audacious crews started breaking windows, taking briefcases, cell phones, watches, sunglasses, radios. "Full service," people joked darkly. "A new kind of crime," sociologists said. And an astute observer—of the kind who traffics in phrases—named them "piranhas."

The teacher called us one by one, and we filed into our new classroom.

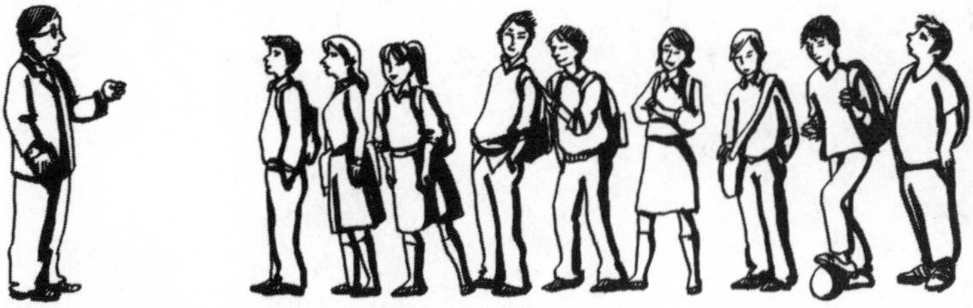

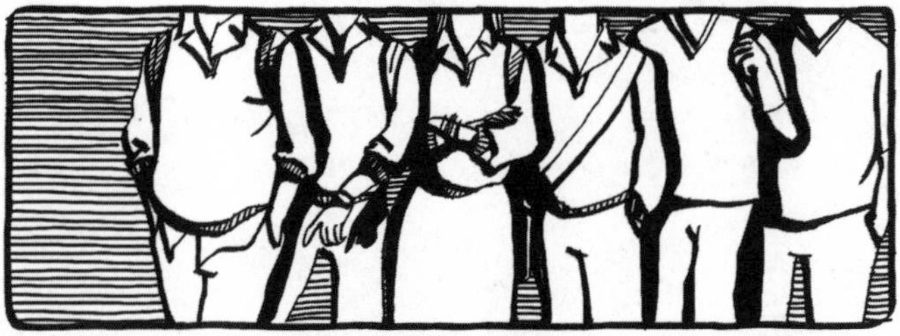

From a distance, I looked like all the others.

My new classmates found me at recess. One kid had a soccer ball in his hands. He kicked it in my direction.

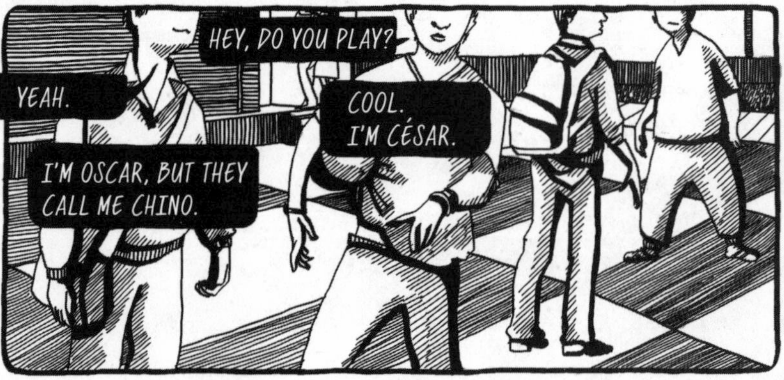
HEY, DO YOU PLAY?
YEAH.
COOL. I'M CÉSAR.
I'M OSCAR, BUT THEY CALL ME CHINO.

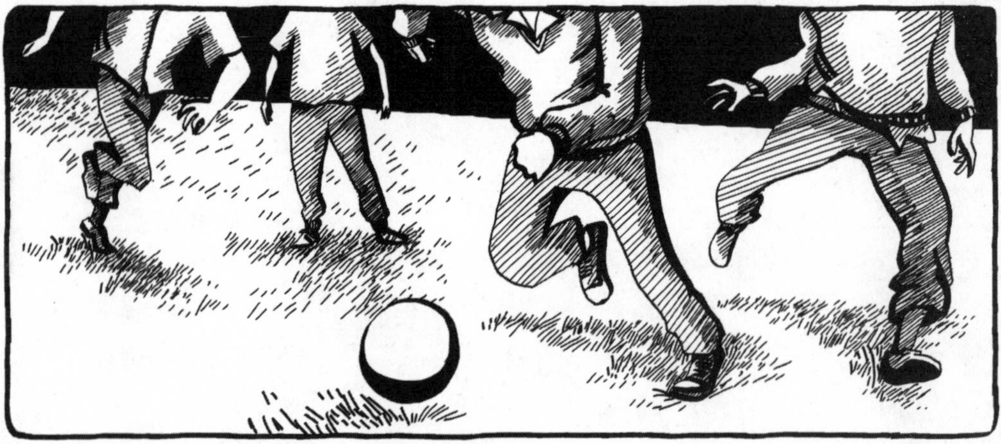

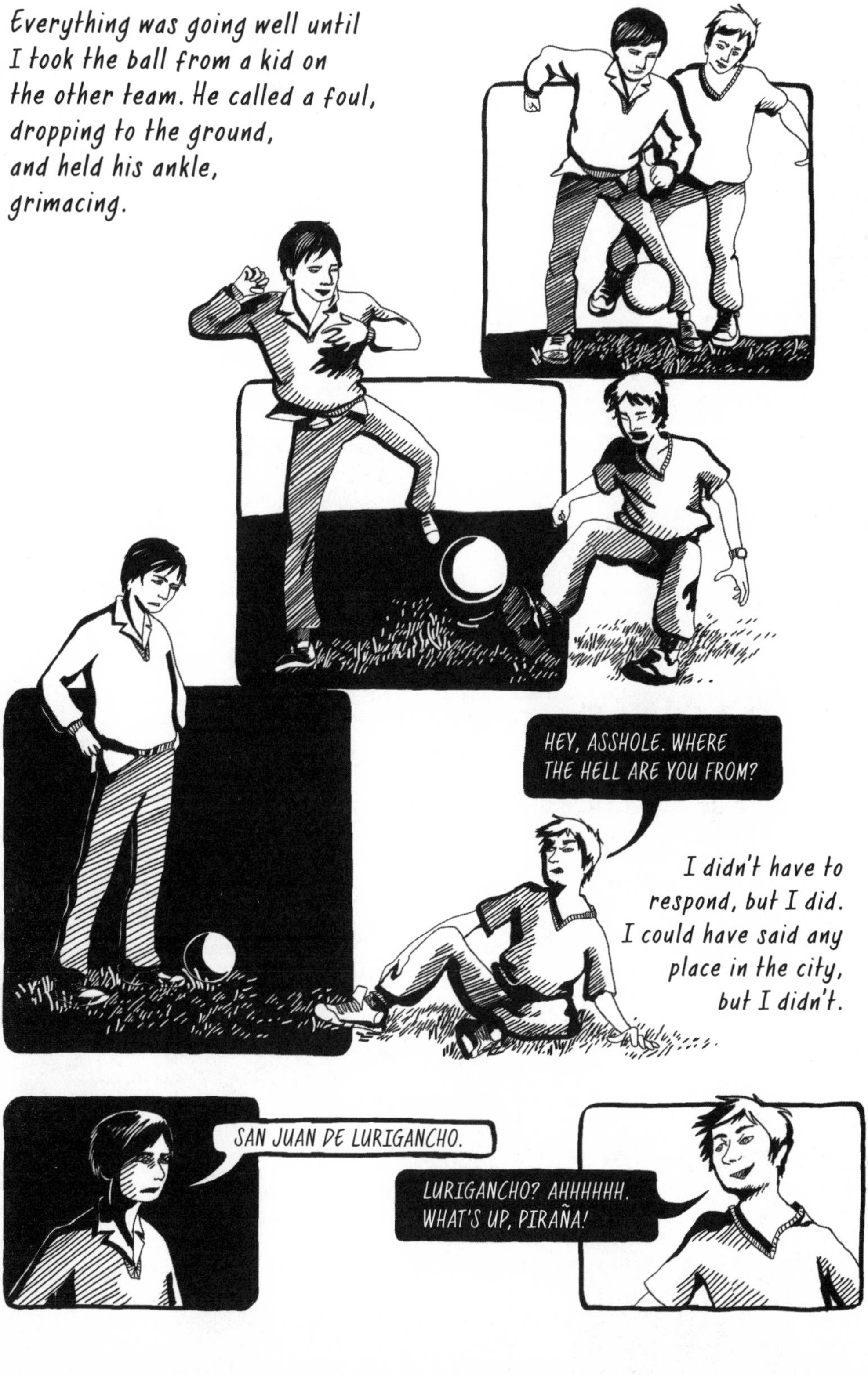
Everything was going well until I took the ball from a kid on the other team. He called a foul, dropping to the ground, and held his ankle, grimacing.
HEY, ASSHOLE. WHERE THE HELL ARE YOU FROM?
I didn't have to respond, but I did. I could have said any place in the city, but I didn't.
SAN JUAN DE LURIGANCHO.
LURIGANCHO? AHHHHHH. WHAT'S UP, PIRAÑA!

I met Toño the next morning at eight-thirty in front of San Francisco. I was still shaking off a hangover. The details of the previous night's conversation were so hazy, I couldn't recall exactly how I had ended up there or what commitments I had made.

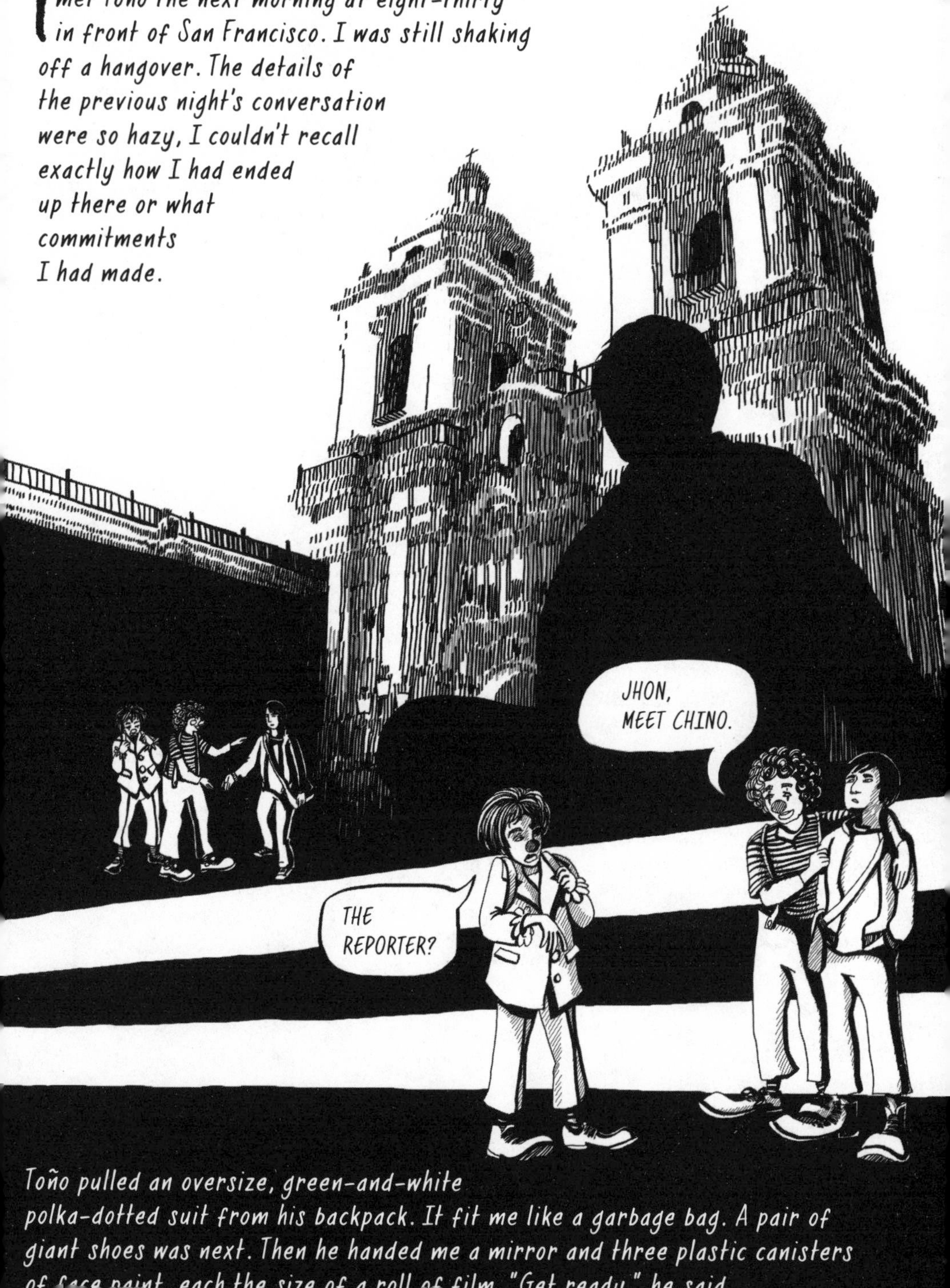
JHON, MEET CHINO.
THE REPORTER?

Toño pulled an oversize, green-and-white polka-dotted suit from his backpack. It fit me like a garbage bag. A pair of giant shoes was next. Then he handed me a mirror and three plastic canisters of face paint, each the size of a roll of film. "Get ready," he said.

I felt outside myself, and I liked it. It surprised me how relaxed I was, and how invisible. Most people walked right by us, without so much as looking in our direction. Jhon and Toño chatted about soccer, I watched and listened in a daydream. We were ghosts in the multitude, three more citizen-employees of the great city, awake and alive on a Thursday morning. We let a few buses pass because they were too empty. Toño explained it was bad luck to start the morning that way. Finally, he signaled to us as a more crowded bus approached.

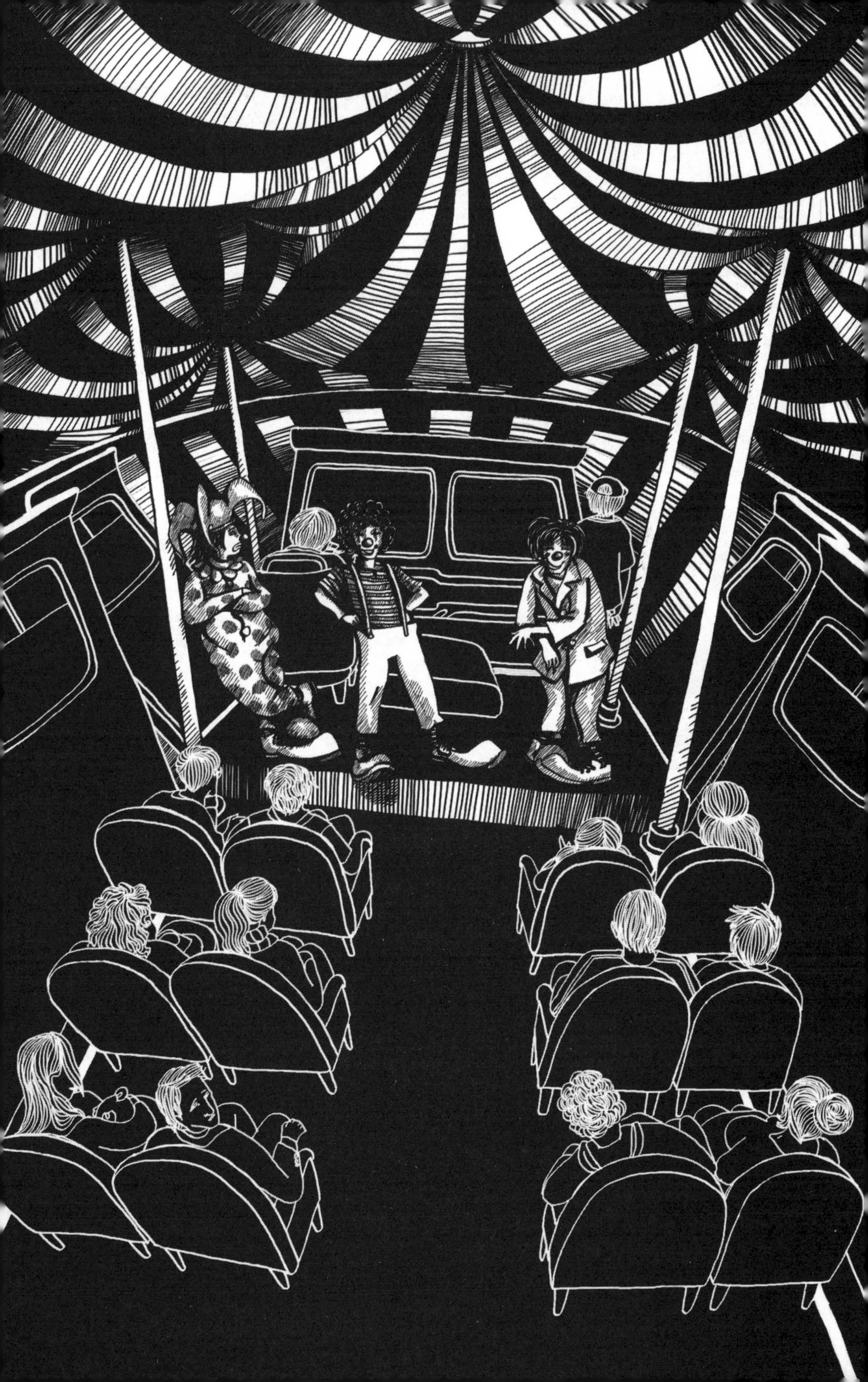

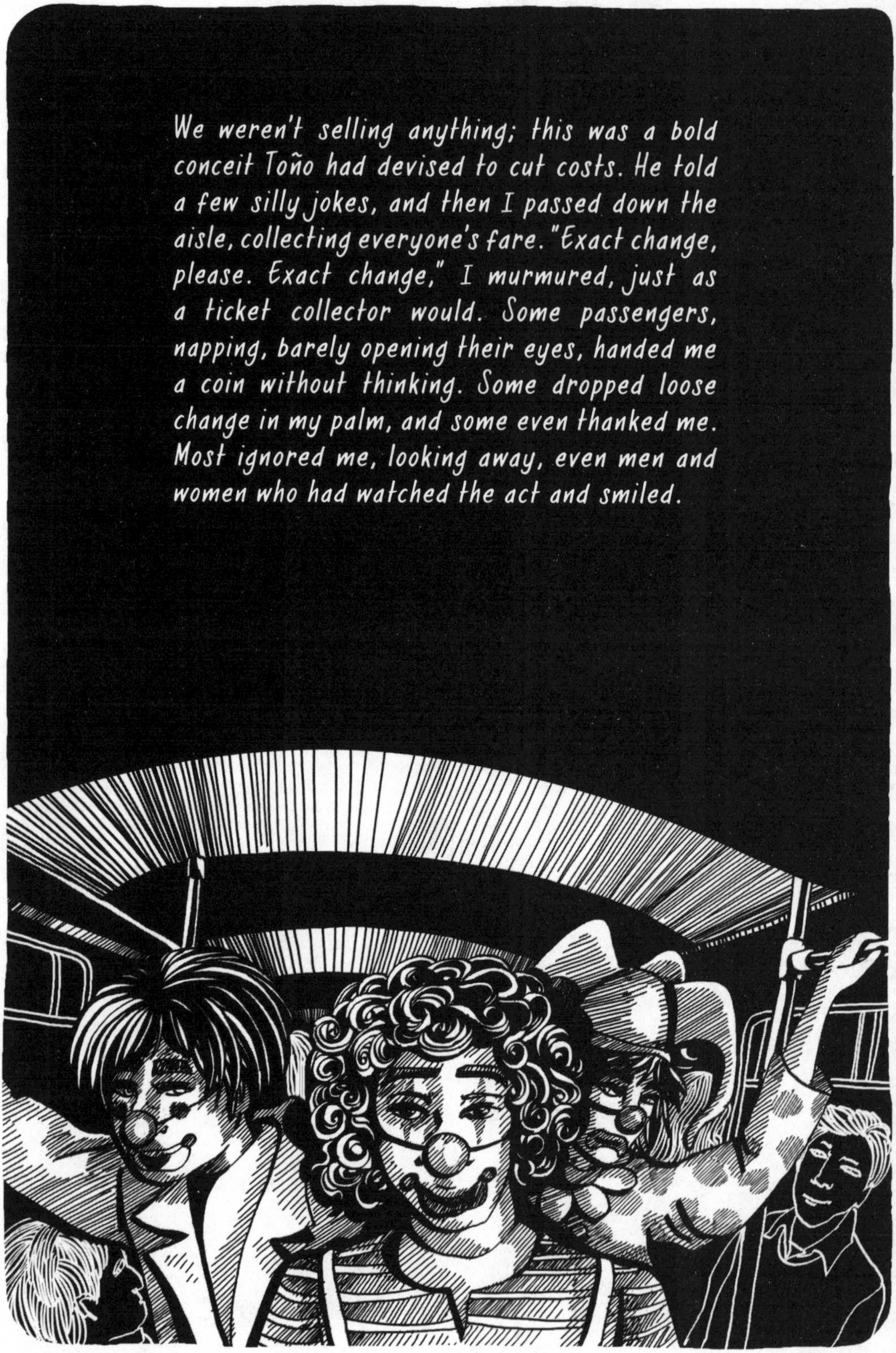
We weren't selling anything; this was a bold conceit Toño had devised to cut costs. He told a few silly jokes, and then I passed down the aisle, collecting everyone's fare. "Exact change, please. Exact change," I murmured, just as a ticket collector would. Some passengers, napping, barely opening their eyes, handed me a coin without thinking. Some dropped loose change in my palm, and some even thanked me. Most ignored me, looking away, even men and women who had watched the act and smiled.

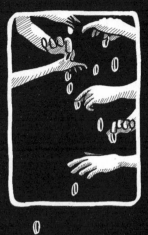
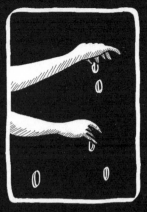

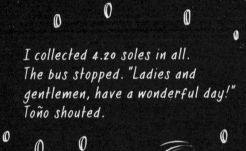

I collected 4.20 soles in all.
The bus stopped. "Ladies and
gentlemen, have a wonderful day!"
Toño shouted.

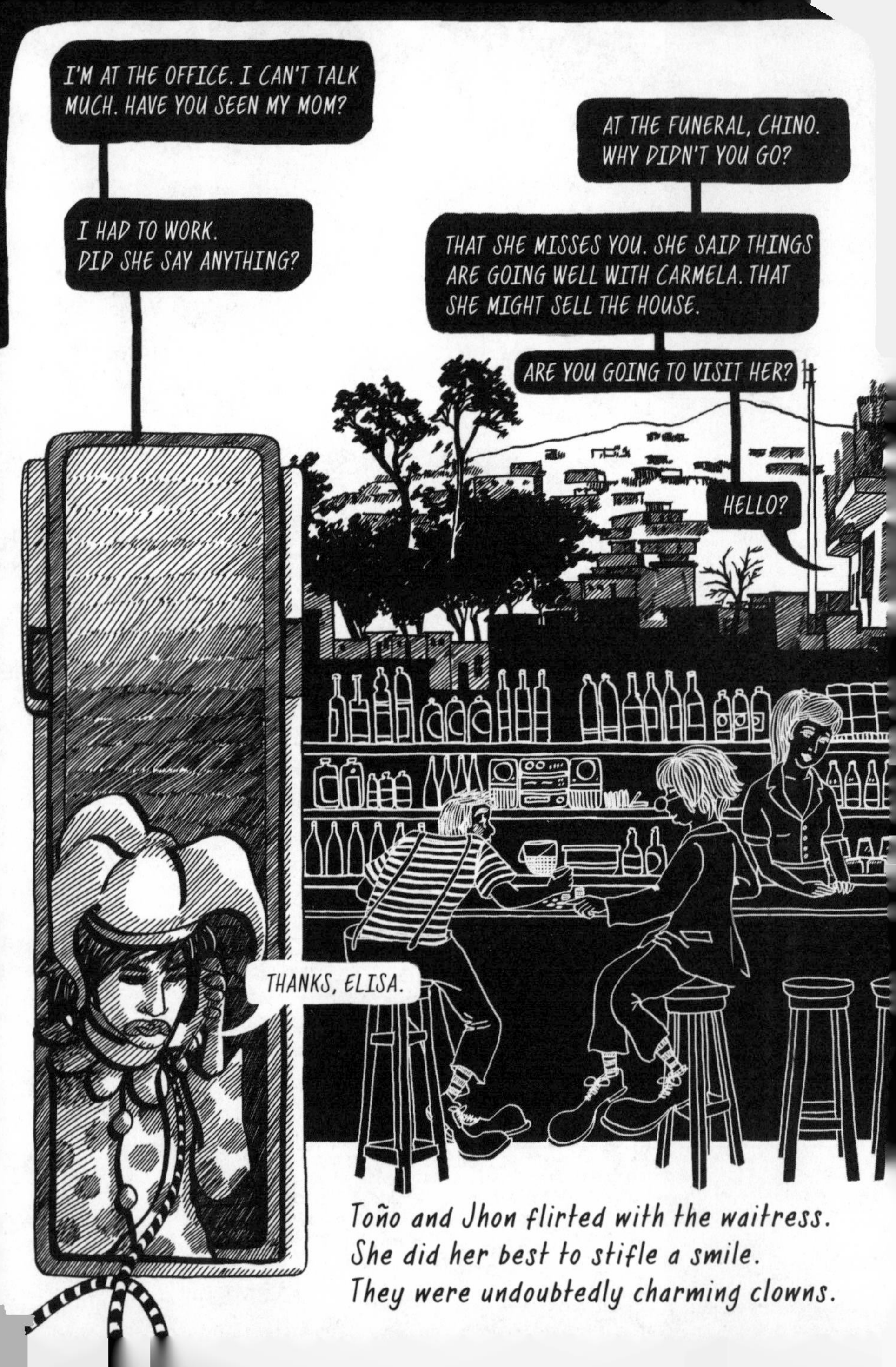
I'M AT THE OFFICE. I CAN'T TALK MUCH. HAVE YOU SEEN MY MOM?
AT THE FUNERAL, CHINO. WHY DIDN'T YOU GO?
I HAD TO WORK. DID SHE SAY ANYTHING?
THAT SHE MISSES YOU. SHE SAID THINGS ARE GOING WELL WITH CARMELA. THAT SHE MIGHT SELL THE HOUSE.
ARE YOU GOING TO VISIT HER?
HELLO?
THANKS, ELISA.
Toño and Jhon flirted with the waitress. She did her best to stifle a smile. They were undoubtedly charming clowns.

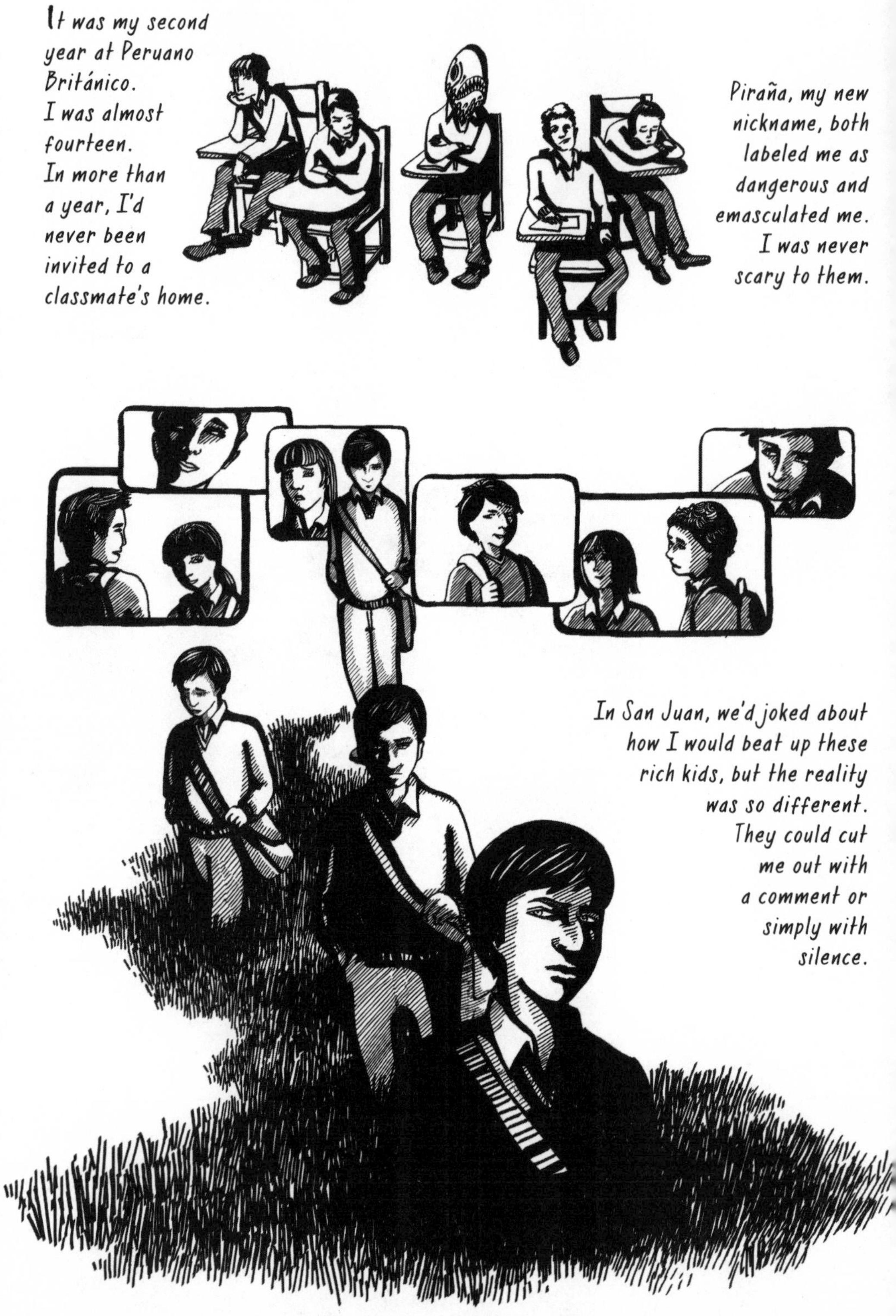
It was my second year at Peruano Británico. I was almost fourteen. In more than a year, I'd never been invited to a classmate's home.
Piraña, my new nickname, both labeled me as dangerous and emasculated me. I was never scary to them.
In San Juan, we'd joked about how I would beat up these rich kids, but the reality was so different. They could cut me out with a comment or simply with silence.

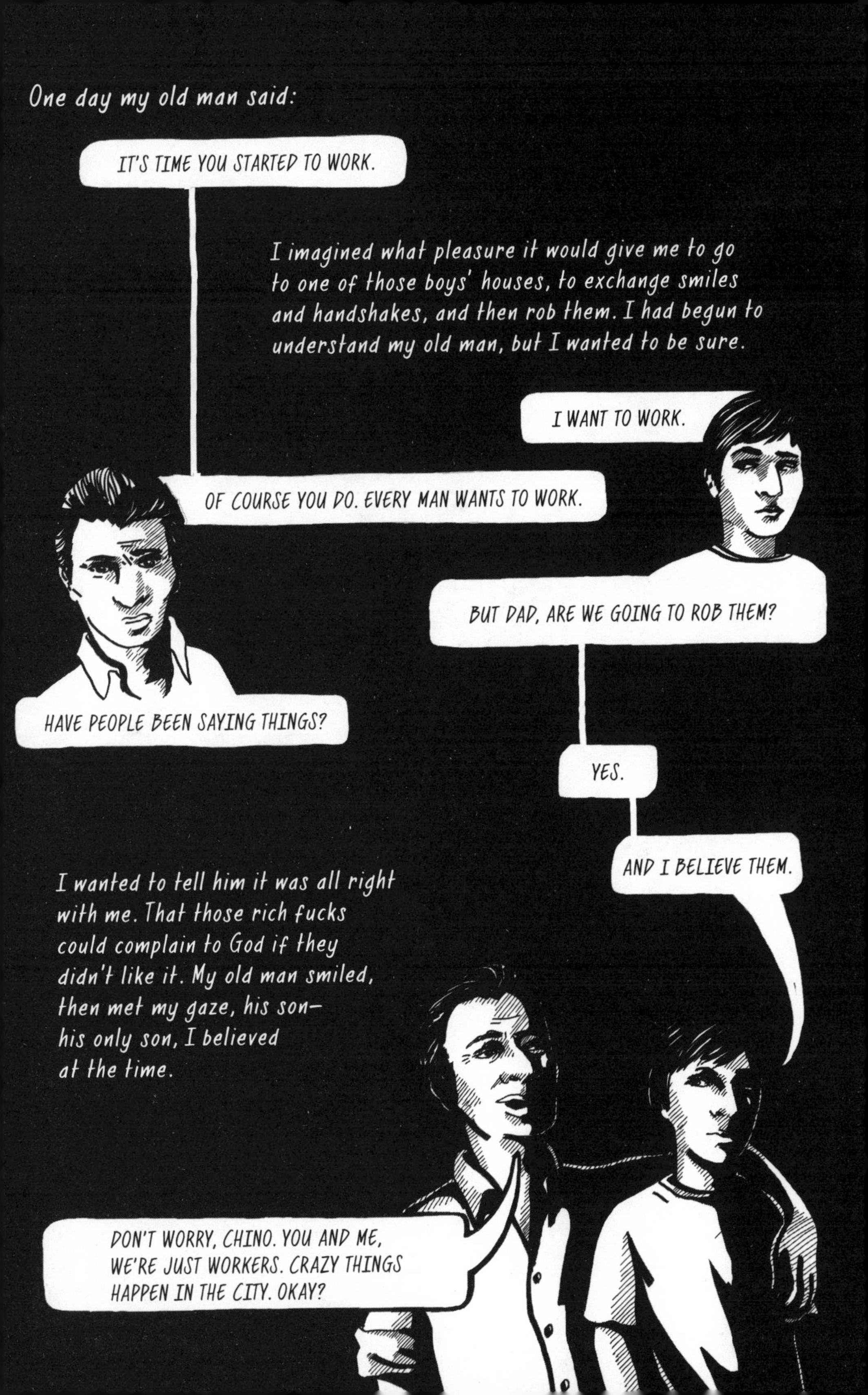
One day my old man said:
IT'S TIME YOU STARTED TO WORK.
I imagined what pleasure it would give me to go to one of those boys' houses, to exchange smiles and handshakes, and then rob them. I had begun to understand my old man, but I wanted to be sure.
I WANT TO WORK.
OF COURSE YOU DO. EVERY MAN WANTS TO WORK.
BUT DAD, ARE WE GOING TO ROB THEM?
HAVE PEOPLE BEEN SAYING THINGS?
YES.
AND I BELIEVE THEM.
I wanted to tell him it was all right with me. That those rich fucks could complain to God if they didn't like it. My old man smiled, then met my gaze, his son—his only son, I believed at the time.
DON'T WORRY, CHINO. YOU AND ME, WE'RE JUST WORKERS. CRAZY THINGS HAPPEN IN THE CITY. OKAY?

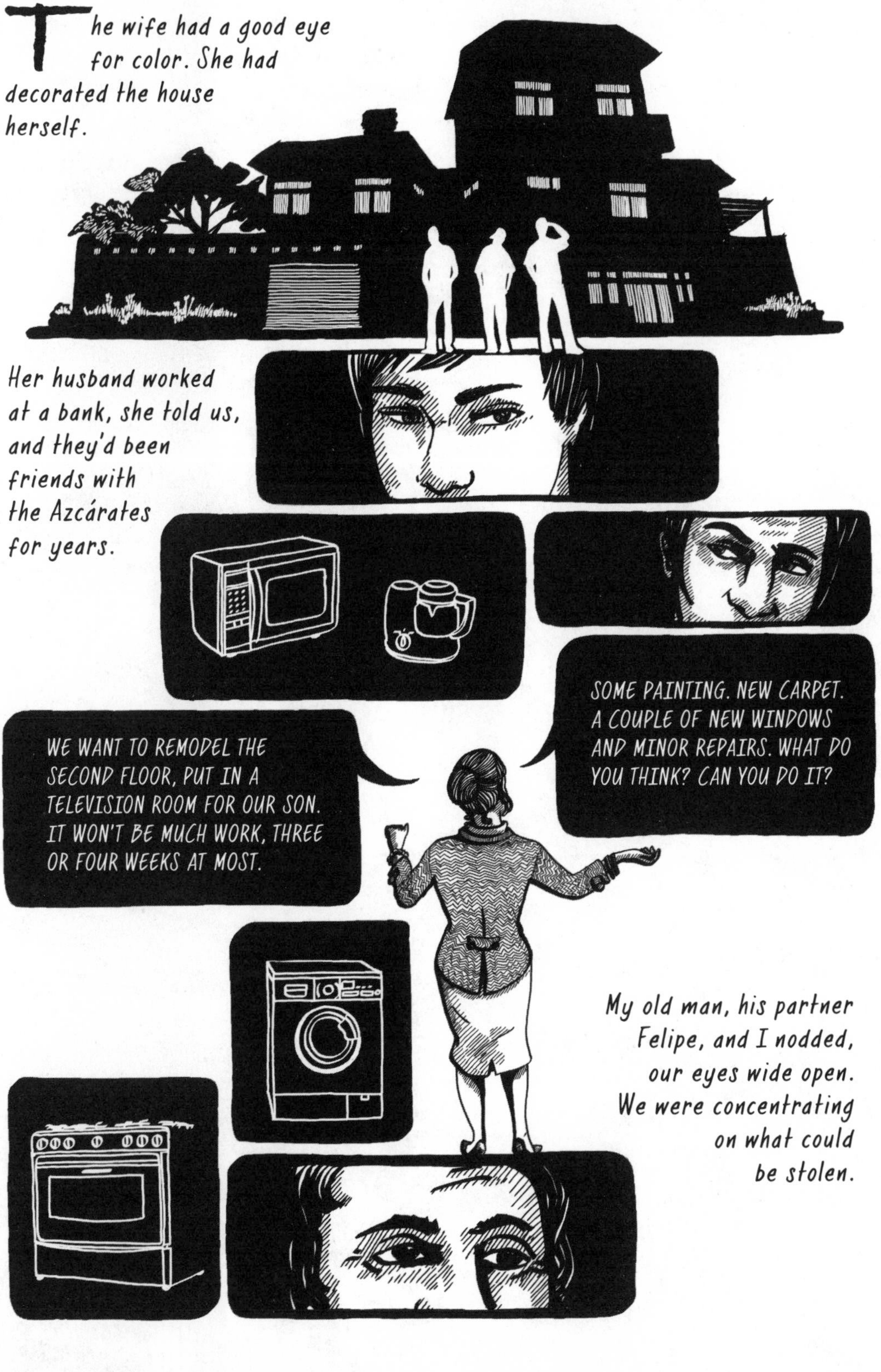
The wife had a good eye for color. She had decorated the house herself.
Her husband worked at a bank, she told us, and they'd been friends with the Azcárates for years.
WE WANT TO REMODEL THE SECOND FLOOR, PUT IN A TELEVISION ROOM FOR OUR SON. IT WON'T BE MUCH WORK, THREE OR FOUR WEEKS AT MOST.
SOME PAINTING. NEW CARPET. A COUPLE OF NEW WINDOWS AND MINOR REPAIRS. WHAT DO YOU THINK? CAN YOU DO IT?
My old man, his partner Felipe, and I nodded, our eyes wide open. We were concentrating on what could be stolen.

I worked on Saturdays, and I saw my dad more there than I did at home. Most of the week he wasn't staying with us anymore. His youngest son would have still been in diapers back then, and surely my mother knew about Carmela by that point.

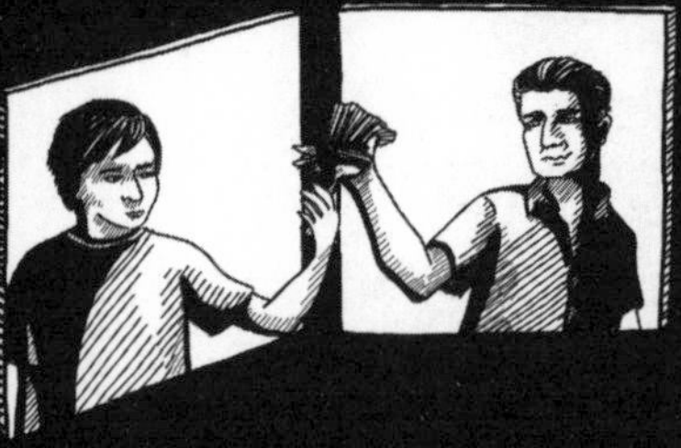

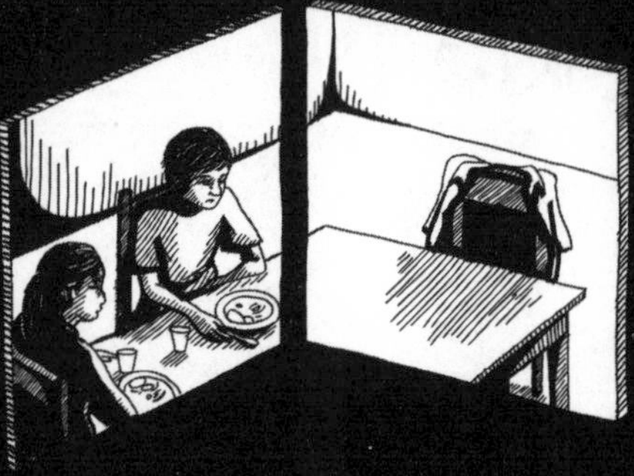

When he came home, they would argue, though I never knew why.

The construction on our house had stalled, the second floor still open air, a thick plastic sheet tied at the corners of three walls.

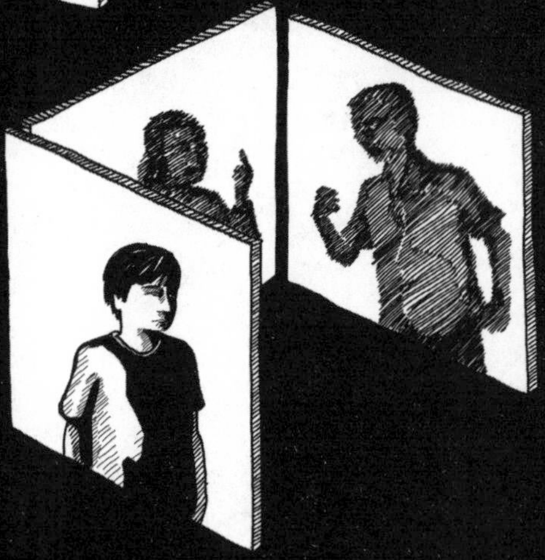

When they were fighting, I retreated there and watched the ridges of the hills draw lines against the sky.

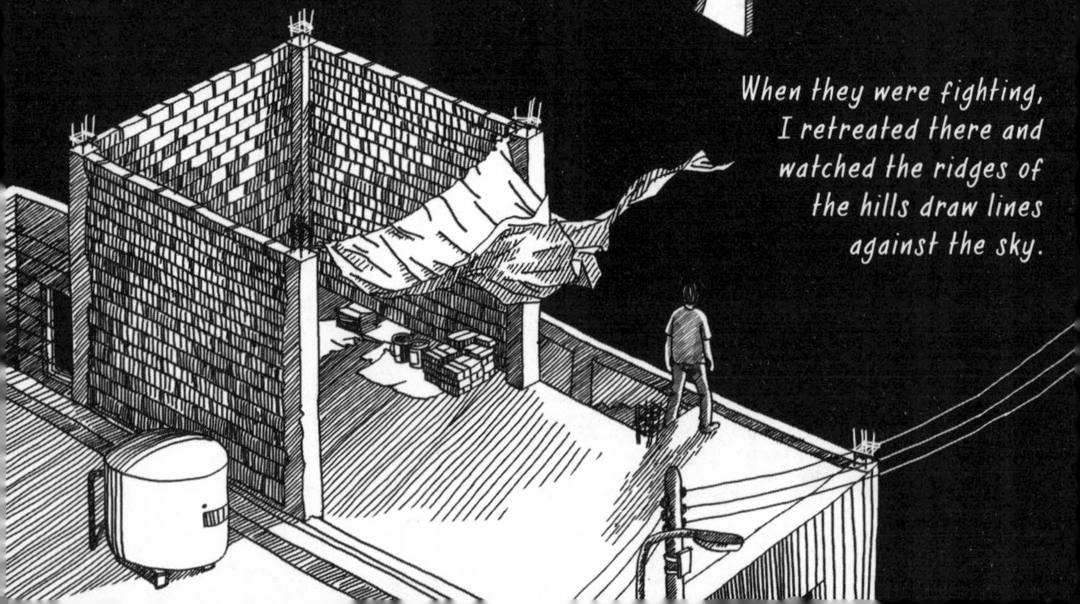

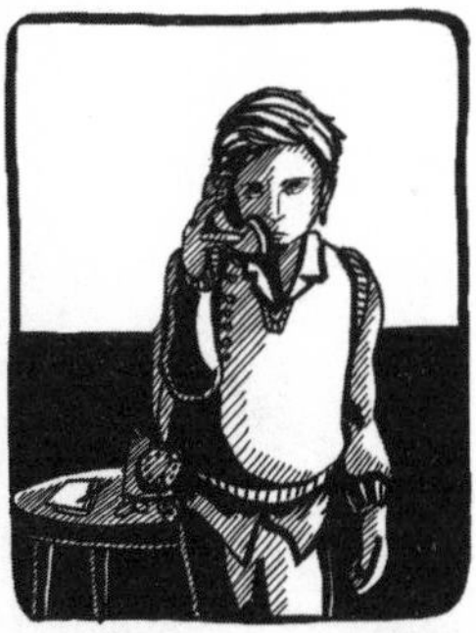

The family we worked for had a son, Andrés, who was a year ahead of me at my school.

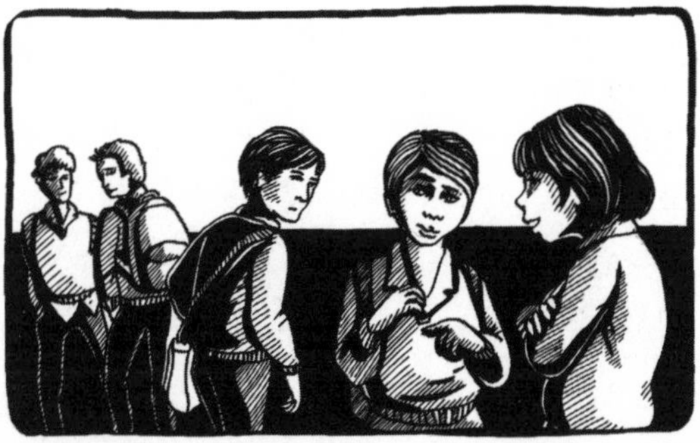

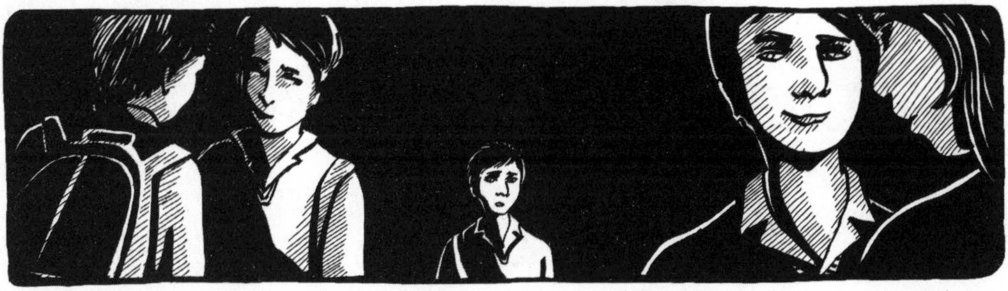

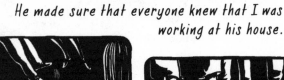

He made sure that everyone knew that I was working at his house.

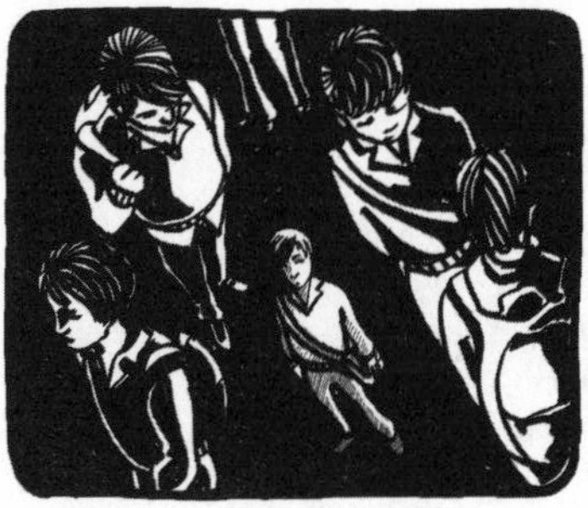

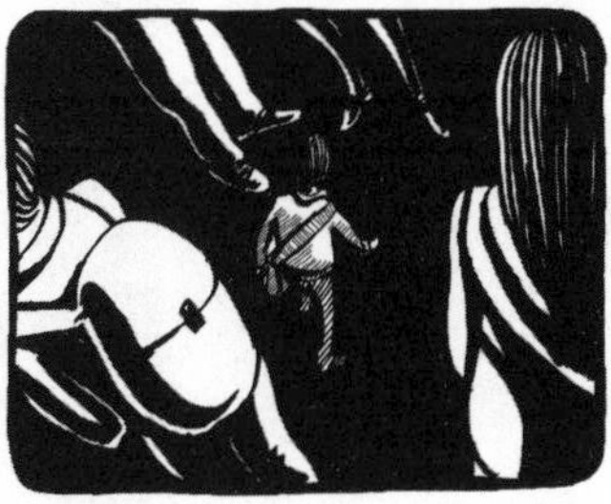

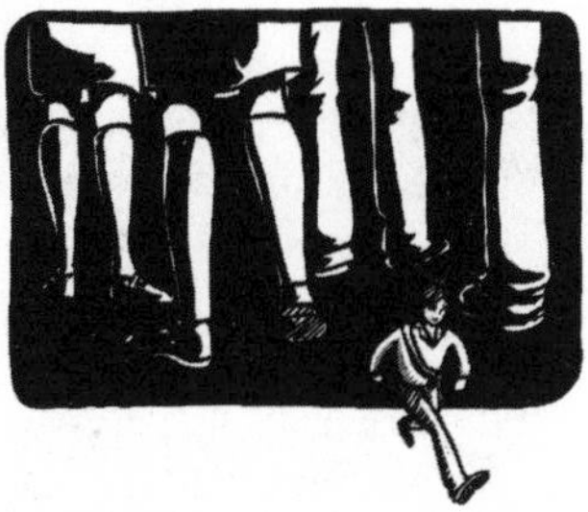

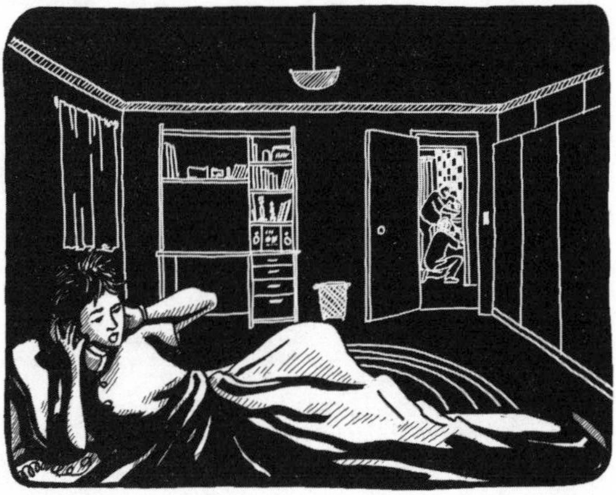

He paraded through the work area, complained of the dust, asked his mother to tell us that the sanding was hurting his ears. He put on a show of power. I bowed my head and pretended not to hear.

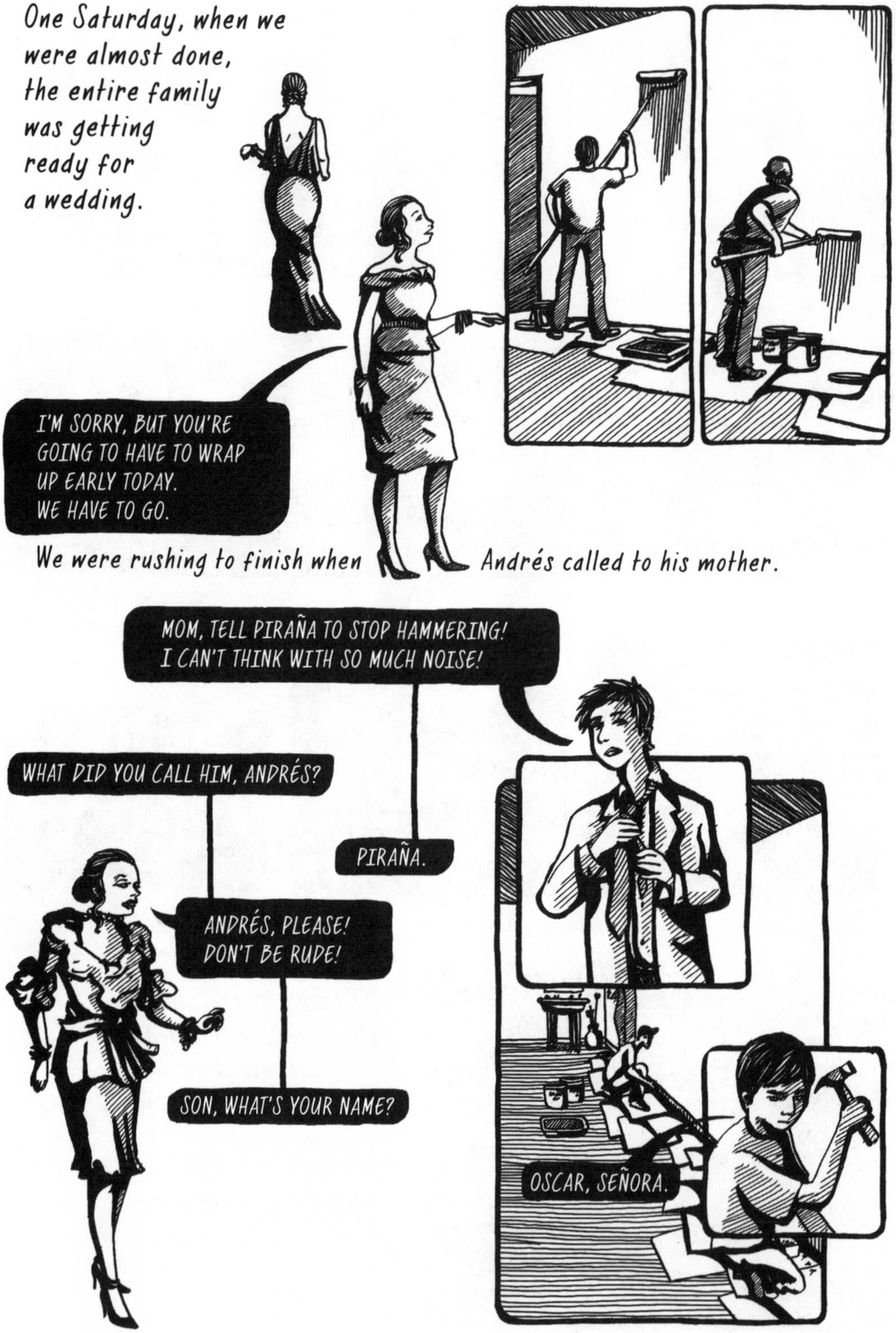
One Saturday, when we were almost done, the entire family was getting ready for a wedding.
I'M SORRY, BUT YOU'RE GOING TO HAVE TO WRAP UP EARLY TODAY. WE HAVE TO GO.
We were rushing to finish when
Andrés called to his mother.
MOM, TELL PIRAÑA TO STOP HAMMERING! I CAN'T THINK WITH SO MUCH NOISE!
WHAT DID YOU CALL HIM, ANDRÉS?
PIRAÑA.
ANDRÉS, PLEASE! DON'T BE RUDE!
SON, WHAT'S YOUR NAME?
OSCAR, SEÑORA.

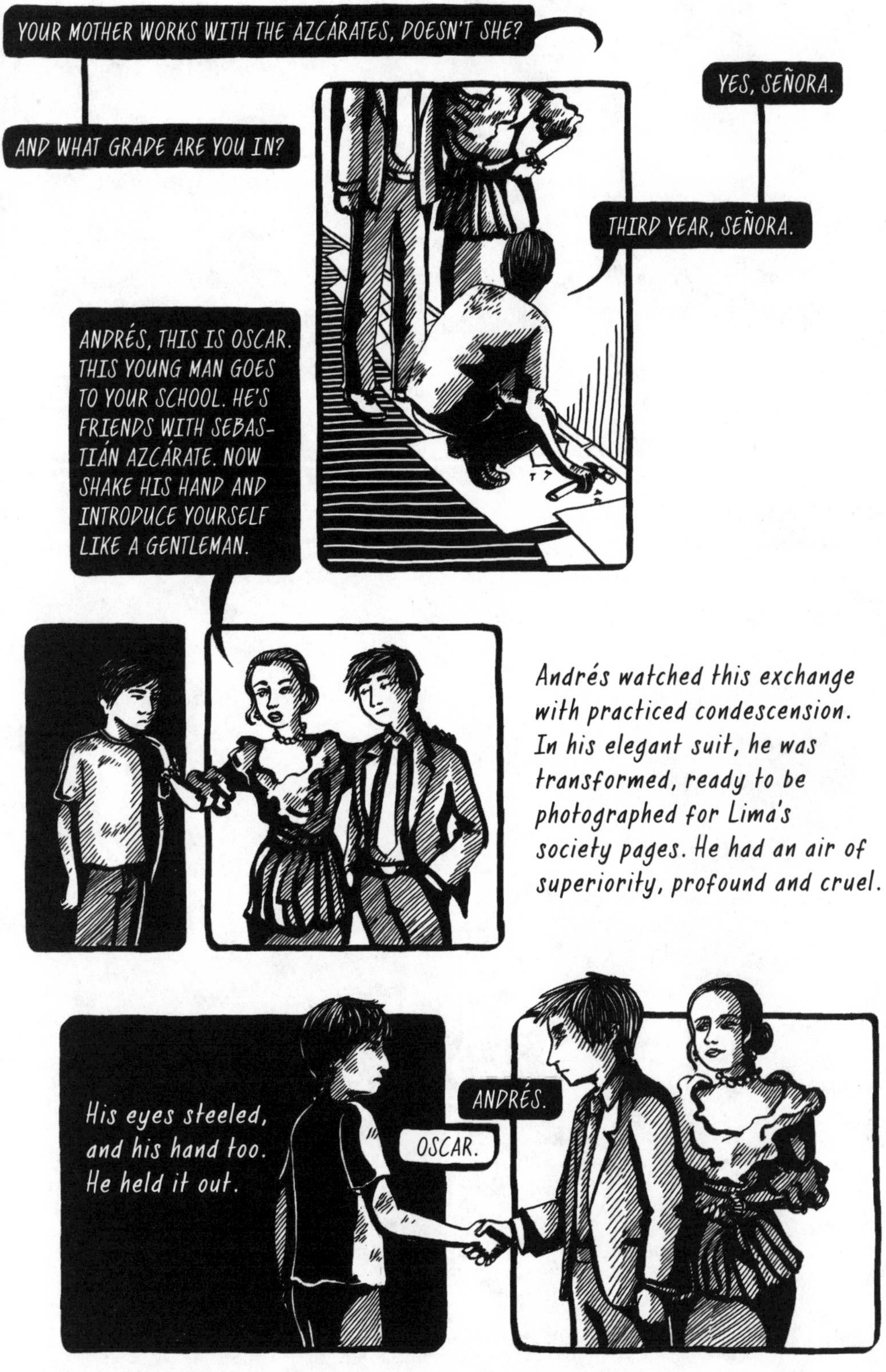
YOUR MOTHER WORKS WITH THE AZCÁRATES, DOESN'T SHE?
YES, SEÑORA.
AND WHAT GRADE ARE YOU IN?
THIRD YEAR, SEÑORA.
ANDRÉS, THIS IS OSCAR. THIS YOUNG MAN GOES TO YOUR SCHOOL. HE'S FRIENDS WITH SEBASTIÁN AZCÁRATE. NOW SHAKE HIS HAND AND INTRODUCE YOURSELF LIKE A GENTLEMAN.
Andrés watched this exchange with practiced condescension. In his elegant suit, he was transformed, ready to be photographed for Lima's society pages. He had an air of superiority, profound and cruel.
His eyes steeled, and his hand too. He held it out.
ANDRÉS.
OSCAR.

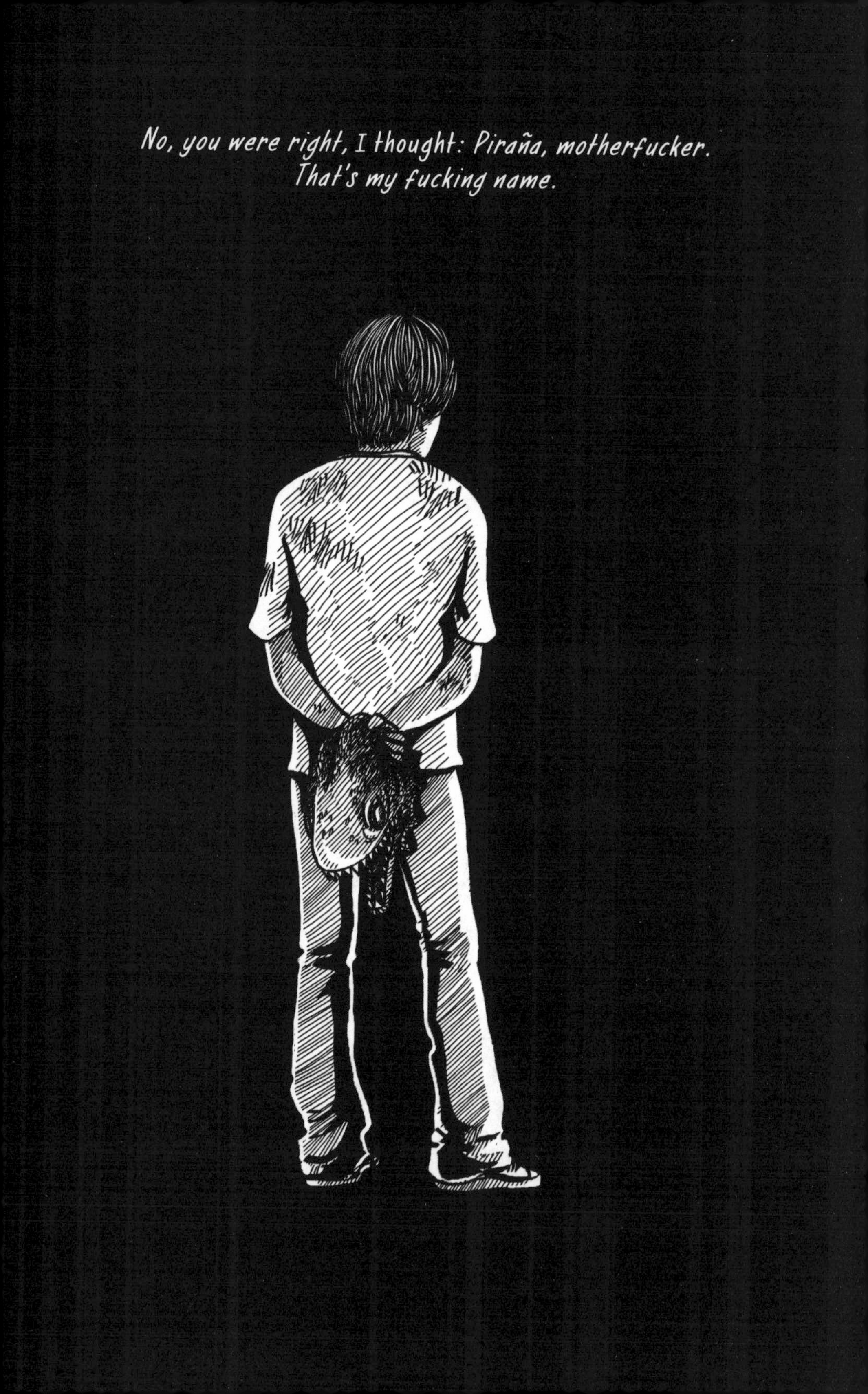
No, you were right, I thought: Piraña, motherfucker.
That's my fucking name.

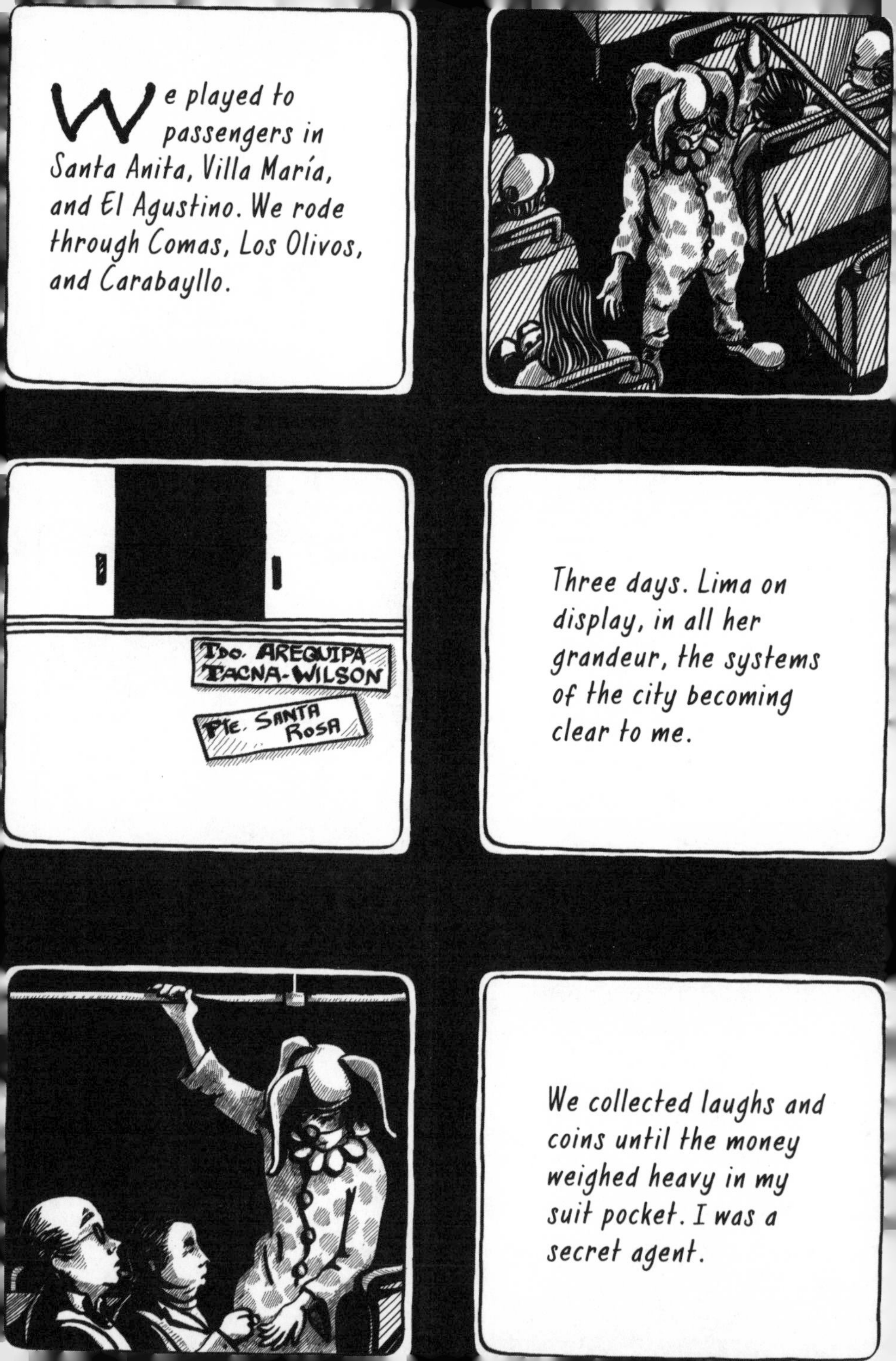
We played to passengers in Santa Anita, Villa María, and El Agustino. We rode through Comas, Los Olivos, and Carabayllo.
Tdo. AREQUIPA TACNA-WILSON
Pte. SANTA ROSA
Three days. Lima on display, in all her grandeur, the systems of the city becoming clear to me.
We collected laughs and coins until the money weighed heavy in my suit pocket. I was a secret agent.

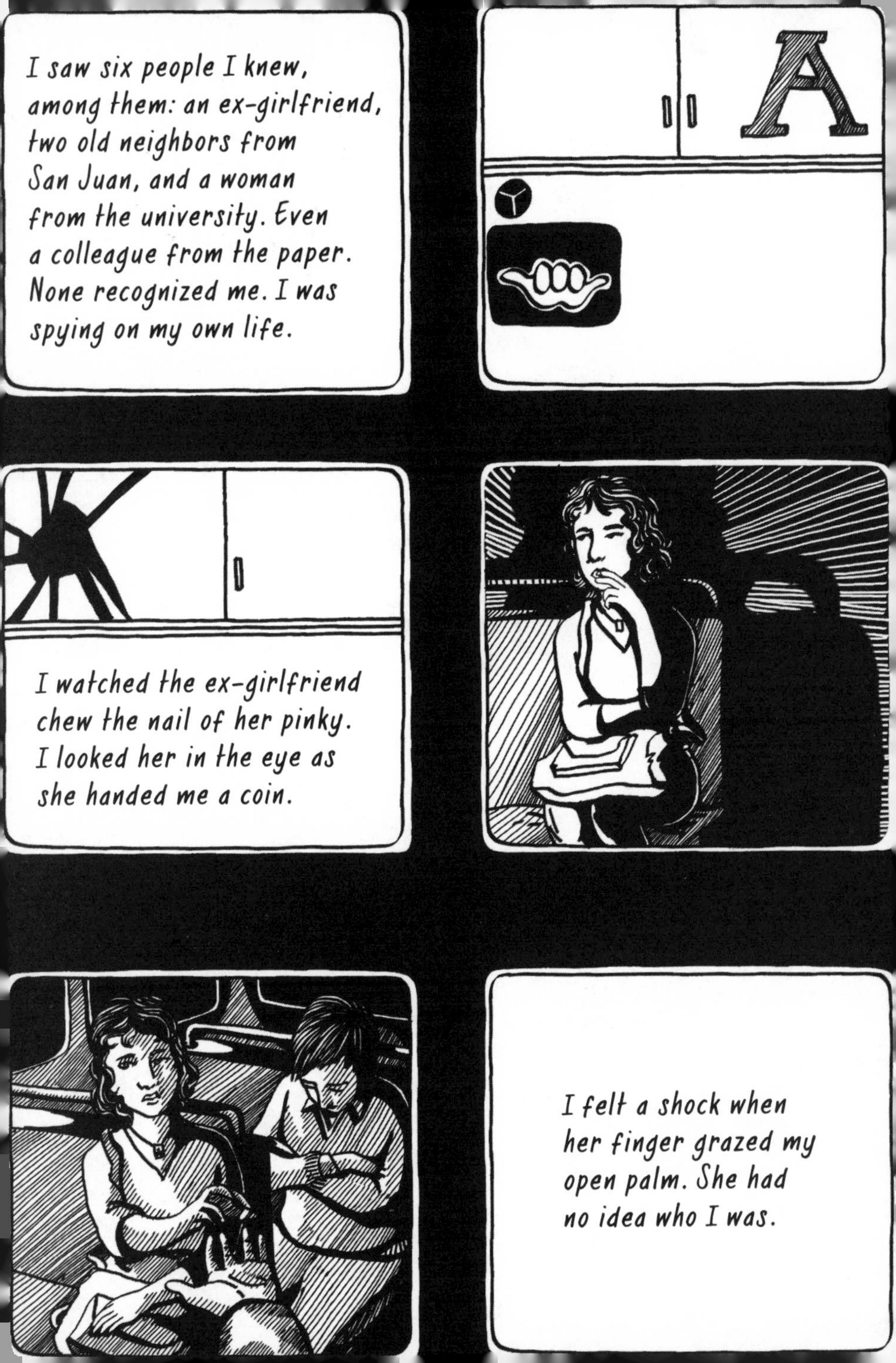
I saw six people I knew, among them: an ex-girlfriend, two old neighbors from San Juan, and a woman from the university. Even a colleague from the paper. None recognized me. I was spying on my own life.
A
I watched the ex-girlfriend chew the nail of her pinky. I looked her in the eye as she handed me a coin.
I felt a shock when her finger grazed my open palm. She had no idea who I was.

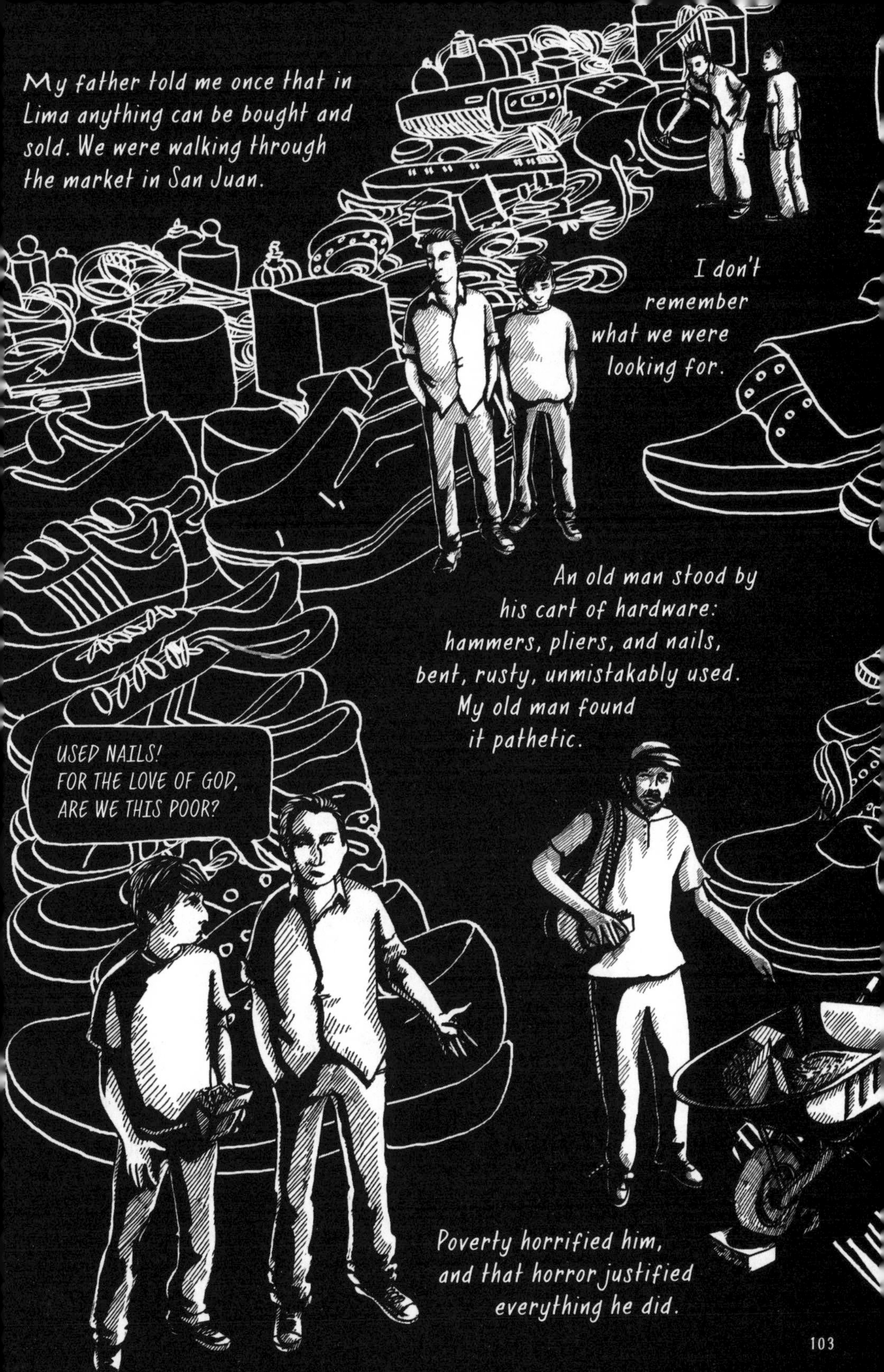
My father told me once that in Lima anything can be bought and sold. We were walking through the market in San Juan.
I don't remember what we were looking for.
An old man stood by his cart of hardware: hammers, pliers, and nails, bent, rusty, unmistakably used. My old man found it pathetic.
USED NAILS! FOR THE LOVE OF GOD, ARE WE THIS POOR?
Poverty horrified him, and that horror justified everything he did.

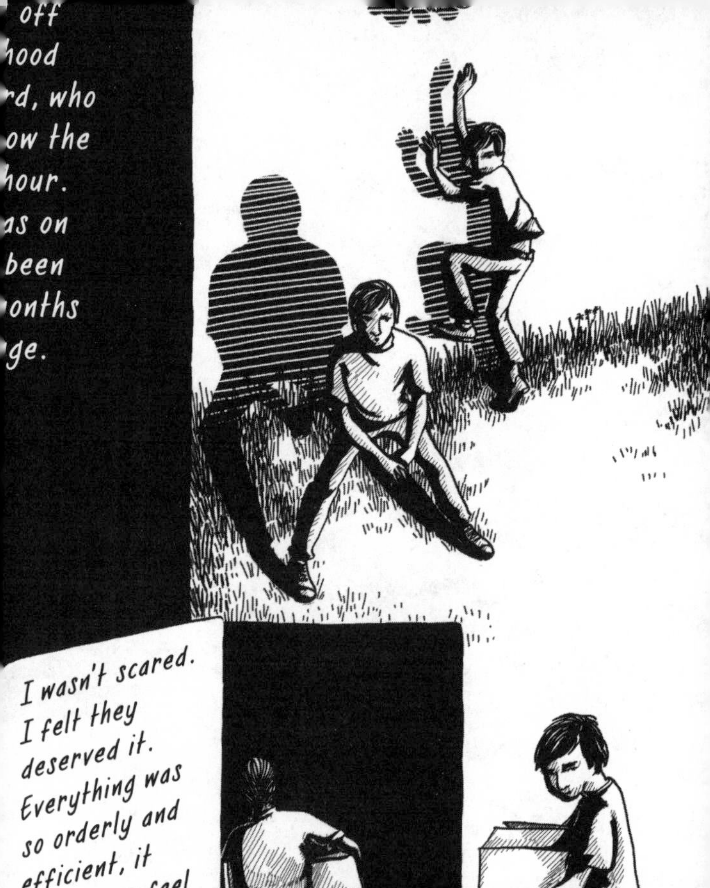
off
hood
rd, who
ow the
hour.
as on
been
onths
ge.
I wasn't scared. I felt they deserved it. Everything was so orderly and efficient, it didn't even feel like a burglary. I did a last run through the house and stopped in Andrés's room.

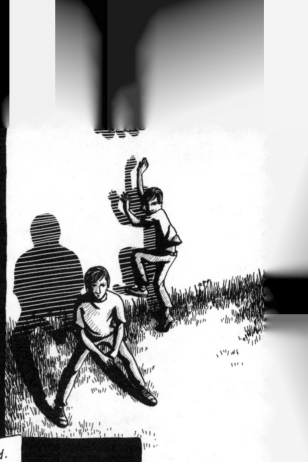

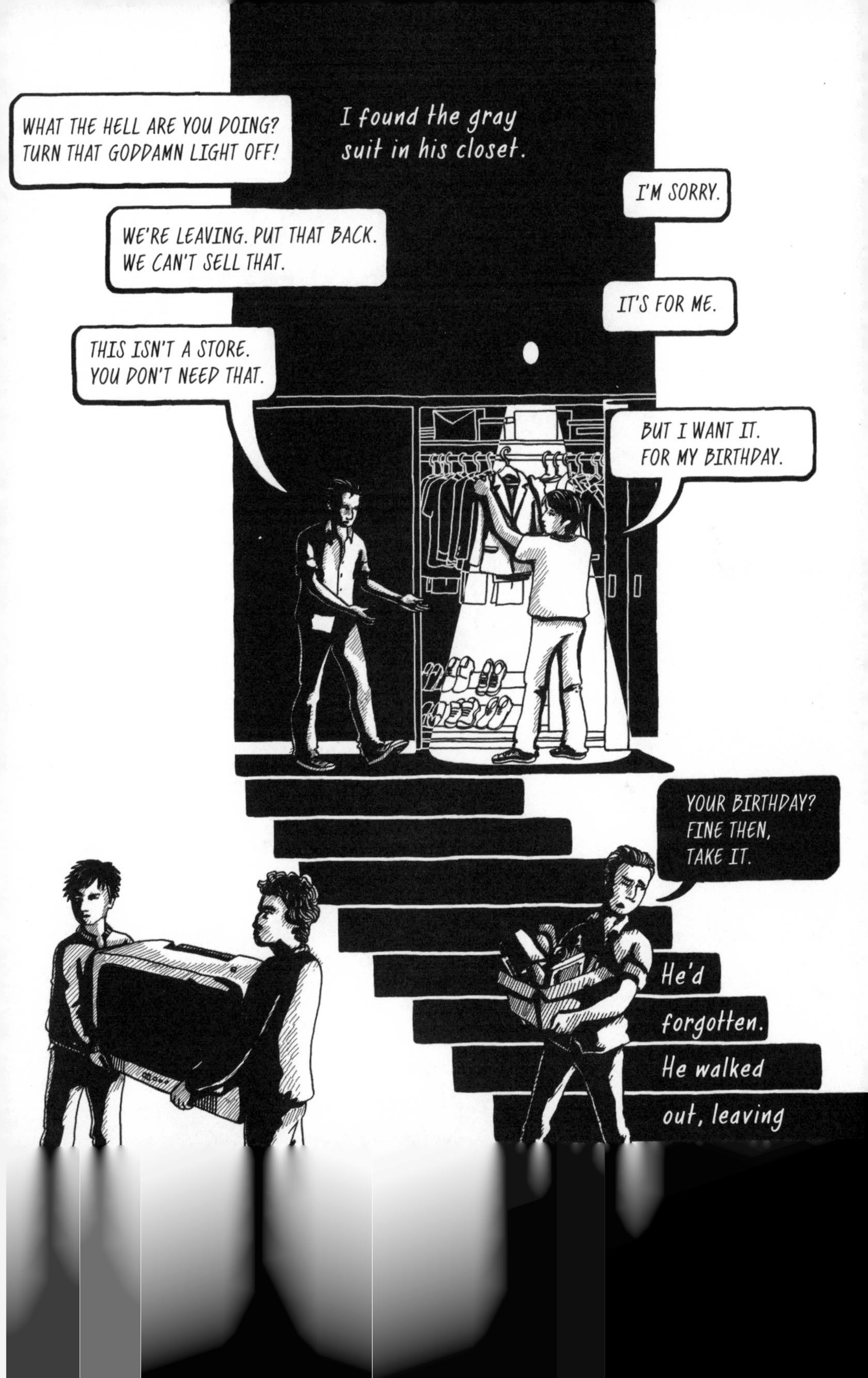
WHAT THE HELL ARE YOU DOING? TURN THAT GODDAMN LIGHT OFF!
I found the gray suit in his closet.
I'M SORRY.
WE'RE LEAVING. PUT THAT BACK. WE CAN'T SELL THAT.
IT'S FOR ME.
THIS ISN'T A STORE. YOU DON'T NEED THAT.
BUT I WANT IT. FOR MY BIRTHDAY.
YOUR BIRTHDAY? FINE THEN, TAKE IT.
He'd
forgotten.
He walked
out, leaving

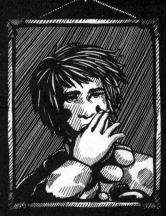

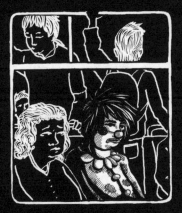

I rode around the city in my green-and-white suit. I didn't reach out to my editor or go to the paper.

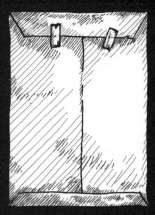

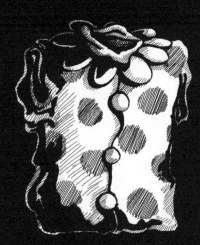

I put my article in an envelope, sealed it, and dropped it in the mail. I broke away from Toño and Jhon, paid them twenty soles for the suit and the shoes and the memories.

PAYASOS S.A.
ALARCÓN-ALVARADO
LIMA-PERÚ
2010
SERIE "A"
MEDIO

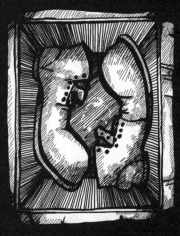

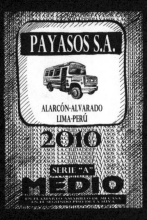

I rode the buses, paying my fare like any other passenger, except that I was unlike any other passenger. I thought about my mother. I knew I would see her.

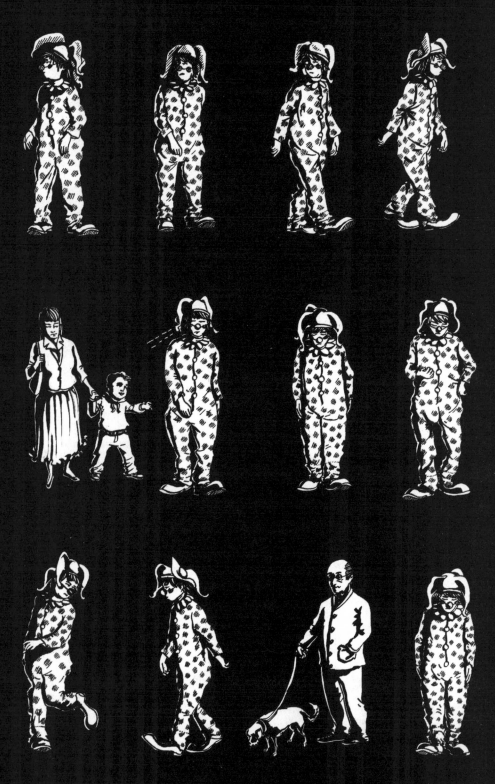

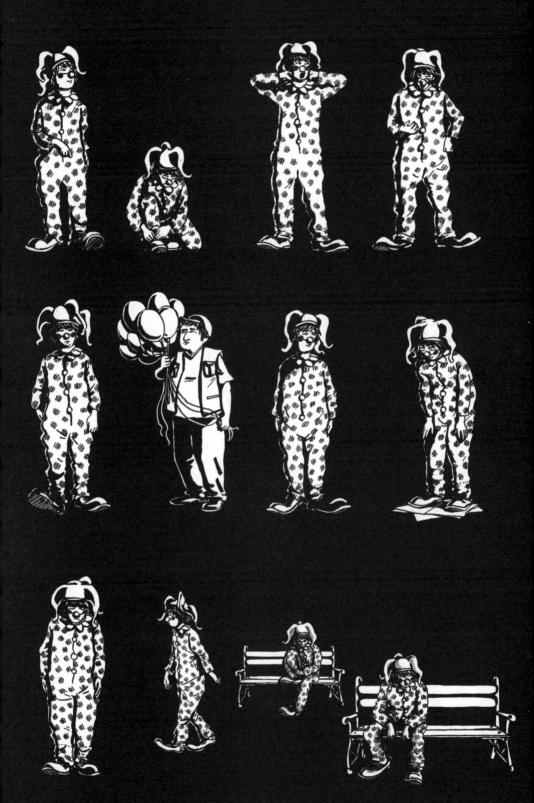

I rode to La Victoria, where the corner kids eyed me, wondering if it was worth their trouble to mug a clown. I walked the narrow streets, my shoes flopping on the crumbling sidewalks. I sat on a bench in front of Carmela's house and waited.

My black brothers came and went from school, from work.

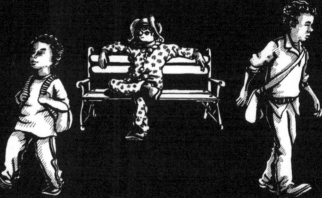

They didn't even look at me. I was part of the architecture.

YOU ALL RIGHT?
JUST RESTING, CHIEF.
YOU LIVE AROUND HERE?
I'M DON HUGO'S SON.
HUGO? CARMELA'S HUGO?

And he left me alone.

Carmela came home carrying dresses, and smiled at me because she smiled at everyone. Her door swung open wide, and from my bench I peered into her world, my mother's new world.

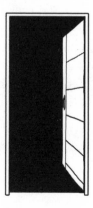

And then things came at me in waves: the street, the house. "I haven't seen you since you were this big," Carmela had said at the hospital. I remembered.

When I was six, Don Hugo had taken me to see his mistress. I'd never seen a black person before. I cried and said she looked burned. She grinned and pinched my cheek. He hit me and told me to be nice to my *tía*. Now I couldn't bring myself to ring the doorbell. I knew she would have been kind, even with me dressed this way. As kind as she was to my mother.

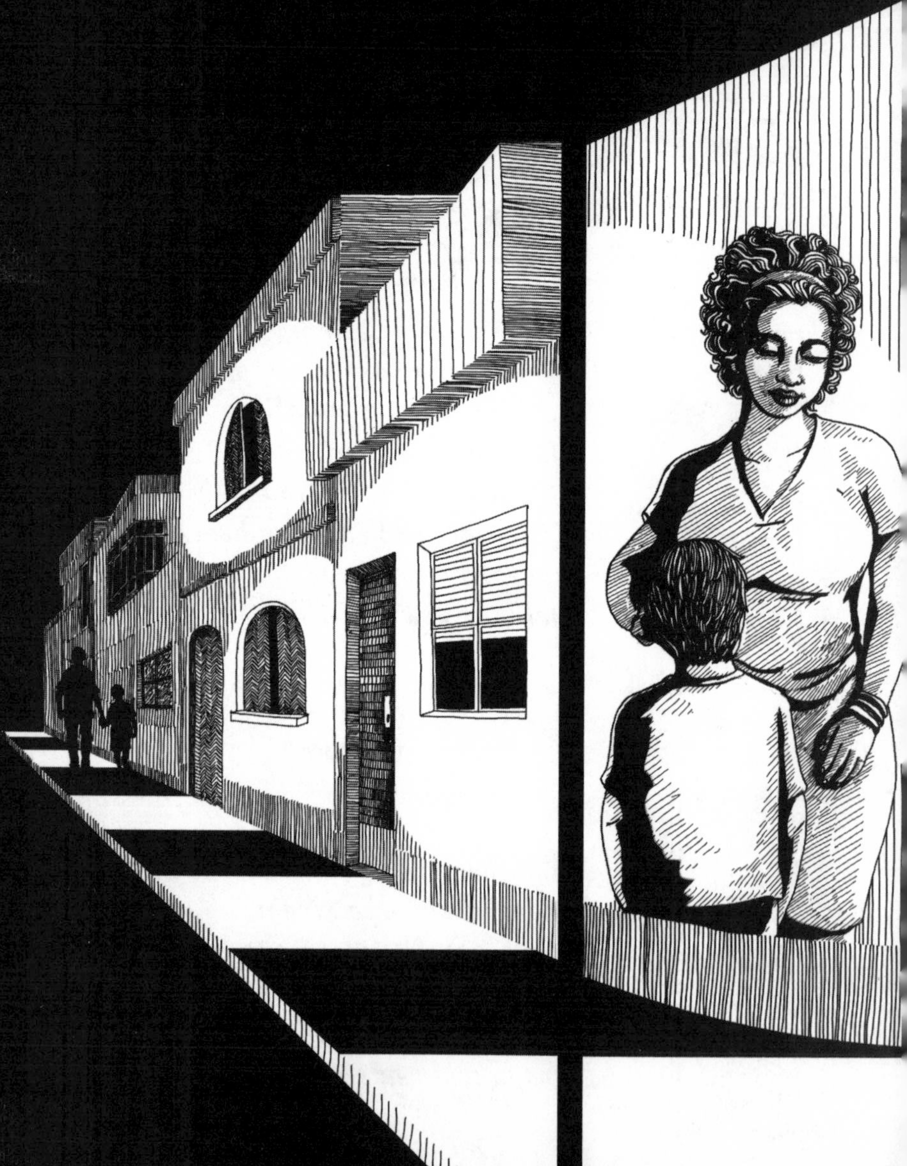

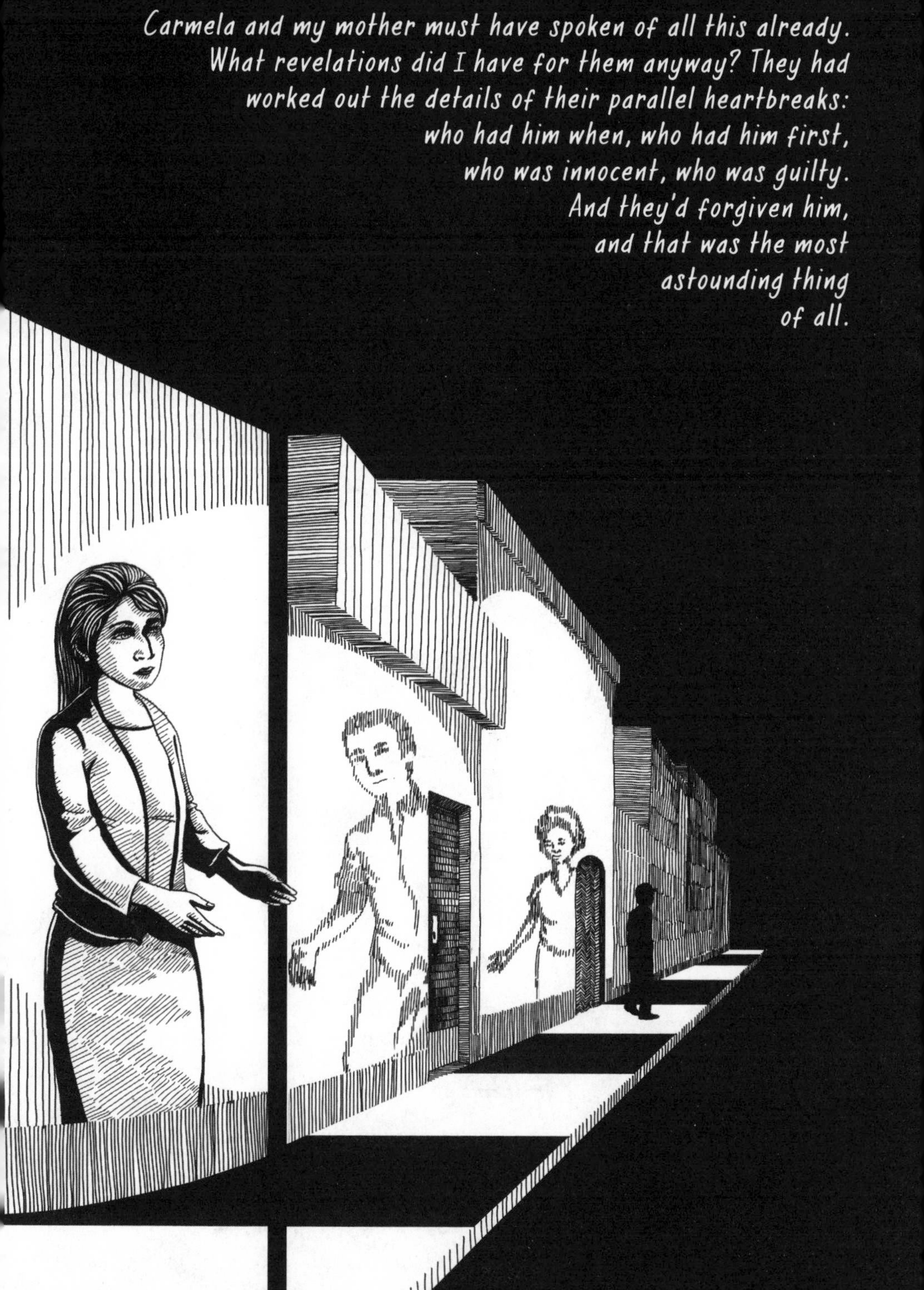
Carmela and my mother must have spoken of all this already. What revelations did I have for them anyway? They had worked out the details of their parallel heartbreaks: who had him when, who had him first, who was innocent, who was guilty. And they'd forgiven him, and that was the most astounding thing of all.

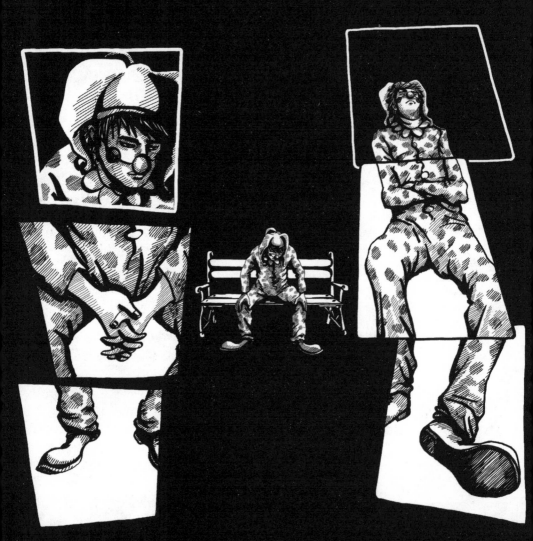

Why were you always forgiving him, Ma?
He told her everything first—about you, about me, about the work
he did and planned to do. He let you swim in darkness, and wonder
at the vacant spaces, and ask yourself what mistakes you'd made.
And then he left us. And you forgave him, Ma.
You forgave him.

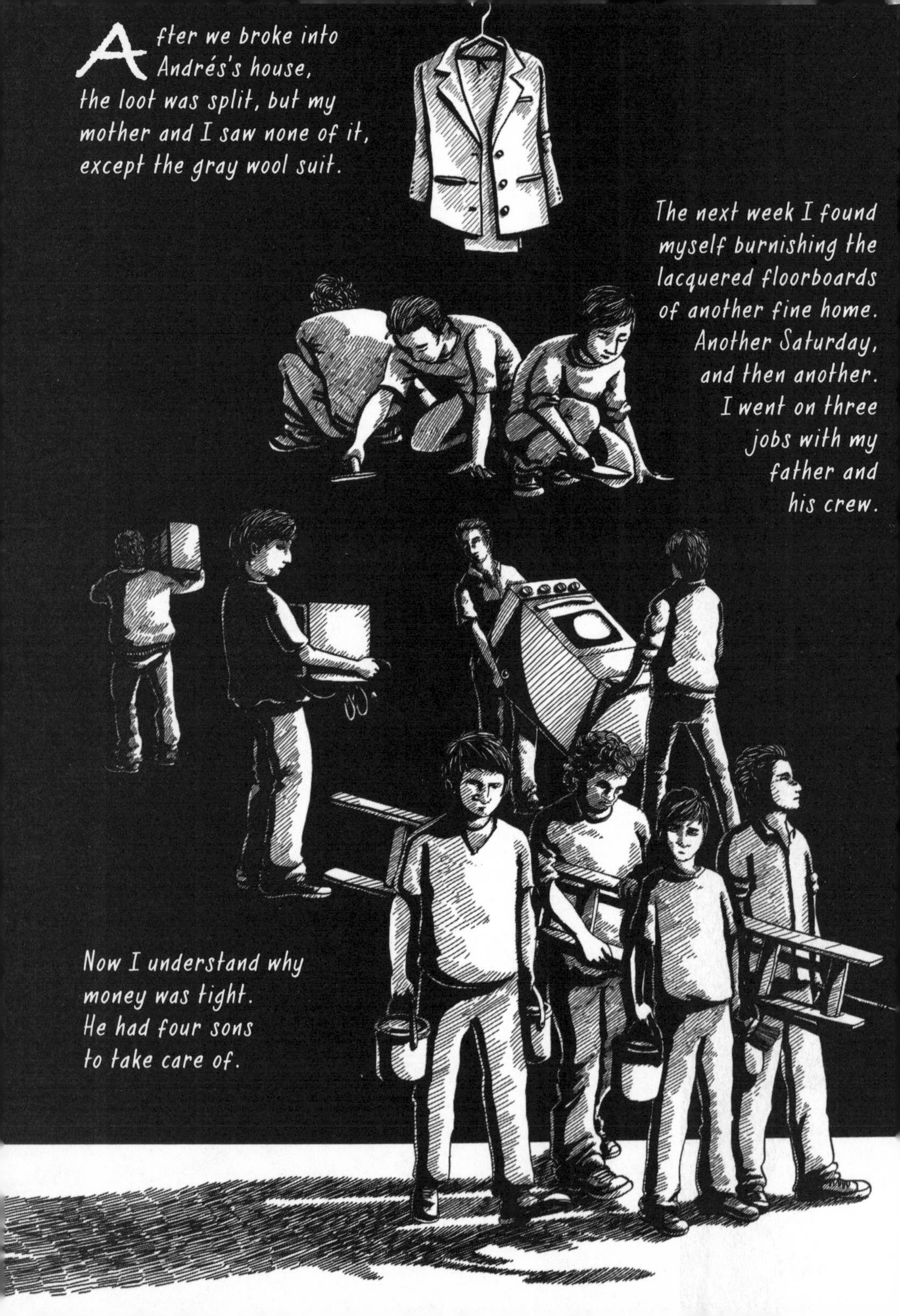
After we broke into Andrés's house, the loot was split, but my mother and I saw none of it, except the gray wool suit.
The next week I found myself burnishing the lacquered floorboards of another fine home. Another Saturday, and then another. I went on three jobs with my father and his crew.
Now I understand why money was tight. He had four sons to take care of.

We'd just finished a two-week job on a house when Felipe came by with the van. I remember thinking it was strange that they hadn't given the place time to cool. I thought I understood the hustle. I asked my father about it.

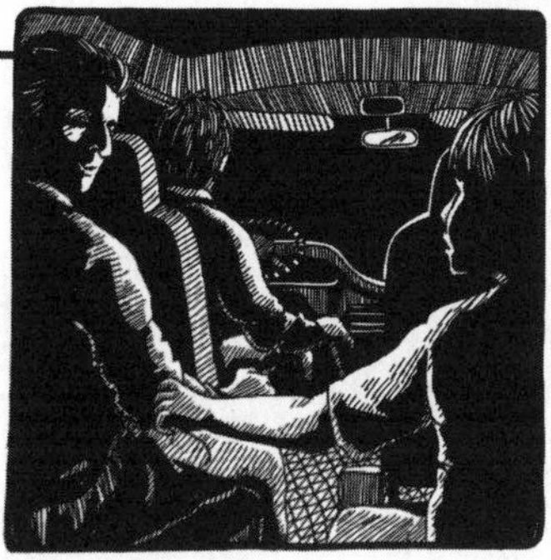

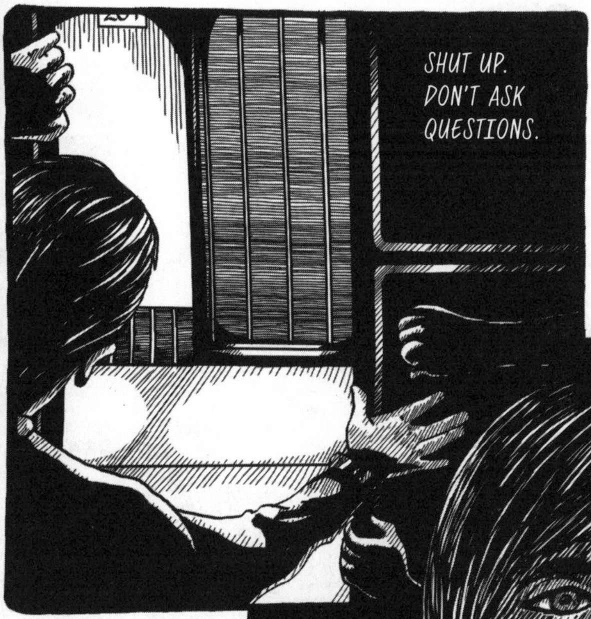
SHUT UP.
DON'T ASK
QUESTIONS.

I had no idea where we were going, but when I got out of the van, I knew immediately.

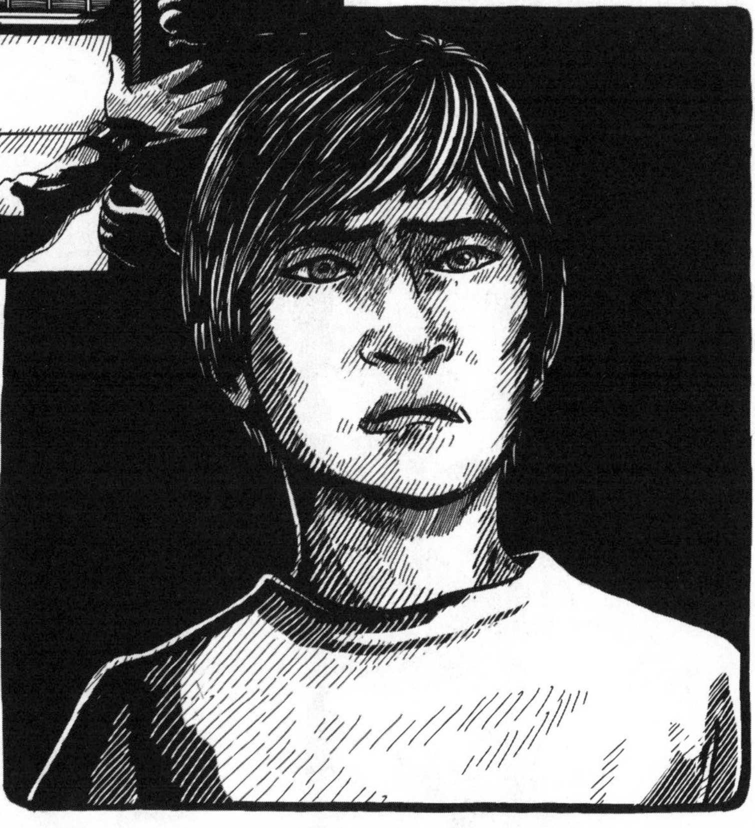

I looked at my father, horrified, expecting some kind of explanation, but he just shrugged. Crazy things happen in the city.

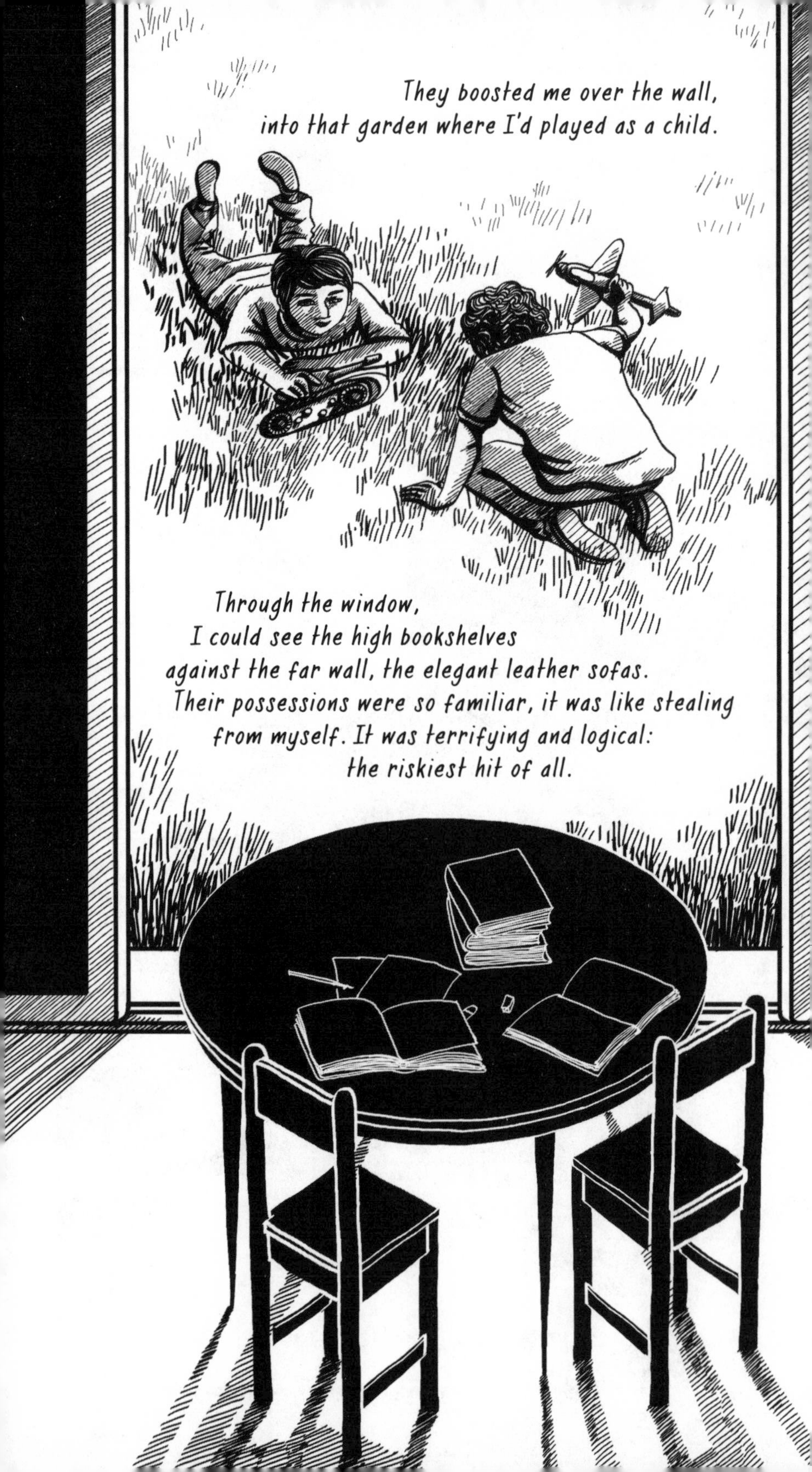
They boosted me over the wall,
into that garden where I'd played as a child.
Through the window,
I could see the high bookshelves
against the far wall, the elegant leather sofas.
Their possessions were so familiar, it was like stealing
from myself. It was terrifying and logical:
the riskiest hit of all.

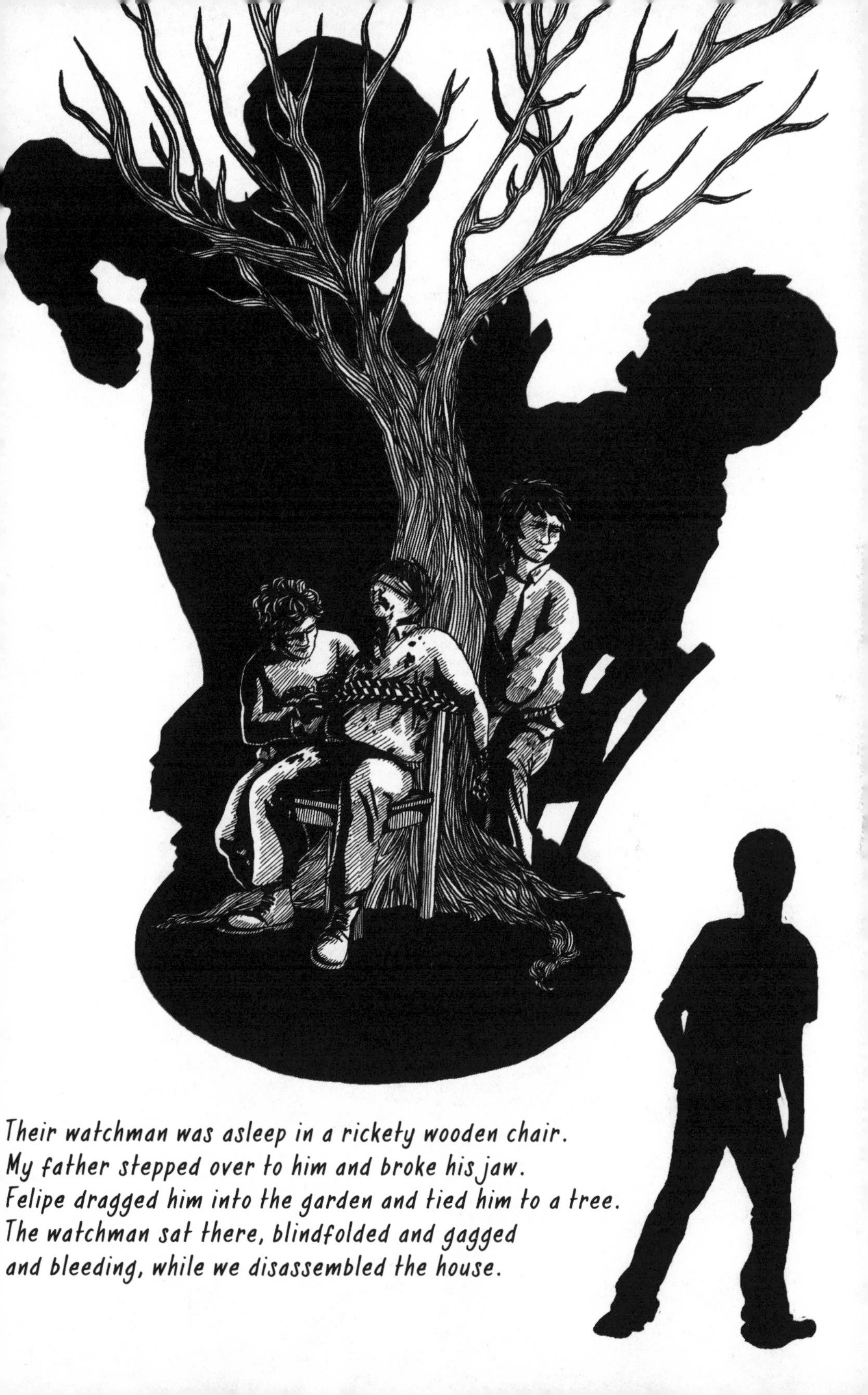
Their watchman was asleep in a rickety wooden chair.
My father stepped over to him and broke his jaw.
Felipe dragged him into the garden and tied him to a tree.
The watchman sat there, blindfolded and gagged
and bleeding, while we disassembled the house.

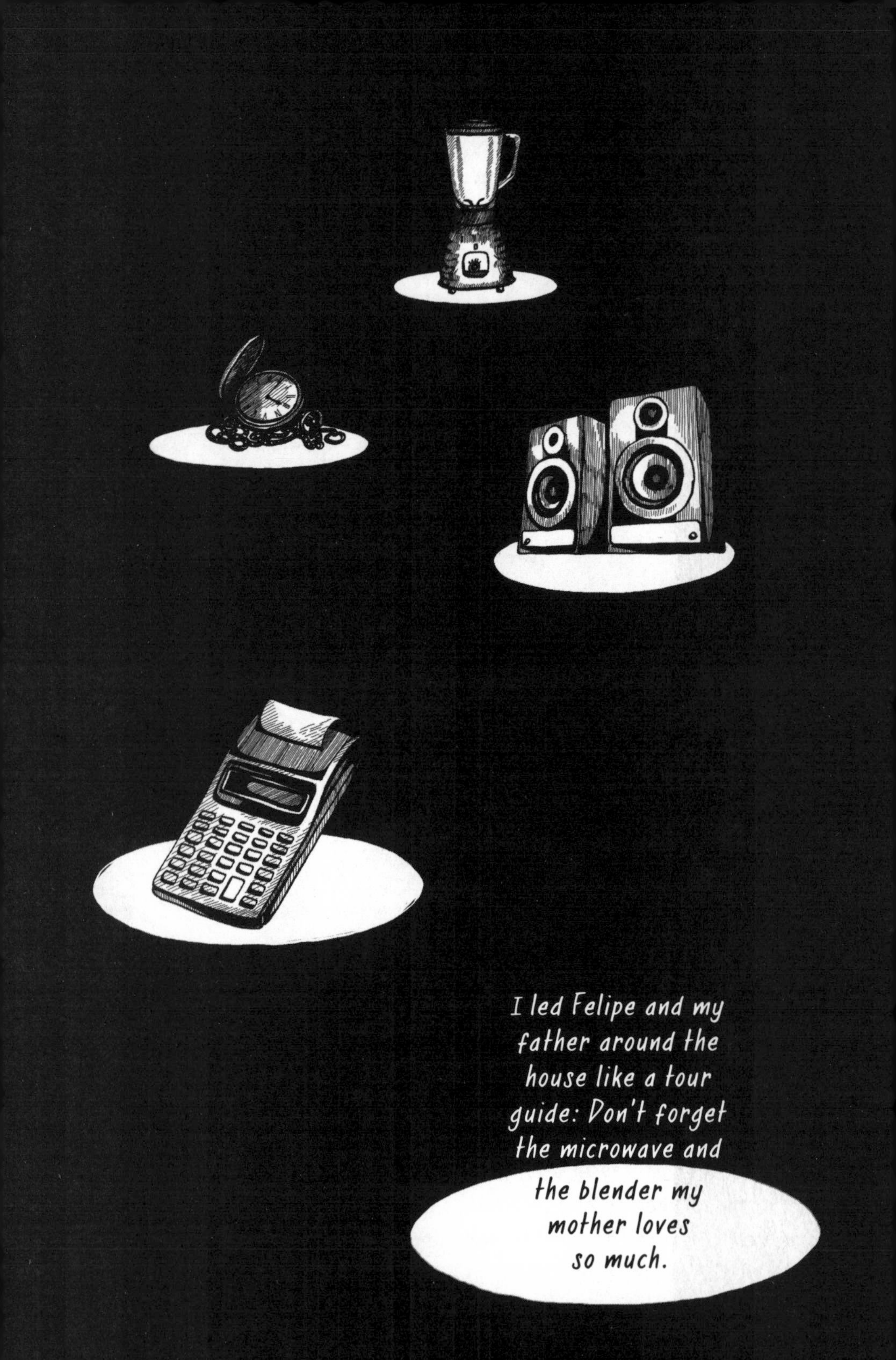
I led Felipe and my father around the house like a tour guide: Don't forget the microwave and
the blender my mother loves so much.

The television with its remote control. Here, the clock and the old engineer's nifty calculator, the speakers from the sound system. There was something beautiful in our silent artistry. Everyone would be a suspect. Whichever members of the crew had worked on the house. And the watchman tied to the tree, bleeding into a rag. The gardener, my mother, my father, even me.

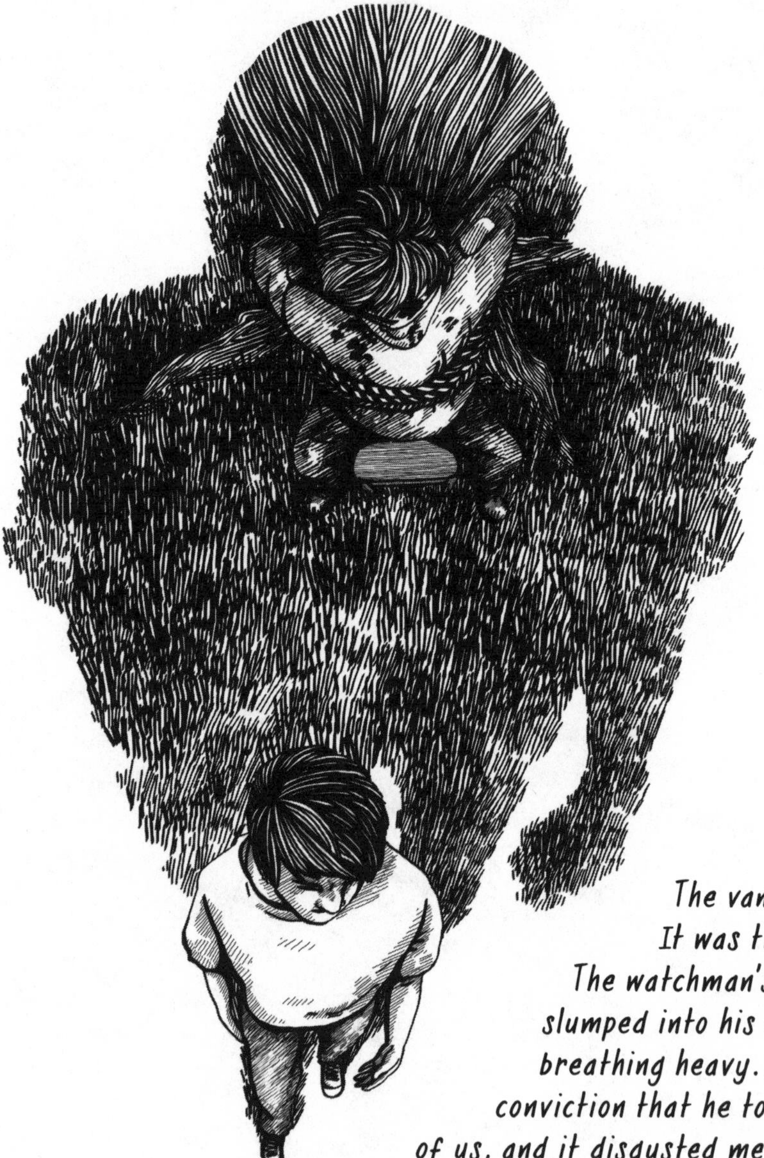

The van was full.
It was time to go.
The watchman's chin was slumped into his chest, his breathing heavy. I felt the conviction that he too was one of us, and it disgusted me. I hocked something viscous and unclean on his forehead. The color of money.

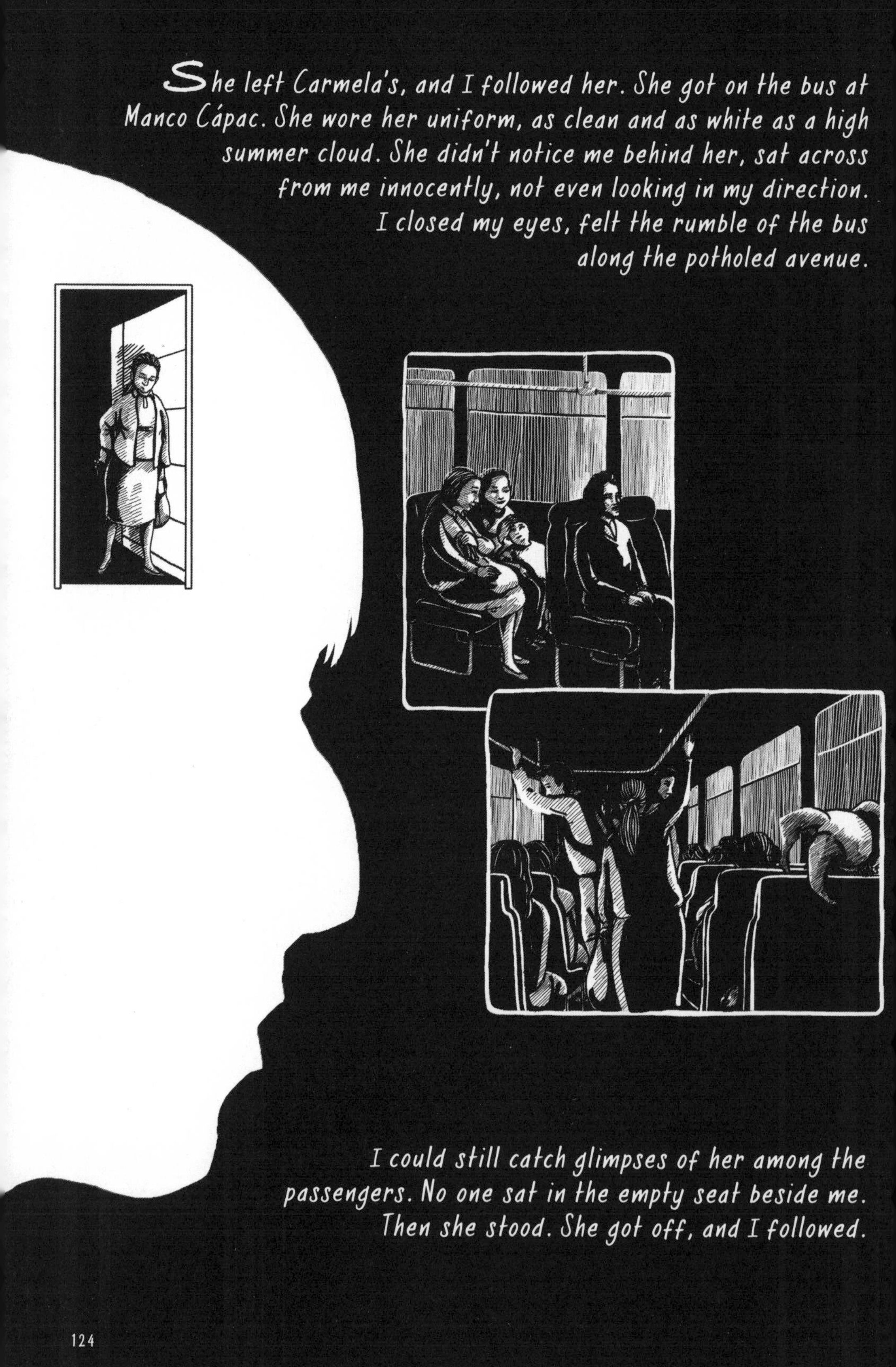
She left Carmela's, and I followed her. She got on the bus at Manco Cápac. She wore her uniform, as clean and as white as a high summer cloud. She didn't notice me behind her, sat across from me innocently, not even looking in my direction. I closed my eyes, felt the rumble of the bus along the potholed avenue.
I could still catch glimpses of her among the passengers. No one sat in the empty seat beside me. Then she stood. She got off, and I followed.

-day home, where I once kept
other company and did my
work on the garden terrace.
pace my father and I had
ed. She had always been safe
. And I had too. They had
doubted us. I trailed behind
ow, an expert in my clumsy
shoes. She walked along the
alk and I marched down the
center of an empty street.
alf turned, and then sped
the sight of me. I rushed to
pace with her.

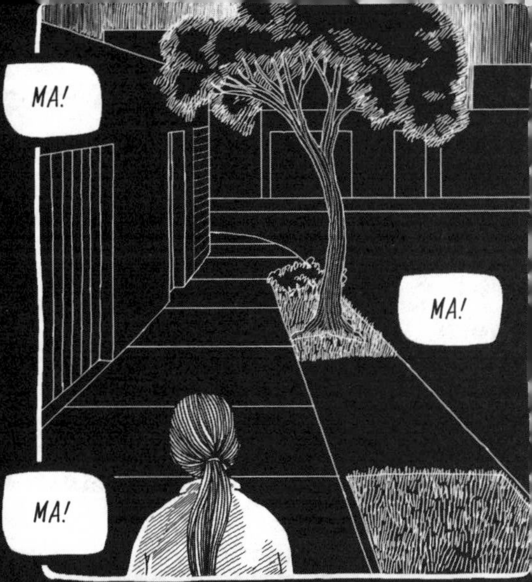
MA!
MA!
MA!

I hadn't seen her since the velorio. I had left her to bury the old man without me. She had held his hand and watched him die. She had put him in the earth and covered him.

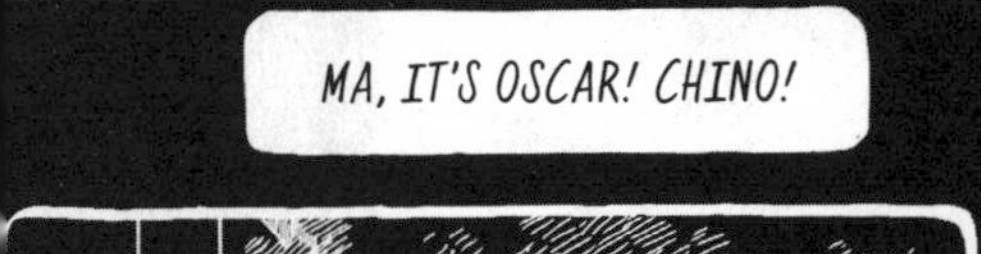
MA, IT'S OSCAR! CHINO!

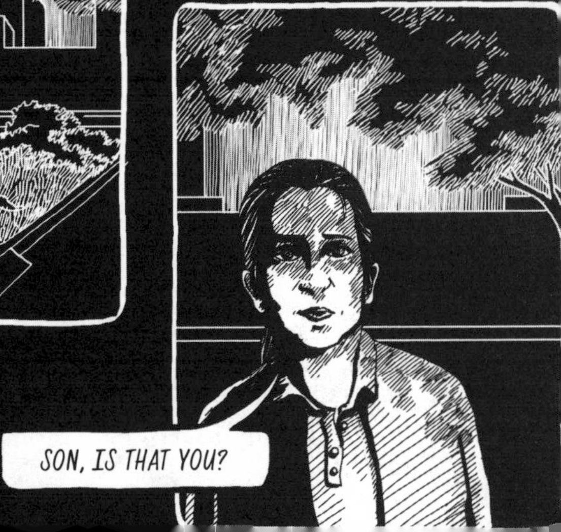
SON, IS THAT YOU?

I'M SORRY, MA. DON'T BE FRIGHTENED OF MY COSTUME. I WAS WRITING AN ARTICLE. I'VE BEEN ALL OVER THE CITY. I EVEN WENT TO CARMELA'S HOUSE, BUT I WAS ASHAMED TO KNOCK ON THE DOOR. I'M SORRY, MA. IT'S SILLY, BUT I NEED TO KNOW SOMETHING.

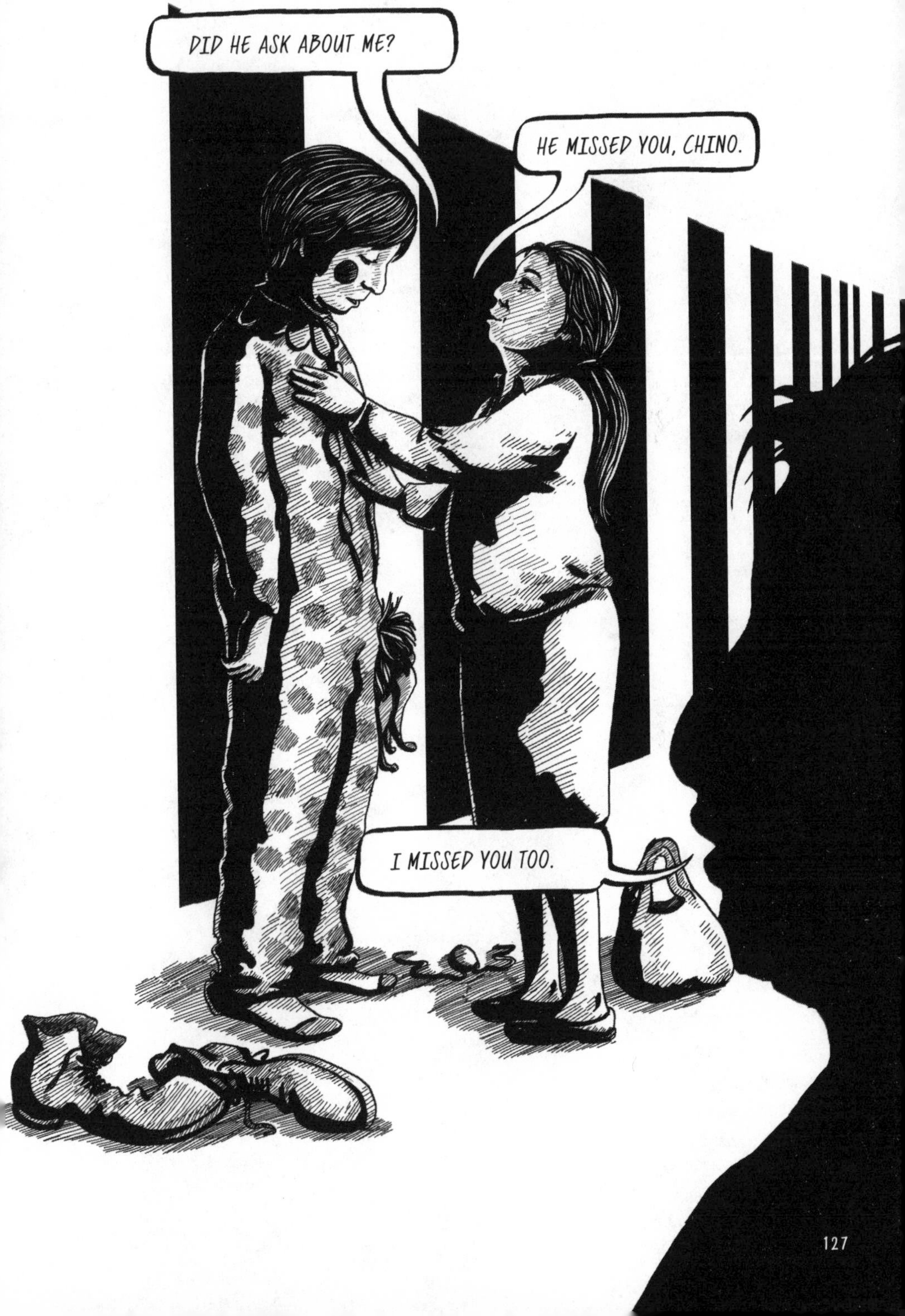
DID HE ASK ABOUT ME?
HE MISSED YOU, CHINO.
I MISSED YOU TOO.

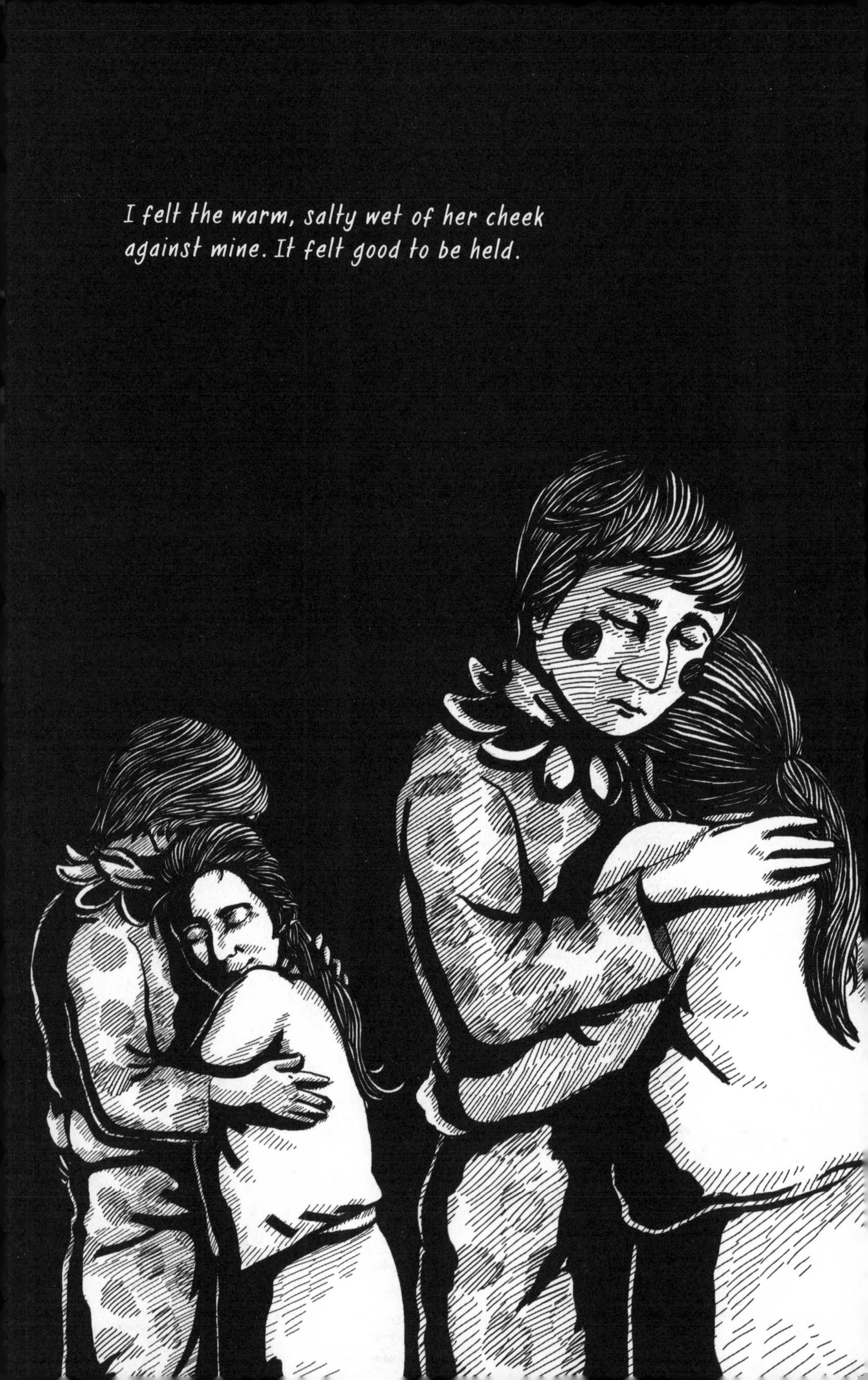
I felt the warm, salty wet of her cheek against mine. It felt good to be held.

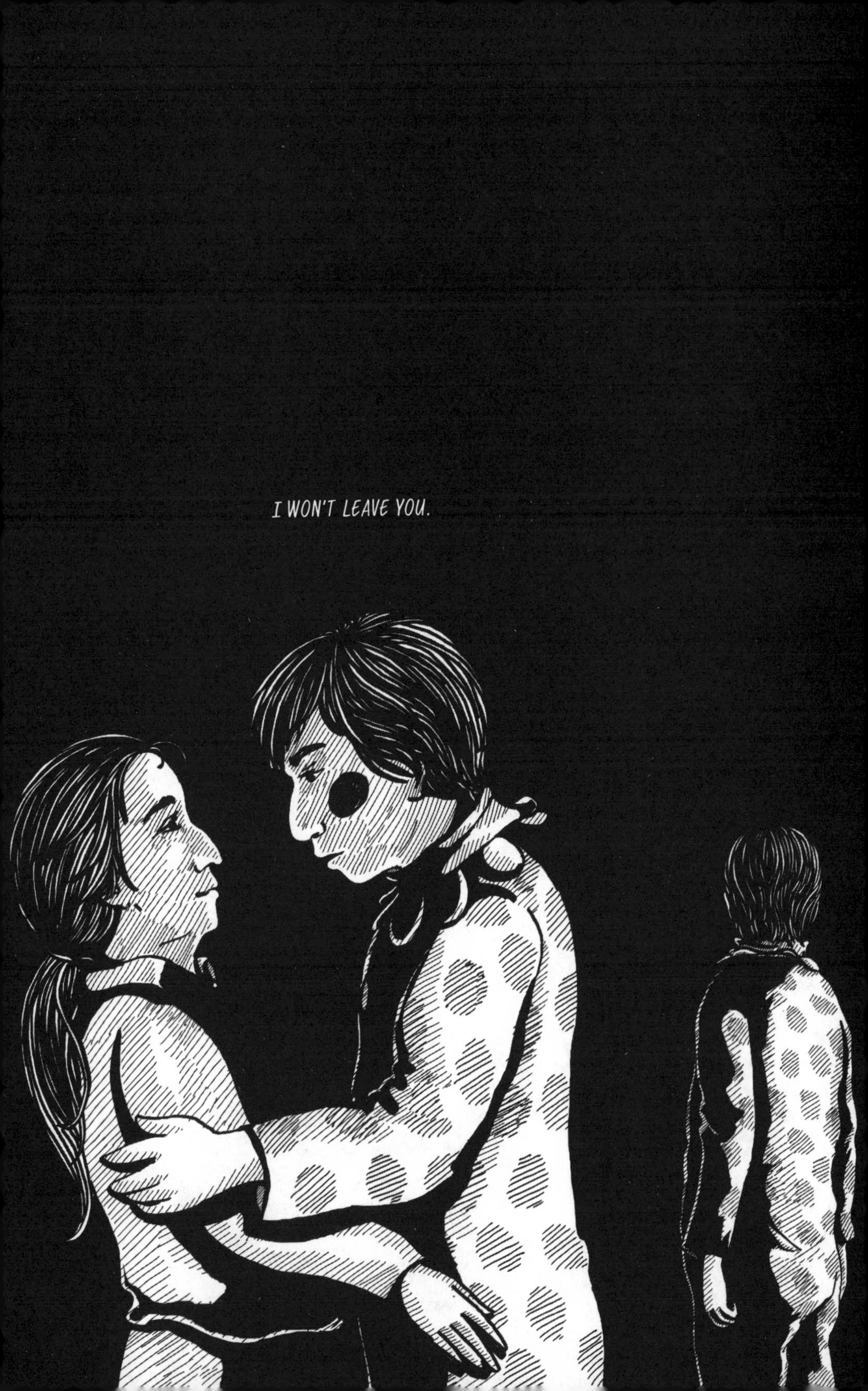
I WON'T LEAVE YOU.

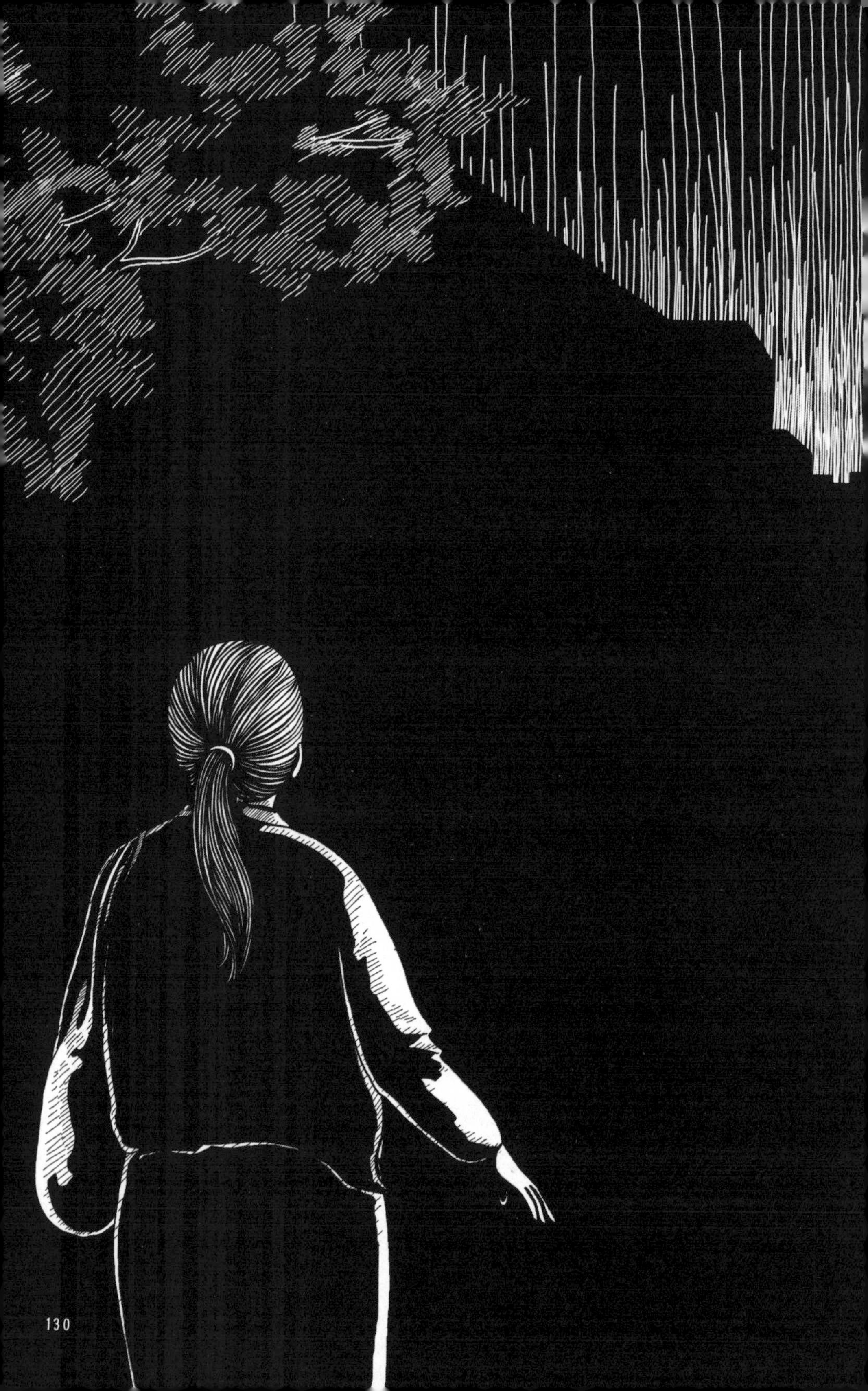

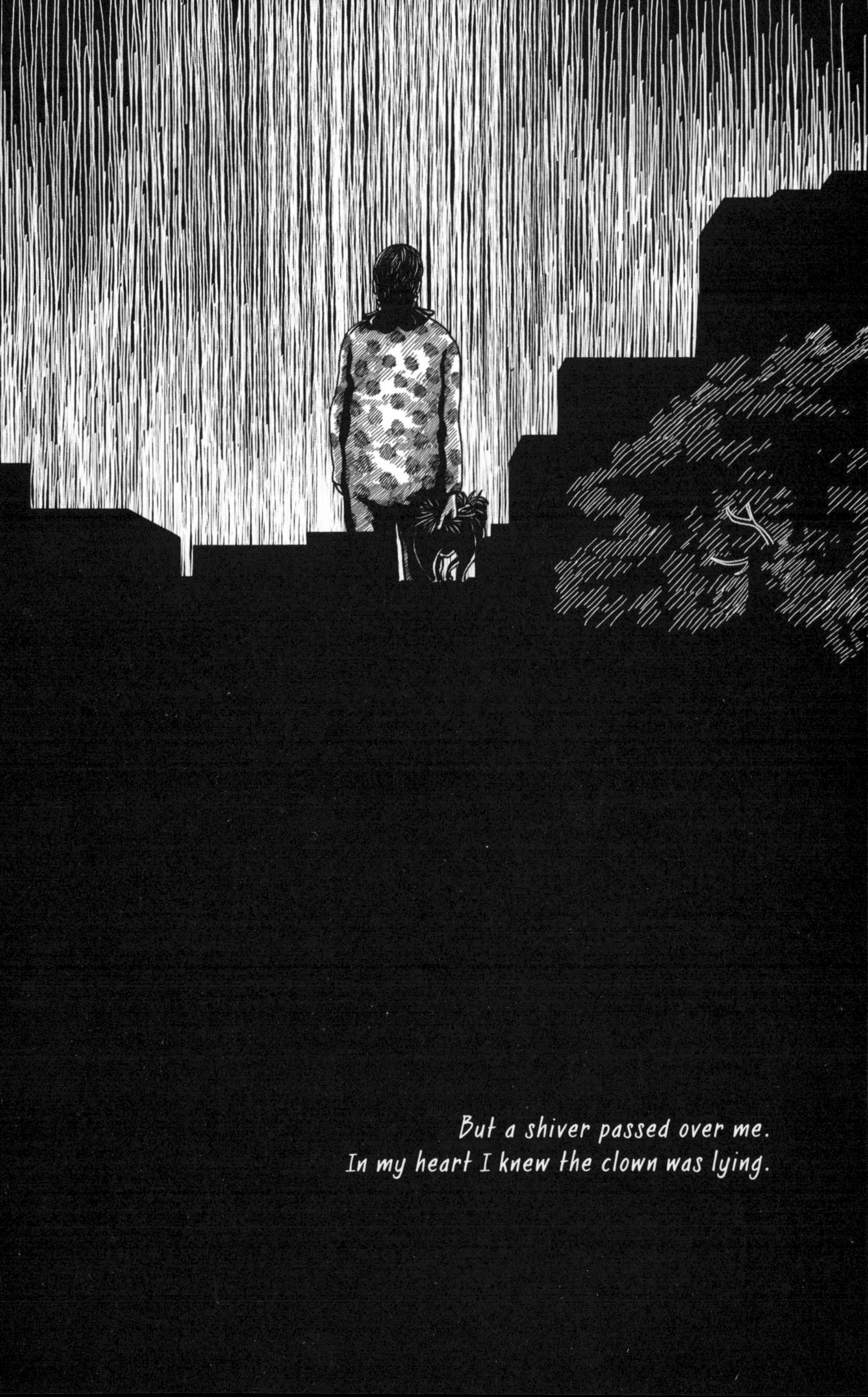
But a shiver passed over me.
In my heart I knew the clown was lying.

AFTERWORD

Sometimes, when the writing is difficult, I go back and look at early drafts of stories I've managed to finish, stories that, in some cases, I'm proud of. The logic is simple: Writing fiction is so unnerving and complex that it's good to reassure yourself now and then, to be reminded that it's possible to be perfectly lost for a month or longer and still find your way out. That it's possible—maybe even necessary—to discard forty pages, or sixty, and not look back. I look through these muddled first drafts and feel relief. It happens, I tell myself. It *has* happened. These primitive versions are inelegant, riddled with false starts and unnecessary asides and characters who will later disappear, but this is all part of the process, missteps that must be overcome in order to arrive at an understanding, however partial and intuitive, of a story's shape.

But the one story I've never been tempted to look back at is *City of Clowns*, in part because I remember the writing of it to have been such a unique and magical experience. The first draft was written in September 2002, nearly twenty thousand words that appeared in three weeks; never before or since have I had such a productive spell, and I don't expect I ever will again. The days were trancelike, the writing automatic and beyond my control. The early drafts are messy, but not tentative. I don't know how, but I was headed, from the first, in the direction of the final scene. This is rare. Everything else I've ever written I've had to fight for, struggle toward, but *City of Clowns* was a different experience entirely.

At the time, I'd just returned from a year in Lima, living and teaching photography in 10 de Octubre, a neighborhood of San Juan de Lurigancho. The work had been wonderful and exciting; I'd made many good friends and learned a lot, but to my shame, I hadn't written a word in twelve months. By the time I arrived in the U.S., I was despairing and, frankly, afraid I would never write again. I moved to Iowa City and rented a room in a farmhouse outside town, a creaky old place on a narrow gravel road, surrounded on all sides by cornfields. I moved in during the last, soporific blast of summer, when the air was still and humid, a soggy heat reminiscent of Lima in February. But unlike Lima, in late afternoon the sky would darken to a blackish purple, crack open, and I'd sit on the porch and watch the storms approach on a stiff, unrelenting wind. I found a trumpet in the basement of the farmhouse, and sometimes, on dry, cloudless days, after hours of writing, I'd sit on the porch and blow into the horn just for the pleasure of disturbing the overwhelming silence of the cornfields. There was no one around to hear me. Occasionally a car passed by, or a tractor. I missed Lima intensely. Missed its noise, its energy, missed its dirty air and its cynical, beautiful people. Conjuring it in fiction became a very necessary distraction from life in this agreeable American college town where I now found myself. I couldn't have written *City of Clowns* while living in Lima. I had to be far from it—as far as possible—in order to concentrate deeply on what the city meant to me.

The story itself is entirely made up, though certain anecdotes are real. Just to give a few examples: A friend called me one day, sobbing. It was my last week in Peru before flying to the U.S. His father had died, and he needed money—urgently—for precisely the same reason Chino needs an advance from the paper at the beginning of the story. I gave him what I could. A few weeks earlier, I'd met a reporter for *La República*, a young man about my age who had written a piece about the youth photography project I was working on in San Juan de Lurigancho. His name was Óscar. We spent an afternoon in 10 de Octubre, and he told me came from a neighborhood just like that one. In a sense, Chino is based on him, or what I gleaned about his life in those few hours we were together. Sometimes I catch his byline in the local papers, but I've never seen him again. And the clowns—every Limeño recognizes these characters, naturally, but some moments I wouldn't have been able to write if I hadn't seen them myself.

Shoe-shine boys walking in protest down Jirón de la Unión, led by a clown on stilts?

I doubt I would have had the courage to make that up.

If this story has always been special to me, it's even more special now that it has been made into a graphic novel with the collaboration of my dear friend Sheila Alvarado. In some ways, I think, this might be its true and definitive form. It is certainly more thoughtful, more deliberate: the original story was written at a furious speed, whereas this version was in the works for well over a year. Every image was discussed and argued about, drawn and redrawn; every page designed and redesigned. In some cases, we went through fifteen versions of a single page. The text too had to be revised: pruned in places, so as not to interfere with the images, transitions added elsewhere. We began talking seriously about this project in November 2008 while in Buenos Aires, and finished a first draft in Lima the following year. After I moved back to Oakland in August 2009, we did a second version and a third, connected via Skype. I'd sit in my apartment, Sheila in hers, and we'd spend hours, entire days, online: drawing sketches, placing text and moving it around, sending PDFs back and forth, or simply holding scribbled pages up to the webcam so that one person could see what the other was talking about. Without a decent Internet connection, this book simply could not exist.

Sheila is the only artist I would have trusted to collaborate with on this project. I cannot overstate the admiration I feel toward her and her work, or how grateful I am for her friendship through the years. When we began, neither she nor I really knew what we were doing, or even how we should approach a task like this. In truth, the more we progressed, the more difficult it seemed. This explains in part why the book took about ten months longer to complete than we'd originally expected. In my case, I had a lot of enthusiasm, but very little practical knowledge about graphic novels. Beyond the occasional *Condorito* or *Asterix*, I never read comics as a kid. In fact, I didn't really think seriously about the art form until 2003, when a friend lent me a copy of Joe Sacco's stunning *Safe Area Goražde*, a brilliant piece of graphic journalism about the war in Bosnia. I'd never seen anything like it. Without exposure to Sacco's work, I wouldn't have been interested in graphic novels at all.

This particular iteration of *City of Clowns* was published in Peru in 2010 as *Ciudad de payasos*, in Spanish, of course. At the time, it was the first literary graphic novel published in the country, something Sheila and I were both very proud of. Now, five years later, it's come to the U.S., and I can only marvel at the strange and circuitous journey the story has had: first, a lived and imagined experience in Spanish, then a text in English, which was then translated back into Spanish, bolstered and transformed with Sheila's illustrations, and now, back into English with those same images and, I hope, the same impact. It's dizzying. I feel very fortunate that a story written in an Iowa farmhouse has had these multiple lives.

—Daniel Alarcón

SKETCHES

Entrada

9:32

eres un payaso
me lo estas preguntando
o me lo estas diciendo, causa?
preguntando chochera
y quien carajo eres tú
oscar vaibe
trabajo para el clarín
El periódico?
¡Maestro!
¡un vaso más.
por favor!

papá
chino
chino
papá

profe
alumnos en formación
acercamiento de torso de chicos
incluido el chino con su maldito de lado
oye

chino
chino

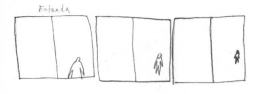

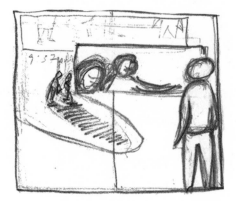

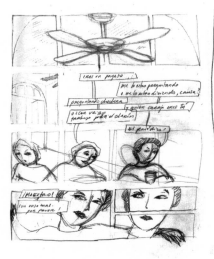

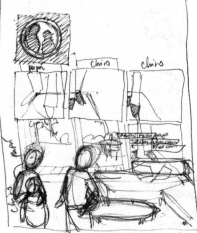

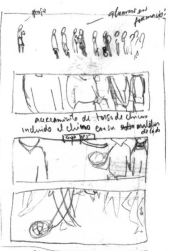

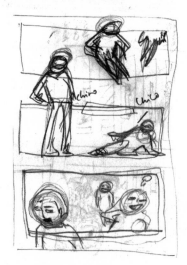

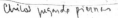

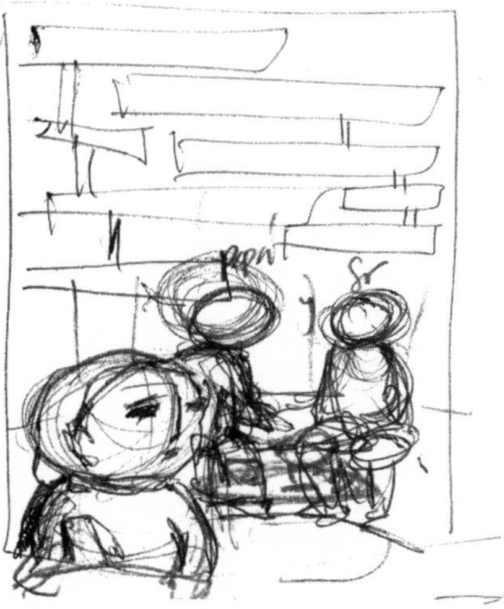

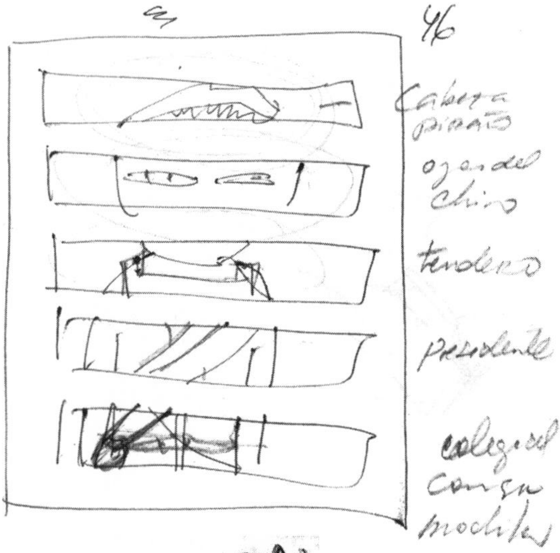
46
tendero
presidente

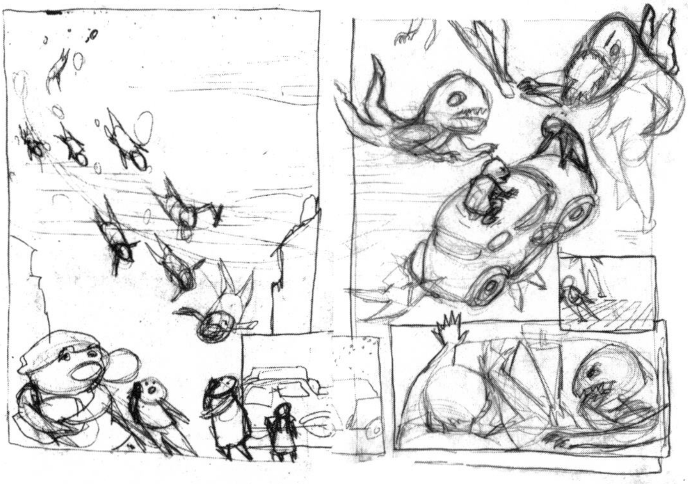

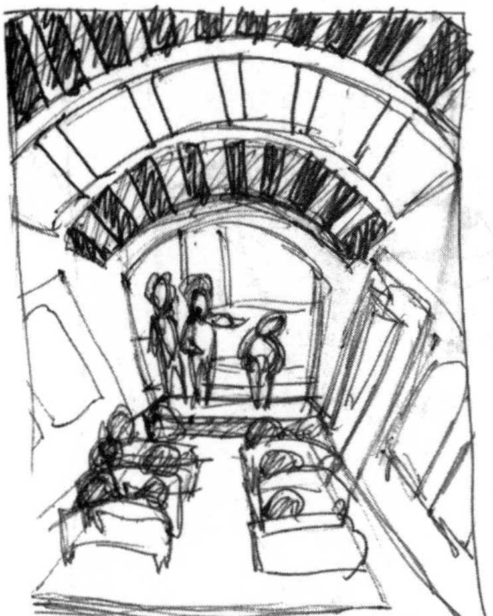

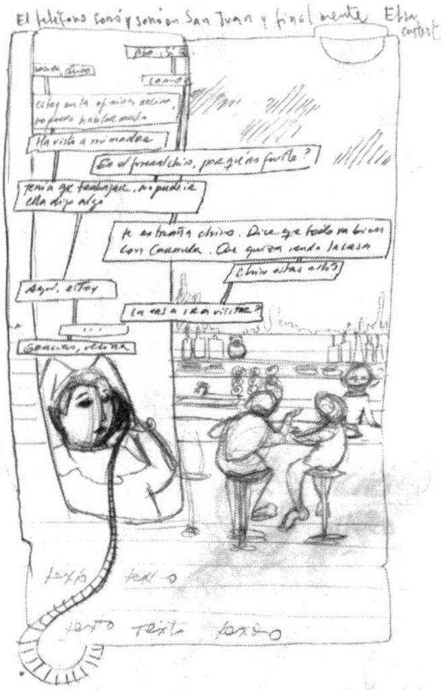
El teléfono sonó y sonó en San Juan y finalmente Elsa contestó
Ha visto a mi madre
Aquí, estoy
Gracias, vecina
texto texto
texto texto texto

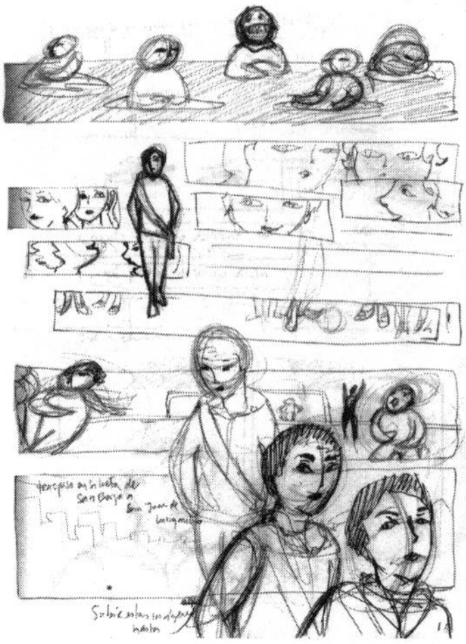

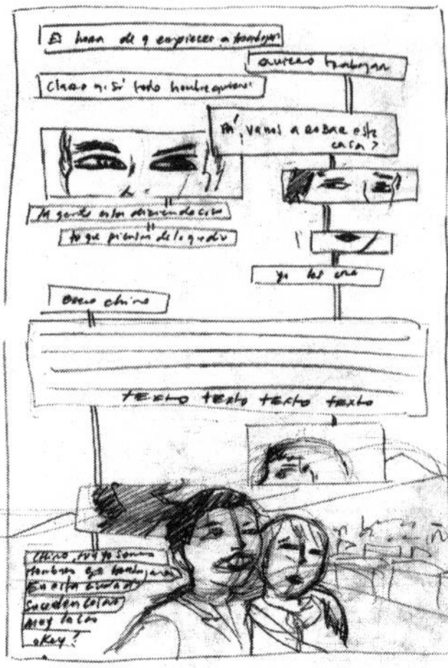
texto texto texto texto

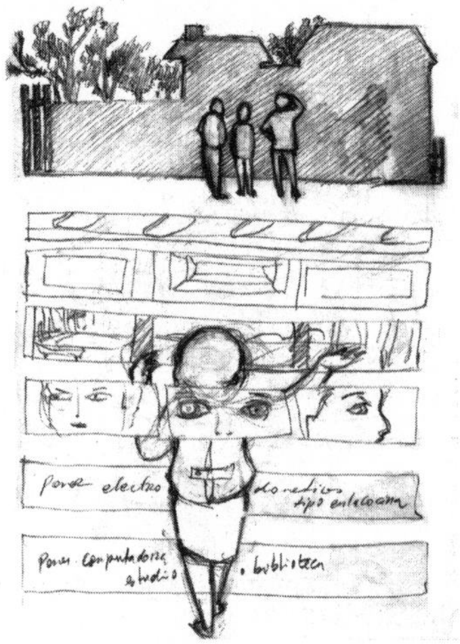

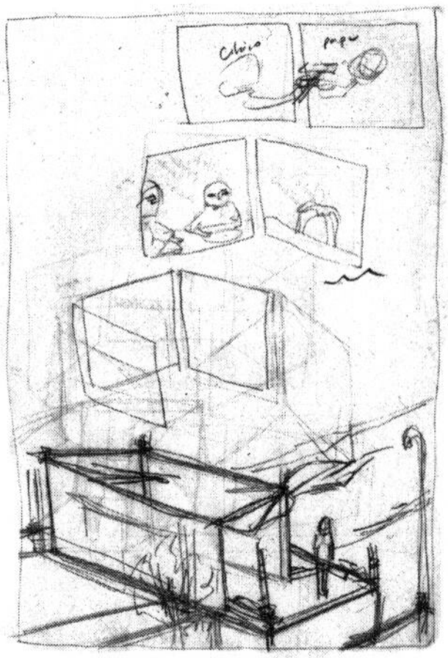

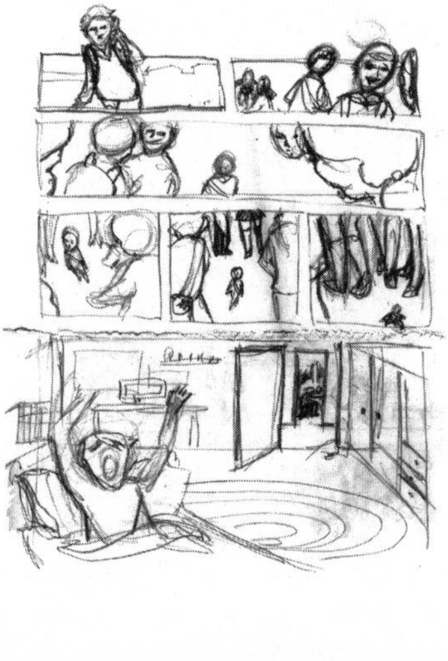

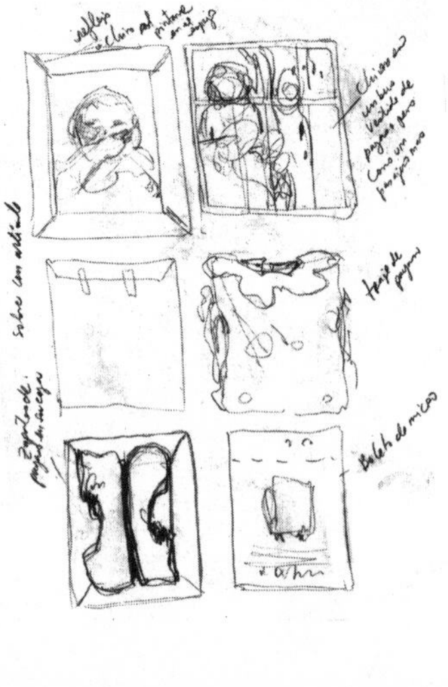

mirando al cielo
Caminando de frente
Hermano menor
Hermano del medio
Hermano mayor

Cocina

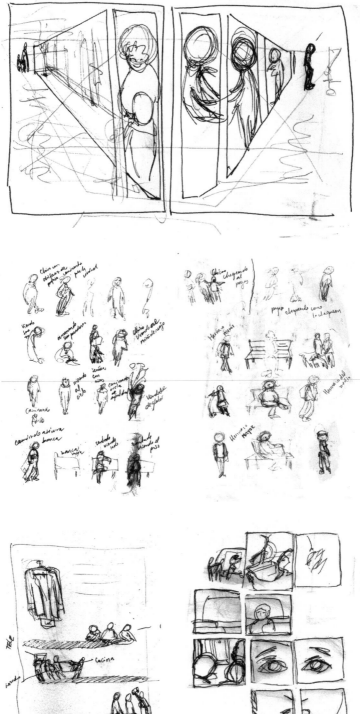